THE CULTURED THUG

by

JONATHAN BOWDEN

EDITED BY GREG JOHNSON

Counter-Currents Publishing Ltd.
San Francisco
2023

Cover design by Kevin I. Slaughter

Cover image: Jonathan Bowden, 6 December 1991
Photo by David Rose, courtesy of J.N.

Published in the United States by
COUNTER-CURRENTS PUBLISHING LTD.
P.O. Box 22638
San Francisco, CA 94122
USA
http://www.counter-currents.com/

Hardcover ISBN: 978-1-64264-011-3
Paperback ISBN: 978-1-64264-012-0
E-book ISBN: 978-1-64264-013-7

CONTENTS

EDITOR'S PREFACE

In August of 2010, I asked Jonathan Bowden to contribute an essay to *Counter-Currents* on the topic "Why I Write." This was part of an ongoing series of articles in which dissidents explained why they chose to take up the pen. Jonathan's contribution was a concise 610 words ending with the paragraph:

> Truthfully, in this age those with intellect have no courage and those with some modicum of physical courage have no intellect. If things are to alter during the next fifty years then we must re-embrace Byron's ideal: the cultured thug.[1]

"The cultured thug" is a golden phrase that resonated with dissidents over the years. It was even adopted as the *nom de guerre* of a video commentator. Thus the phrase leaped to mind when I was searching for a title to tie together this rather disparate collection of eight speeches and four reviews. But the title fits, because all of these works embody Bowden's fusion of intellectualism and vitalism.

These pieces fall into four groups. The first three transcripts deal with British culture: Shakespeare, Elgar, and British sculpture beginning in the bronze age. The next two transcripts deal with American writers: H. P. Lovecraft and Robinson Jeffers. Then follow three transcripts of talks dealing with the Left: Orwell's *Nineteen Eighty-Four*, the Soviet gulag, and feminism. Finally, the book ends with two book and two film reviews written for *Counter-Currents*.

The "British Sculpture" transcript accompanies a video of Bowden flipping through a book and discussing the images. Due to issues of space, image quality, and copyright, we could not include the images here. You can, however, watch the original film as well as a new version with much-improved images

---

[1] Jonathan Bowden, "Why I Write," in his *Pulp Fascism: Right-Wing Themes in Comics, Graphic Novels, & Popular Literature*, ed. Greg Johnson (San Francisco: Counter-Currents, 2013), p. 166.

edited by Buttercup Dew at the Jonathan Bowden Archive (jonathanbowden.org)

In editing Bowden's transcripts, I introduced paragraph breaks and punctuation for maximum intelligibility. I dropped filler words, omitted false starts, and corrected slips of the tongue. I left sentence fragments intact but corrected the subject/verb disagreements common in spoken discourse. In the transcripts, ellipses indicate where Bowden's train of thought changed direction before completing a sentence. I capitalize the names of artistic movements like "Modernism." In Bowden's written pieces, I left his sometimes-eccentric capitalization practices unchanged. Occasionally, I added in the first names of less famous people. I added corrective, bibliographical, biographical, and explanatory notes where needed, but I tried not to be too pedantic. (None of the notes are by Bowden.) The passages that appear in quotation marks in Jonathan's speeches are, of course, usually his paraphrases, not exact quotes. I use single quotes for paraphrases, double quotes for actual quotes. If you wish to consult the original recordings at the Jonathan Bowden Archive, you will see that nothing extraneous has been added and nothing essential removed.

I wish to thank everyone who helped bring this book to press: Michael Woodbridge, Jonathan's literary executor, for his imprimatur and encouragement; Michèle Renouf, Matt Tait, and others who recorded and circulated Jonathan's speeches; my heroic transcriptionists, including V.S., Lee and Donna Hancock, and Buttercup Dew; Millennial Woes and his brain trust for his help with difficult words in the transcripts; Buttercup Dew for laying out the book, correcting the transcriptions, annotating the texts, and preparing the index; J.N. for the cover photo and Kevin Slaughter for his cover design; and James O'Meara for his proofreading. Any remaining errors are my fault. Finally, none of this would have been possible without the readers, commenters, and donors at *Counter-Currents*.

This book is dedicated to the other Greg.

Greg Johnson
August 5, 2023

Shakespeare*

We're here today to talk about William Shakespeare, one of the greatest artists, writers, and playwrights that has ever existed in our race—the Aryan or Indo-European people—or, to be truthful, in any other group on this planet. Shakespeare lived during the Elizabethan period and wrote over fifty plays. He was an artist who was also an active actor and jobbing writer. For him, the work was part of the craft that he did in and around theatres, which he helped to own and manage.

Shakespeare has become integral to Western culture, and to English and British culture in particular. But there is a degree to which many liberals at the present time find a lot of his work to be problematical. There are elements in all of the plays which do not fit in well with contemporary discourse. If we look at a play like *The Taming of the Shrew*, for example, even the title itself is "sexist" and doesn't fit in with allegedly politically correct nostrums of this period.

Let's go right to the heart of the most controversial metapolitical area involving Shakespeare. Metapolitics is cultural struggle. It's the politics of culture, rather than of narrow, sectarian, and party interest. Race and discourses about ethnicity are central to the Shakespearian experience. They occur in early works like *Titus Andronicus*; they occur throughout the *oeuvre*; they center in *Othello*.

Traditionally *Othello* has always been played in our theatres by a white man blacked-up, in the manner of Laurence Olivier. Now, he's a blackamoor, in some ways a Negroid Arab, but he's nearly always played as a black or African individual in the British or Western theatre. But as things have moved on, we now have a viewpoint manifested from post-1960s British drama in particular that *Othello* is a "racist" play. This means that non-

---

* Transcript by Lee and Donna Hancock of Jonathan Bowden's talk on William Shakespeare, which you can listen to at the Jonathan Bowden Archive, https://jonathanbowden.org/.

white actors, traditionally. have started to take up the role and perform *Othello* thereby.

But later on, possibly in the last ten to fifteen years, pioneered by Dobbs from the Yorkshire Playhouse for example, there is a view that, because this play is "racist," even to have a non-white in the leading romantic part isn't good enough. So what now happens is that a rather liberal-minded white actor, not blacked-up, plays Othello in order to fit in with new linguistic and mental and moral conceptions as regards this part.

Now, why go to all of these difficulties? Why consider that this play is in any way difficult to understand or ethically appreciate? The real reason is that there is a critique of miscegenation at the heart of this particular play, even though Othello and Desdemona are treated as tragic characters in love. Iago, the villain of the piece, without any question, and based upon certain Machiavellian philosophical precepts of which Shakespeare was generally aware at that time, and coming out of Tudor discourse before him, makes Iago into a real villain. He is the agent of evil, of malevolence, of forces of destruction or non-creativity.

Shakespeare is always true to the moral caste of a character, and puts himself in his place. He's shallow, but he's an egotist. He's puffed up with the splendor of self and with glory. He wishes to debase and destroy, yet at the same time feel his own power in the quickness of the struggle. But he is also an agency of fate, of what ancient Greeks would have called Atë, negative fate, a destructive identity which comes, in their religious system, from the Furies.

He destroys and tears down and mutilates morally and, ultimately, physically these two characters—Othello and Desdemona—because they have contracted into a union outside their own racial kind. Because Shakespeare is coming out of a post-Medieval conception, even though the country has formally rejected Roman Catholicism as the state religion and turned to a mildly Protestant or Anglican dispensation under Henry VIII and his successors on the throne.

In this way of thinking we have a situation which says that all of the races are created by God. But at the same time, they should remain separate or entire. There is always a discourse—

as with Leni Riefenstahl's photos from the 1960s of the Nuba in the Sudan—of estrangement and difference and differentiation about "the other." In Nietzsche's thinking at the end of the nineteenth century such an idea will be called the "pathos of difference." It is, in many ways, an aristocratic mode of thought. It is quite alien to the egalitarian and liberal-Left values which dominate British and Western European and North American culture at the present time.

So we see in this particular play a medley of ideas which have come to seem unacceptable to present-day opinion, but which were totally integral and centered in the culture out of which Shakespeare came. But *Othello* isn't the only play where these alleged problems come to the fore.

Titus Andronicus was an early work and is a violent tragedy of revenge. Sometimes the number of bodies, as with John Webster's play *The Duchess of Malfi*, at the end of the dramaturgy, leads a modern audience to giggle, because there's so many corpses around the stage. There's almost a Grand Guignol or Punch and Judy element to the number of people who die, and their deaths are treated with a certain levity, often after sword fights and stabbings and so on, which had the pit in the Globe at the height of the Elizabethan Age on their feet, roaring and cheering and throwing nuts and orange peel about. Because people went to this theatre the way a proportion of our people today go to a soccer match.

Now, in *Titus Andronicus*, Tamora who is the queen of the Goths, has a black lover—Aaron—and this symbolizes her outsider status, her status as a demon and a Lilith who tortures Andronicus' family, and, in the end, is done to death. Much of the blood dramaturgy of this particular work is based on Seneca and is based upon Roman tragic drama which draws upon the Greeks. The Elizabethans had Greek tragedy out of Rome via a discourse of modernity that came through Erasmus and from the Italian Renaissance.

So, in a way, Shakespeare and John Webster and Christopher Marlowe and Thomas Kyd and all the other great Elizabethan playwrights are working their way back to the beginnings of our tragic art and sensibility through Romanesque examples which have been handed down to them, or across to them, by the Italian Renaissance. We're particularly looking, ultimately, back to Sophocles—less Euripides, really—but primarily to Aeschylus. Now, at the heart of the *Oresteia*, which is the beginning of all tragic Western drama, there's a blood sacrifice and a feast, particularly involving the house of Atreus and revenges that went on there in this part of south-eastern Mediterranean Europe two-and-a-half to three thousand years ago.

This is then filtered through Romanesque tragedy via Seneca in the play *Thyestes*, which was glossed by Caryl Churchill in the 1980s in quite a famous Royal Shakespeare Company performance. And this then comes forwards to the use of revenge as a motif for early and bloody Elizabethan tragedy. There was a very famous version of *Titus* by Peter Brook, who was highly influenced by Antonin Artaud's idea of the Theatre of Cruelty in the 1960s and late fifties, and it partly was based on the Stratford production from the early 1950s which made Laurence Olivier's name. That production catapulted Olivier to great star status and ultimately led him to become the first major principal of the National Theatre, first at the Old Vic and then to be based on the South Bank.

Those are two of the plays that deal with the nature of race in a way that makes them very relevant today, given that a multiracial society for the last fifty years has been created around us.

The other play which liberals, in many ways, do not "like" is *The Merchant of Venice*. This is a play which is allegedly "anti-Semitic," but much less so, even if we admit that it might be, in comparison to Marlowe's *The Jew of Malta*, for example, which really is a piece of puppet adult theatre and Grand Guignol, deliberately made as a theatrical potboiler by Marlowe, in comparison to a play like *Tamburlaine*, to make money. Because these were playwrights who were interested in getting the public in. They weren't just writing for a small, little intellectual elite. They were drawing in an entire culture: the aristocracy, the burgess orders, whores, soldiers, the plebs. *Everyone* went to the Globe, and there are parts of the play that appeal to each part of the audience.

The Merchant of Venice was put on in the late 1980s by Trevor

Nunn's company at the National. There's one black character of a minor cast in that particular play. A third of the characters at the National were black. And there was an apology at the end of the play for the Holocaust, which I don't imagine had occurred five hundred years ago when the play was actually conceived. Now these things are done and, sometimes, quite mainstream modern-day instances of this material are done without any cognizance of politically correct rhetoric at all. But these things are done because people are ashamed and embarrassed and self-estranged from their own culture and from the manifestation of their own ethnicity in — in this respect — high culture.

Now, if we move on from race as a motif of otherness and otherworldliness and outsider status to look at the sexual politics of these particular dramas, you can look at the relationship, complicated though it be, between the three daughters and Lear in the play that bears that name. Shakespeare set *King Lear* before the Christian era, and morally in the atmosphere of King Canute, as it were, because he wanted to explore certain ideas which were non-Christian.

Lear is the harshest play — in terms of its moral theory of life, in terms of its eschatology and its belief in ultimate moral human purpose — that Shakespeare ever wrote. During one particular period, the end of *Lear* was actually changed by a man named Nahum Tate in the seventeenth century because people found the ending too harsh and too violent; yet again, an example of the fact that Puritanism or philistinism has always interfered with Shakespeare and his direct appeal to audiences after the immediate Jacobean and Elizabethan periods. Today the form of Puritanism and censorship that's involved is of a liberal-Left variant, but it wasn't always so.

There are three daughters that Lear has and very foolishly, as every contemporary[1] listener of the play would have known, he divides his kingdom between them — one, two, three; Cordelia, Goneril, Regan. Goneril and Regan are out for themselves and are wolves and animals who want to tear Lear down and reduce him to penury and madness on the heath with his fool — the only

---

[1] Contemporary to Shakespeare.

one who's foolish enough or brave enough or moral enough, depending—to stay with him, together with Edgar who, in a sense, is Gloucester's fool in the subplot of the play.

There's one scene in that play—the blinding of Gloucester—where he is made to physically suffer, which is one of the most remarkable and cruelest acts in world theatre. But it in turn goes back to Sophocles in ancient Greece and is brought forward. Sophocles wrote a trilogy called the Theban plays in which Oedipus blinds himself because he accidentally murders his father and commits incest with his own mother, Jocasta. Now, Shakespeare factors that forward to the blinding of Gloucester by the sadist Cornwall when he shouts, "Out, vile jelly! Where is thy luster now?" And Gloucester is sent away to throw himself metaphorically and actually off the cliffs at Dover with his son Edgar.

Shakespeare is never frightened of violence or of cruelty or of patriotism or of warfare, but they are *never* gratuitous. Much of contemporary culture which masquerades as mass entertainment often involved motifs endlessly repeated, because they're always in the human mind, of sexuality and violence. But the problem with a lot of this material is it's not connected to anything organic and therefore it doesn't *mean* anything and is just shallowly superficial and pornographic in the worst, rather than the best, of senses. With Shakespeare these things are always bred in the bone and related to language and related to ideas and structures of being and meaning, which is why they've resonated with people, in all groups actually, but principally our own, all over the world.

If one moves to another play like *Macbeth*, *Macbeth* has been criticized by feminist critics, particularly in "New Wave" or second-generation feminism in the 1970s, because of the portrayal of Lady Macbeth. She is more staunch than Macbeth, more ruthless, more feminine in a vindictive way, more of a Hecate, more of a Lilith, more of a woman who keeps things with her touching stone, who gives him the daggers in reality and metaphorically so he can go in and stab Duncan under their roof, which of course is a blasphemy against honor and the code of hospitality, whether in the Scotland of Macbeth's day or the England of

Shakespeare's Elizabethan Renaissance.

There's an extraordinary painting by Henry Fuseli[2] in the Tate which shows the aftermath of the murder of Duncan and his two stewards. When Macbeth, who's been brought up to the nature of the deed by his wife Lady Macbeth, comes out with the two daggers and holds them up before her, steaming and reeking with blood and with gore, and to one side she's there — the Gorgon — almost in see-through white like a ghost, wrapped in silk, looking very much like a Medusa in certain images on coins and shields which have come down to us from ancient Greece.

Now, in this play there is an understanding of the dialectic and the interrelationship between a man and a woman in a ruling marriage where he's been elevated to being Thane of Cawdor by Duncan. But . . . "Thane of Cawdor? Why not king of *all* Scotland?" when he can take it with *power* outside morality, which ultimately leads, in the concourse and cavalcade of the play, to murder after murder, to the return of ghosts of those that he's slain, and ultimately to nihilism and to moral despair at the end of the drama, "signifying nothing."

Now, it's important to understand that Shakespeare cannot be fitted easily into any box — a liberal or allegedly politically correct one at the present time, or an illiberal one, or an ultra-conservative one. With him all voices are the flow-through of his own artistic consciousness and imagination. He is a pure playwright, perhaps the purest that's ever lived, which is why he has in some ways become universal in his present moral currency. And that's because when he has a character before him on the page, he thinks himself totally into that character and what they are, what their values amount to. The philosophy which may animate them at any stage of their being flows through him onto the page. It's *pure* theatre, even though it's rooted in the ideology of the period where he lived and wrote and worked and acted.

Because he acted in nearly all of his plays. He performed in a lot of the sword fights. He directed people. He took plays by John Fletcher that were half-made, such as *Pericles*, and he reworked them to make them slightly better. Of other manuscripts

---

[2] Henry Fuseli (1741–1825), *Lady Macbeth Seizing the Daggers*, 1812.

he probably worked on, we know very little, like *Edmund Ironside* and so on, that were worked over by him. He was always coming to material, basing much of what he said and wrote *Holinshed's Chronicles*[3] and building it up into new tabernacles of force and ecstasy and energy. This is particularly seen in the patriotic plays, quintessentially *Henry V.*

Henry V—which was made into a famous wartime propaganda film in 1940–41 at the behest of Winston Churchill with Laurence Olivier in the lead, a magnificent sort of traditional British cinema film, seen in its own terms—is a quintessential play of English radicalism and patriotic forethought. It's a statement of warlike intensity where these Norman nobles war back upon the France from which they ultimately came to seize large chunks of it for England and to force a union between the English and French royal houses. It's a play which to this day is nakedly patriotic in its feel and which many liberals internally dislike as a consequence.

William Hazlitt, the well-known liberal writer of the early part of the nineteenth century, wrote a debunking essay about *Henry V* along these lines. Ezra Pound responded to that in a different spirit, for example, in the twentieth century about one hundred years on.

Now, in all of this it's important to remember that Shakespeare had a cosmology and a feeling of life. The Elizabethans believed that there were static globes or spheres above us ascending to the heavens and to God. They also believed that life was classical and proportioned in a way that we, thinking about physical processes of pure energy, don't really believe the world—biologically or otherwise—now to be.

They also believed that not only was man God's creature, but he was at the center of everything, and at the center of life on this earth was England, which is why Shakespeare internalizes the idea that the Elizabethan monarchy and its culture had moved away from the Papacy and from Roman Catholicism.

---

[3] *Holinshed's Chronicles of England, Scotland, and Ireland* (1577; second ed., 1587) is a three-volume, multi-author history of the British Isles.

The real point about having a Christian religiosity, or *any* religiosity for ourselves in these islands at Shakespeare's time, was to have a national version of the European culture. This is the foundation point culturally of the British state before it goes out to the world, in the Empire, which will become the largest empire that the world has seen since Rome up to the present time. That empire only really begins to die fifty years ago in our society, in the lifetimes of some of the people reading this text.

Now we have a situation where liberal ideas have come in over the last fifty to sixty years and, in turn, have retrospectively reoriented everything and see everything in their own terms and in accordance with their own lights.

Othello is seen as a tragic and romantic hero who doesn't point out the dangers of race-mixing but is, in a strange way, a validation of that which was once decried.

Titus Andronicus is seen as a pithy comment in a supererogatory way on the nature of the revenge tragedy, upending it, producing so many bodies, and having so much militancy of blood and struggle that there's a degree to which the whole thing becomes a bit of a joke and can be considered as such and is treated as a bit of a sadist ballet by people like Brook in his well-known version of it with Olivier forty-plus years ago.

We have a situation where the *Taming of the Shrew* is considered to be a "reactionary" play and is played up to the hilt in order to demarcate our present feelings of feminism and sexual egalitarianism in relation to that which once was.

We have a situation where some of the battle scenes in *Julius Caesar* are considered so far back that they don't need to be considered seriously in relation to contemporary violence and slaughter.

We have a play or, in this case, a long poem which is dramatic and theatrical but is still a poem — *The Rape of Lucrece* — which can never really be viewed without irony because you have a member of the Roman aristocracy who is raped by a dissolute individual descended from the royal House of Tarquin, which was the key early monarchy in Rome before it became an aristocratic republic. And she is raped and done down, and her husband avenges the rape by killing the rapist, namely Tarquin-ius. But at the same time, she, dishonored, kills herself because of the cult, not of the virgin, but of the marital virgin, in other words, of the woman who only gives herself to one man within marriage.

Now, this is really, and has been regarded for the last two-hundred-fifty years, never mind the last fifty years, in increasingly liberal ideas, as a ridiculous notion which moderns, so to say, can't really get their heads around. There was a famous painting of this incident by Tintoretto[4] whereby Lucrece is raped by Tarquin, or you begin to see the early stages of that. Benjamin Britten made a chamber opera of these very events and of certain textual elements of Shakespeare's work in the 1950s, halfway through the cycle of operas which for him was to end with *Billy Budd*, which is based on a novella by Herman Melville.

Now, Shakespeare brings to bear in all of this and in all of the plays which we haven't even mentioned. Even though we've been through *Othello* and *Macbeth* and *Lear* and *Titus Andronicus*, and we've looked the *Rape of Lucrece* and other works. Shakespeare brings to bear the entire weight of a culture which is animated through him and in him and in his language. Most people find the language, at times, when they first confront it, a bit of a bar or something that they have to leap over. But, in actual fact, the language is the key to the nature of the entire work. Even Trevor Nunn, whom I've criticized for certain of his PC variants of Shakespeare's dramaturgy when he was head of the National Theatre in the mid-to-late eighties and the early 1990s said, "In the end, all you have is the text." An unusual source for it, but Steven Berkoff said much the same in relation to *Macbeth*.

You can pare away everything. You can have even a minimalist set. You don't have to play in Elizabethan period *à-la* the Globe, but you can have the text before you semiotically as a living document because of its *power*, because of its magic, because of the almost incantatory nature of the language which is used. It's a special type of language. It's called technically iambic pentameter. This is the register in which he wrote. But it is designed to heighten experience and to distil emotion and to make of it

---

[4] Tintoretto (Jacopo Robusti, 1518–1594), *Tarquin and Lucrece*, 1578.

blood and bone poetry that speaks to us and to our race and to all people for all time.

Language is key to all meaning in Shakespeare. Let's have a look at certain key passages, certain dramatic moments and aporia within some of the plays that I've mentioned so far.

Now is the winter of our discontent
Made glorious summer by this sun of York;
And all the clouds that lour'd upon our house
In the deep bosom of the ocean buried.
Now are our brows bound with victorious wreaths;
Our bruised arms hung up for monuments;
Our stern alarums changed to merry meetings,
Our dreadful marches to delightful measures.
Grim-visaged war hath smooth'd his wrinkled front;
And now, instead of mounting barded steeds
To fright the souls of fearful adversaries,
He capers nimbly in a lady's chamber
To the lascivious pleasing of a lute.
But I, that am not shaped for sportive tricks,
Nor made to court an amorous looking-glass;
I, that am rudely stamp'd, and want love's majesty
To strut before a wanton ambling nymph;
I, that am curtail'd of this fair proportion,
Cheated of feature by dissembling nature,
Deformed, unfinish'd, sent before my time
Into this breathing world, scarce half made up,
And that so lamely and unfashionable
That dogs bark at me as I halt by them;
Why, I, in this weak piping time of peace,
Have no delight to pass away the time,
Unless to spy my shadow in the sun
And descant on mine own deformity:
And therefore, since I cannot prove a lover,
To entertain these fair well-spoken days,
I am determined to prove a villain
And hate the idle pleasures of these days.
Plots have I laid, inductions dangerous,

By drunken prophecies, libels and dreams,
To set my brother Clarence and the king
In deadly hate the one against the other:
And if King Edward be as true and just
As I am subtle, false and treacherous,
This day should Clarence closely be mew'd up,
About a prophecy, which says that "G"
Of Edward's heirs the murderer shall be.
Dive, thoughts, down to my soul: here
Clarence comes. (*Richard III*, act 1, scene 1)

In peace there's nothing so becomes a man
As modest stillness and humility:
But when the blast of war blows in our ears,
Then imitate the action of the tiger;
Stiffen the sinews, summon up the blood,
Disguise fair nature with hard-favour'd rage;
Then lend the eye a terrible aspect;
Let pry through the portage of the head
Like the brass cannon; let the brow o'erwhelm it
As fearfully as doth a galled rock
O'erhang and jutty his confounded base,
Swill'd with the wild and wasteful ocean.
Now set the teeth and stretch the nostril wide,
Hold hard the breath and bend up every spirit
To his full height. On, on, you noblest English.
Whose blood is fet from fathers of war-proof!
Fathers that, like so many Alexanders,
Have in these parts from morn till even fought
And sheathed their swords for lack of argument:
Dishonour not your mothers; now attest
That those whom you call'd fathers did beget you.
Be copy now to men of grosser blood,
And teach them how to war. And you, good yeoman,
Whose limbs were made in England, show us here
The mettle of your pasture; let us swear
That you are worth your breeding; which I doubt not;
For there is none of you so mean and base,

That hath not noble lustre in your eyes.
I see you stand like greyhounds in the slips,
Straining upon the start. The game's afoot:
Follow your spirit, and upon this charge
Cry "God for Harry, England, and Saint George!" (*Henry V*,
sct 3, scene 1)

This is from the *Rape of Lucrece*. This is after the deed:

To this well-painted piece is Lucrece come,
To find a face where all distress is stell'd.
Many she sees where cares have carved some,
But none where all distress and dolour dwell'd,
Till she despairing Hecuba beheld,
Staring on Priam's wounds with her old eyes,
Which bleeding under Pyrrhus' proud foot lies.

In her the painter had anatomized
Time's ruin, beauty's wreck, and grim care's reign:
Her cheeks with chaps and wrinkles were disguised;
Of what she was no semblance did remain:
Her blue blood changed to black in every vein,
Wanting the spring that those shrunk pipes had fed,
Show'd life imprison'd in a body dead.

On this sad shadow Lucrece spends her eyes,
And shapes her sorrow to the beldam's woes,
Who nothing wants to answer her but cries,
And bitter words to ban her cruel foes:
The painter was no god to lend her those;
And therefore Lucrece swears he did her wrong,
To give her so much grief and not a tongue.
"Poor instrument," quoth she, "without a sound,
I'll tune thy woes with my lamenting tongue;
And drop sweet balm in Priam's painted wound,
And rail on Pyrrhus that hath done him wrong;
And with my tears quench Troy that burns so long;
And with my knife scratch out the angry eyes

Of all the Greeks that are thine enemies.

"Show me the strumpet that began this stir,
That with my nails her beauty I may tear.
Thy heat of lust, fond Paris, did incur
This load of wrath that burning Troy doth bear:
Thy eye kindled the fire that burneth here;
And here in Troy, for trespass of thine eye,
The sire, the son, the dame, and daughter die."

Shakespeare is quintessentially English and British but belongs to all Western, white, and European people throughout the world. There's a great attempt now to dumb down everything and to place all things upon a cultural level. Shakespeare, amongst many other authors, stands out against this prevailing trend. But if we lose what he says across half a millennium to us, we will have lost a core, integral, linguistic and racial part of what it is to be English, to be British, to be white, to be European. His language isn't old or fustian and archaic or fuddy-duddy. It's immediate and strikes through to the hearts of men and women. In love, in hate, in war, in peace, in belief, in the absence of belief, to read Shakespeare is a revolutionary act in an age where people say we have no culture but the culture of globalism, and where all groups and all usages of language are deemed to be of equal merit.

Counter-Currents, December 19, 2014

EDWARD ELGAR*

We're here today to talk about Edward Elgar, the great composer of the English renaissance in modern music—by which I mean twentieth-century music. There's an enormous gap in our island's musicology between Elizabeth's time—when some major, largely Roman Catholic, polyphonic composers like William Byrd and Thomas Tallis and the first John Taverner[1] and Davenport[2] and others came to the fore—and Henry Purcell. Purcell lived in and around the time of the Great Fire of London from the restoration of the Stuart monarchy after the interregnum of Cromwell and the Civil War until the turn of the 1700s. He died, like John Keats, of tuberculosis, so it is essentially believed.

Purcell was a great genius of structure and order and composition and is described somewhat loosely as the English Mozart. Byrd and Tallis looked back through what for them was the modern idiom of polyphony to medieval plainsong and chant and high Christian Catholic music. We factor forward across two centuries basically, from 1700 to 1900, and there is not really an English composer of universal—never mind European—significance.

People come and go, and there are academic composers like Hubert Parry and so on towards the end of the nineteenth century, with whom Elgar was initially compared. But in actual fact, apart maybe from Arthur Sullivan's Irish Symphony in 1864, there is not too much to speak of. What fills the musical landscape of our society during those two hundred years is largely French and Italianate musical theatre and opera, which, paradoxically, had begun back under the culture of the Puritans in the English

---

* Transcript by Lee and Donna Hancock of Jonathan Bowden's talk on Edward Elgar, which you can listen to with musical examples at the Jonathan Bowden Archive, https://jonathanbowden.org/.

[1] There is only one John Taverner (c. 1490–1545), but he is often confused with John Tavener (minus one "r") (1944–2013).

[2] There is no English Renaissance composer named Davenport. Bowden may have confused John Dunstaple (c. 1390–1453) with Francis William Davenport (1847–1925).

Civil War where a lot of theatre, including Shakespeare, was banned. But musical performances which were non-liturgical and non-religious were allowed. Therefore, women with large busts and bodices and so on, would perform secular pieces on stage, completely at variance with many Puritan ideas, but as long as it wasn't religious it was okay. And that type of musical drama-turgy dominated our musical life for two hundred years. And the view grew up on the continent that during the great era of largely Germanic symphonies, defined principally by Mozart and by Beethoven, we'd reached a position in England where there really was no music that was at all interesting or of universal import to the European civilization. Certainly, any music that could be talked about was parochial.

Elgar completely redefines the nature of English music, Eng-lish classical music, and high art music of a British character. He's also not a lone genius because, partly opened up by his example, there come several generations of composers who contain indi-viduals like John Ireland, who was heavily influenced by him and Arnold Bax and Arthur Bliss, who wrote a lot of ballet scores, and eventually Benjamin Britten and Michael Tippett, despite his Left-wing views, and Harrison Birtwistle and William Mathias, a Welsh composer of largely choral works, many of them put on by the BBC Third program as it was. Sir Peter Maxwell Davies at the present day — who looks to postmodernity, but also to very early and even pre-Baroque musical styles to draw inspiration from, and then goes back up to the present day again to complete his cy-cle of eight symphonies and who lives up in the Orkney Islands — is a continuation of a tradition that really began with Elgar.

Elgar moves English people in a way that no other composer — certainly none of those that I've just mentioned — really does. He speaks emotionally and from the heart and subjectively to the im-pressionism of the English. There is something slightly magical and indefinable about his musicology, whether people are listen-ing to the imperialist sort of performances like "Land of Hope and Glory," like "Rule Britannia" orchestrated by him, like *Pomp and Circumstance*; whether they're listening to things to do with Vic-toria's jubilee; or whether they go much deeper into works like the first two finished symphonies or the third symphony which would be finished from impressionistic notes long after his death by a contemporary, middling, and rather academic composer;[3] or whether they're listening to *Cockaigne*; or whether they're listening to *The Kingdom*; or whether they're listening to the mysticism related to his own personal Catholic faith of *The Dream of Gerontius*, his music draws English people in, in a way that really words cannot define.

There's an interesting story that I'd like to share with you just for a moment that shows you the power of Elgar beyond all political and social affiliations as regards Englishness. Tony Banks is, in many ways, a very decadent and Left-wing politician who has just left the House of Commons saying he despises most of his constituents who happen to live in a part of east London called Newham. Sixty percent of them are black, so I don't know what that says about Banks' particular take on all that. But he was a very Left-wing member of the GLC[4] under Livingstone in the 1980s.

When Thatcher shut that local authority down for internal political reasons within the British establishment—she didn't like the way Livingstone was introducing taxes into London and so on, and was under business pressure to do so—the GLC on their final afternoon played Elgar throughout the three or four hours when the bailiffs were coming in to turf them out of what was then County Hall, which is now a private sector tower block.

And they played the *Enigma Variations*, and you had people like Banks who, in many ways, has been party to political and social programs and processes that have torn most of what this country once was down over the last thirty to forty to fifty years—and he's just one individual. But you have him in tears over the *Enigma Variations*, which represents the quintessence of Englishness. And you see the power even in the most unlikely places that this music has when it's particularly manifest in relation to

---

[3] Anthony Edward Payne (1936–2021).

[4] The Greater London Council, founded 1965 and dissolved in 1986 with the devolution of administrative powers to local boroughs. Ken Livingstone of the British Labour Party took up the post of Leader from 1981 until its dissolution.

our nationality.

There is something about the Worcestershire countryside; there is something about England, greenness and lushness and sweetness and harshness; there is something about the weather; there is something about the insularity both as a source of strength, of imaginativeness, of fairy-tale lights, of romantic and imaginative introspection, but also sentimentality, which is there in this man's music and which, really, is in no one else.

People like Purcell were great composers of the European type who happen to be English. But Elgar is a great English composer who is largely self-created because, unlike Vaughan Williams and unlike Bax, who draw on a lot of Celtic folklore — but both of them went back to folk traditions that pre-exist higher or classical forms of white or Indo-European or Aryan music — Elgar created out of his own person; he created for himself and in terms of his own deep emotional longing and desires. He also created in a very impressionistic way.

After a day's teaching, for example — because that's what he did to survive for most of his adult life — he would play on the piano. He would play in an almost sort of stream of consciousness and free association way. He would note things down, how certain conjunctions of the diatonic register, certain forms of tonal composition, would work. He'd play them over to the wife again and note more down. He'd go away and stick things to the backs of chairs in his study and so on and see that there would be an overlap between that piece over there and this bit over here, and, gradually, the texture of a larger work would be built up step-by-step organically, almost like pottering about your garden essentially in terms of his mental musicianship.

He was a very good violinist, a very good cello player when he was young. He didn't really master any other instruments, but he became a major conductor of his own and other music, because British music was beginning to burgeon then, as I've already mentioned, towards the end of his life. He also hired many individual virtuosi and people who could actually play many of his pieces. It's important to realize that there were several Elgars and that in many respects he was a very private man. His Tory, indeed, ultra-Tory politics and imperial manner and "Blimpishness" together with figures like Conan Doyle, Kipling, and Rider Haggard and so on, many of whom in that Edwardian and Victorian era he was deeply, personally associated with and were friends of his, can give people the wrong impression about him.

There is a certain Leftist distaste for Elgar or for the politics of imperialism, with which he began—Victoriana, with which he can be associated. But at the end of the day, he was a radical rather than a purely conservative, in the sense of restorationist, figure. He's a man who wanted to bring forward a deep, romantic sensibility and articulate it through an individual vision of genius.

Now "genius" is a concept itself which is unfashionable today, as is beauty, but Elgar believed in both. But true to a lot of English and British visual art, personhood and individual character—character above all—was supremely important. Elgar was, in many peoples' minds, whether bohemian or otherwise, an eccentric. Amongst anglers, amongst people who like to row, amongst people who like to cycle in the countryside around where he lived, there's a degree to which even amongst these rather more conventional and slightly staid, inartistic types he always stood out as a bit of an eccentric. Whereas amongst the artists he often brought to them the manner of the Victorian drawing room and the imperialist granduncle. So he existed as a "straight" amongst the bohemians and an alternative person amongst people who were of a more conventional and bourgeois register.

Like all artists he existed between worlds, because the great point of an artistic sensibility is observation and analyzing life from without, because although his music is primarily about emotional sentiment, art is not a matter of sentiment. It's not about emoting or sentimentality. Art is a hard, ultimately, rather than a soft discourse. Deep down it's more objective than subjective. It's the objectification which is what art is about, creating objects out of emotion. Science is about the objects of the natural world, of that which can be ratiocinated from the front of the brain, whereas all artistic matters are about emotion and lie deep in the recesses of the back brain in particular. But there's a science of them, there's a logic to them, there's a knowledge of them and how the processes which connect with people's emotions and are translated into form actually work. And music of all forms—which in some ways is why it's always the most difficult to talk about in my view — is the form which is beyond all of the others because its language, its semiotic, is universal for human beings within and beyond race. It's almost the one art form that can impact on all minds and on all states of consciousness.

Apart from the completely tone-deaf and deaf from birth there's virtually nobody who cannot be moved by music. One pauses to think here that the greatest musician in the European classical tradition is Beethoven who was deaf for a significant proportion of his life and can hardly play properly towards the end, but the music was pure inside, and a lot of it was done by sight in terms of actual reading and close reading of the score. There are musicians to this day who actually relate more to the eye and the text, if you like — they're textualists — rather than the ear, although for nearly everyone, of course, who works in the area it's a combination of the two.

Now, Elgar epitomizes certain forms of Englishness which, for a long time, stood rejected at the heart of the continental culture. English music, even its revival, through Bax, through Bliss, through Vaughan Williams, through Ireland, through Tippett, through Britten, through Britten's operas via Elgar, even looking back to people like Sullivan and Parry and so on, and forward to modernists of a certain moment like Birtwistle and not Mathias, but certainly Sir Maxwell Davies. Despite all of these and despite the recognition that continental musicology has given to them, and large books by Germanic critics like Ernst Naumann and others that have now been written about English music in the twentieth century, there is still this slight belittling of English musicology in continental sensibility, this sort of view that it's all a bit Leonard Constant Lambert and a bit more, that it's too saccharine, and it's too sweet, that it lacks Germanic rigor and harshness, if you like, in these great architectural cathedrals of sound that someone like Bruckner creates, or pure concern with form or the expression of very lurid and over-the-top operatic emotion, that somehow there's a certain quaintness to it, a certain shyness, a certain internal privacy, a certain softness and sweetness. This is, at times, a continental view of English music.

But this music that is Elgar's — which is, racially speaking, a combination of Germanic and Celtic strands musically, within one particular personality — creates a feeling that English people respond to with deep sonorousness in joy and in sadness. And there is certainly joy and power and pageantry in Elgar's music. But there's also sadness as well. Because reading the life closely and with an eye upon the text you can really sense that there's a bit of a sine curve in Elgar's personality, and there are deep troughs as well as there are great ecstasies.

There is the fact that after a major period of creation like the second symphony, he needed to rest up and couldn't do very much creating for a quite long time. After his wife died, I think in 1920 or thereabouts, there's a great falling away. And apart from occasional pieces — an unfinished opera I think based on King Henry VIII — until his death, there wasn't too much done. Elgar also realized that after the Great War there had been a high point of what critics would call jingoistic patriotism with which he had become partly associated, let's be frank. And there was a great falling away of interest in his music during the 1920s. Although no one, even his detractors, would say that he wasn't actually very, very significant.

One piece that I would like to talk about in particular is *The Dream of Gerontius*, which is based upon a personal impression of Elgar's religious ideas. His Roman Catholicism has never really been pushed that much, although no one's particularly shied away from it in relation to his own specific biography. But it was there, and in an artistic way it was reasonably central to his life. His Catholicism had very little to do — if not nothing to do — with sectarianism. But what it was, was a personal religious tradition of transcendence, of the belief that you go beyond the body completely, which can lead in that theology to a disrespect for the body.

Now, *The Dream of Gerontius* is based upon a poem by Cardinal Newman, who was an important convert from the high Anglican Church to the Roman Catholic Church in England in the middle of the Victorian period, indeed the high Victorian period. He led a movement out of the clerisy of Oxford University at the time called first the Oxford Movement and then the Tractarians. To many people this is rather dry and archival and archaeological material, so to speak. But in the Victorian period for somebody important or for a group of people led by Newman to convert from the Anglican dispensation, which has now largely collapsed in our culture. Let's face it, who listens to Rowan Williams now? For them to go over from that to Rome was an earthquake. It was a decisive change, and it set people wondering what was happening to English Protestantism, so to say, in the nineteenth century.

The most mystical poem of a high Gerard Manley Hopkins type that Newman wrote was *The Dream of Gerontius,* upon which Elgar bases his particular work. There's an interesting metaphoricization of this piece in the Elgar Museum, which is a private sector museum based near Worcester. They're very odd there, if you want to film about all this. You've got to pay quite a lot to go in there and so on and so forth. We went around the cottage where he was born which is turned into a museum.

But an American contemporary sculptor, modern but traditional in casting, has done a metaphoric vision in stone,[5] three dimensionally obviously, of *The Dream of Gerontius,* and there's a figure, which is the soul, leaving the corpse, leaving the body after death. And none of us knows what happens technically when a body dies, but there's a certain energy which is obviously in it goes. Because a cadaver is just an inanimate object whereas anything that has organic life in it is so qualitatively different to that which doesn't, that something is there that's gone. The big question, of course, is where and what energy there has gone.

But in this particular relief the energy is going up out of the body. There are various sorts of devilish, satanic creatures reminiscent of Hieronymus Bosch and so on clawing around the bottom or the pedestal of the sculpture, trying to drag the spirit down into matter, into the present day, into the somatic, into the bodily. And there are angels, or angelic figures of some description — because it's not an explicitly Christian sculpture actually — moving the spirit upwards and outwards and towards the light.

And Elgar is always concerned with, if you like, certainly in this piece, a certain lightness and a certain delicacy of touch;

---

[5] Jeffrey Rouse, *The Dream of Gerontius.* Bowden mistakenly refers to it as being a stone relief, but it is actually bronze.

strength with delicacy; music related in some way to the spirit of dance, although he never really explicitly wrote for the dance the way Bliss did with pieces like *Checkmate* later on, now which have been revived towards the end of the twentieth century by Sir Vernon Handley and his influence at Liverpool Philharmonic, for example.

I see Elgar as essentially a deeply individuated and traditional artist who is subjective, emotional, sweet-tempered, slightly melancholic, very, very English, and concerned primarily with transcendence. But there are also great moments of joy and that martial patriotism that the English have and which is a sort of pageantry. I've always been struck by elements of English nationalism within the British context and how they differentiate it from how the more Celtic parts of the British peoples, such as the Irish, the Scottish, and the Welsh, evince their own national feeling. There is in the English a slight softening or understatement of a more radical position and the need emotionally to express a radical feeling of patriotism and self-regard by using perhaps slightly softer tones and terms.

And this is why, in comparison to very militant expressions of national feeling, English people can stand to attention to things with tears in their eyes and tears streaming down their faces and with extreme emotion — and, sometimes, with very held-in violence as well — that relates to these types of emotional forms that touch them very, very deeply and very much at the heart. It is that sort of belief that you can do an extraordinary thing and you don't really necessarily want to be praised too much for it, at least in public afterwards. It's that slight diffidence in the expression of that which otherwise would be radical which characterizes partly the depth of Elgar's music, partly the fact that it's a certain English sensibility unmasked, and there are certain cultural criticisms of the English viewed outside in that see ourselves, see the English people, as in part wearing a mask. Elgar's music is the emotional expressiveness of the English people unrepressed and without a mask, with deep sonority relating to private and yet personal experiences of a general and generic character. It is also expressive of the European civilization in high art music, but it is totally concentrated in the sensibility of these islands.

You can also hear a voice—a musical voice and a musical personality—coming out of this music from first to last. And when BBC Radio 3 in alliance with the Proms at the Royal Albert Hall produced the third symphony which is made up from scraps—absolute scraps and notes chucked about his study basically and pasted together by essentially an academic musicologist—immediately people realized it was him living again almost a century later, certainly seventy years later. And that voice, that sensibility, that sureness of note and pitch and tone came through yet again. And although maybe the "third symphony" has had much less impact than the first two, never mind the *Enigma Variations*, never mind *The Dream of Gerontius*, never mind the personal and impressionistic motifs based upon his friends like Jaeger[6] and, later on, the composer Richter[7] who took him up . . . Notice again the Germanic influence that, although understanding the difference between the English and the Germanic, nevertheless cleaved to the English voice which was new and original and put the music of England and, later, Britain in its entirety back upon the map of European civilization two-hundred years after the death of Henry Purcell.

Counter-Currents, November 11, 2014

---

[6] August Johannes Jaeger (1860–1909), to whom the Nimrod movement of the *Enigma Variations* was dedicated.

[7] Hans (Johann) Richter (1843–1916).

BRITISH SCULPTURE*

Welcome to this brief film about English and British sculpture.

STONEHENGE

Let's begin right at the beginning with something which can't really entirely be described as a sculpture, but it's Stonehenge, an enormous and a sort of semi-celestial monument the better part of four thousand years old.

Grim, chthonian, profound, a pagan cathedral, freestanding. The Christianity of two thousand years left it alone, and in a strange way the English and British monumental tradition in stone begins with this piece. There's an extraordinary leap as well across the better part of four millennia to modernist sculpture which, Henry Moore-like, epitomizes the primitive and the fierce and the primeval and even the tribal.

So, let's begin this analysis of what we have done three-dimensionally in the arts with the first cathedral that has come down to us on these islands from the ancient world.

THE TORRS PONY-CAP[1]

Here we move on in time to a Celtic horse-mask from southern Scotland circa 200 B.C. or thereabouts. Slightly dented now as it comes down to us, pre-Germanic in feel, ancient Celtic. The symbolism of snakes, almost, and swirls and that patterning that Celtic art so beloves. Obviously, it's an item that comes from the battlefield and is essentially a piece of armor to protect a horse or to signify the power of a horse. In it we see something of pre-

---

* Transcript by V. S. and Buttercup Dew of a video documentary by Jonathan Bowden, which can be seen at the Jonathan Bowden Archive (https://jonathanbowden.org/) in both the original version and one with much improved images edited by Buttercup Dew. The headings are editorial insertions.

[1] The Torrs Pony-Cap was found between 1820 and 1829 in the county of Kirkcudbrightshire, Scotland. The original image Bowden presents is missing the horns found with it.

Germanic Britain, of a Britain that is yet to be influenced by Romans or people of Germanic ancestry. A Britishness that is differentiated in terms of how we perceive it the better part of two thousand years on.

Many of these items, small and large, particularly coins, have come down to us, often elongated, often with slightly surreal shapes. Celtic craftsmen weren't interested in realism, and their art was essentially not abstract but mystagogic and followed from the nature of their legends and their myths.

GORGON FROM THE TEMPLE OF SULIS MINERVA, BATH

Here we move forward to the influence of the Roman civilization on the British Isles. This is a particularly British interpretation of a classical legend. It's the head of a medusa, the snakes as hair swirling around the actual physiognomy of the piece. Yet this piece is not really Italianate. It's not that classical in feel. It's very British and even English. It was found in Bath in the West Country, and it comes to look, to my mind, as a sort of heavy piece: solemn, fiercely etched, non-classical in its lineaments, a sort of transliteration of Romanesque art into British terms. We've taken their material and interpreted it in accordance with our craftsmen, and you can leap forward almost to the images on the outside of steeples in the Middle Ages from this type of art. Fierce, slightly primitive: you can almost sense an Italian of the era would wince. But we've taken it into ourselves and made something different out of it.

ROMANO-CELTIC HEAD FROM THE BON MARCHÉ SITE, GLOUCESTER (LEFT)[2] & HEAD OF ANTENOCITICUS (RIGHT)[3]

Here we have something in the same era. A British variation on a Roman theme. Two images for the price of one. One of them extraordinarily modernist looking. The one on the left as you look at it could almost be a piece by Elisabeth Frink, say, from the

---

[2] Romano-Celtic head statue, first century CE, found at the Bon Marché site in Gloucester.

[3] Stone head of Antenociticus, second century CE, found near Condercum in Benwell, west Newcastle upon Tyne.

middle of the twentieth century.[4] But again these are British takes on Roman ideas about their gods, one from Gloucester and the other from Northumberland. One thing you will notice about them is their heaviness, their three-dimensionality, their earthy solidity. There's a certain absence of classical lightness, but there's an ur-primeval and deeper consciousness, a more Northwestern European consciousness not a Southern European one. Again, we've taken Roman cultural archetypes, motifs, and forms into ourselves, and our craftsmen have obeyed their Roman masters, but in a sense, they have produced something which is irredeemably British.

RUTHWELL CROSS[5]

Here we have a Northumbrian Christian cross leaping nine centuries forward from the last exhibit. Very Christian, slightly Romanesque, smallish figures outlined in semi-relief against the texture of the cross as it goes up. To my mind, there still seems to be certain pre-Christian iconographic elements to the piece. The thing that strikes me though is that differentiated from the Celtic art that we looked at before, but very much in spirit with the more Roman art that we evaluated a moment previous to this, there's a solidity to the piece, a strength, an insularity, and a grandeur which goes through all British three-dimensional art whether Celtic, Romanesque, Christian, explicitly pagan, Restorationist, modernistic. This sense not of heaviness, but of the gentility of strength and of a sort of residential power to three-dimensional space.

CHRIST FROM ROMSEY ABBEY[6]

Here, moving on in time, we sense a Saxon and an explicitly Germanic influence in Christian English art, as we can now call it. The sculpture is still embedded on a wall, on a plane. It's part-

---

[4] Elisabeth Frink (1930–1993), known for modernist figure and portrait sculpture.

[5] The Ruthwell Cross, probably dating from the seventh century, in the village of Ruthwell, Scotland.

[6] Eleventh-century carving at Romsey Abbey.

ly relief, but as you can see from its three-dimensionality, the figure of the crucified Christ wants to come out of the wall and is almost, one could say fifty percent, three-dimensional. It's not going to take too much for it to burst out of the wall, off the cross, and be a configured figure in its own right. Again we see not just a Christian influence ideologically and theologically but that element of profundity and heaviness and truth to materials and prior solidity which I believe is a quintessential part of English and British three-dimensional form. It's interesting that these things remain extant no matter the change in historical period or the overlying culture. We pass from a primeval paganism to a Celtic influence to an influence of imperial Rome to an influence of early Middle Ages Christianity, and yet some of the abiding ethnic themes that lie behind the delineation of three-dimensional art remain the same.

QUEEN ELEANOR OF CASTILE[7]

Here we move slightly forward in time to an extraordinary image which could be said to be the beginning of the high art sculptural tradition in England as it has come down to us as it will be interpreted by critics like William Orpen[8] in the early part of the twentieth century just gone. This dates from 1290 and is an effigy made by William Torell. One of his first ones, a life-size bronze, it's an extraordinary piece. Imagine that it's incredibly heavy, highly wrought, the full length of a man's course, metallic, powerful. But again you have amidst the finery and appurtenances of the form a strength, a physical power, a solidity even in repose. Ideologically, it's supposed to show the redemption of a Christian and knightly grace in death. But I think it very much relates too in its three-dimensionality many of the images that we've seen before. So powerful even in its metallic form that it survived the better part of a thousand years and will probably

[7] William Torell (fl. 1291–1303), Tomb Effigy of Queen Eleanor of Castile (1241–1290), Queen of England as the first wife of Edward I (1239–1307), Westminster Abbey.

[8] William Orpen (1878–1931) was a popular and successful portrait artist and prolific war artist during the First World War. It is unclear what critique or critical work Bowden is referring to.

be extant a thousand years from now. This is the bringing together of stoicism in form, grace, solidity as to material, truth to materials (to use a modern slogan), and the quiet power of the English three-dimensional tradition.

KING RICHARD II[9]

Here we have an image in bronze again, highly weathered, of Richard II, the subject of a Shakespeare play. Again, very much seen in a Christian vogue, a Christian knightly monarch looking slightly meek and humble, how you were supposed to look in the era. Very strongly three-dimensional. Good line. Powerful, squat nature of the features and upper shoulders. He's depicted slightly as an apostle. But again these are part of the conventions of the period. But again we return to this theme of compactness, stoicism, truth to material, and solidity. In all of English and, to a slightly lesser extent, British sculpture there is this deep, quiet, and reverberating sense of power in the depiction of the face, the upper body, or the entire frame.

THE RESURRECTED CHRIST[10]

Here we have an image from the fourteenth century from Cambridgeshire from a provincial church. It strikes me as a very Germanic image, this one, almost completely three-dimensional, but with a certain element of relief. But the relief becomes ever more studied, ever more withdrawn. The figures are bursting through into three-dimensionality. This is a scene of the ascent of the Christ after death after the resurrection. He appears both as a victim and as a monarch or celestial king. The Roman soldiers, who actually look like Medieval warriors of the time because those are the forms or archetypes upon which the anonymous sculptor is drawing, fall back in amazement and consternation before this risen being, who's almost sort of walking out

---

[9] Nicholas Broker (c. 1350–1426) and Godrey Prest (fl. 1377–1395), Tomb Effigy of Richard II (1367–1400), Westminster Abbey.

[10] This polychrome alabaster panel depicts Christ with a crown of thorns stepping on a Roman soldier (in thirteenth-century English armor) as he exits the tomb.

of the relief to what is perceived to be a semblance of glory.

JULIUS CAESAR[11]

Here we have a terracotta from the 1510s. It doesn't really relate to pure English art that much, but what we see here is an
opening out in the Tudor period to continental influence. So,
we're dealing with a sort of re-Europeanization or a return of the
sculpture of the ancient world in the form of a bust relating to
Julius Caesar.[12] But it's the opening to intellectual ideas on the
continent. And although you could say that in the Middle Ages
we internalized lots of continental ideas, here are Italian sculptors coming over at the behest of the court structures of the day
to bring High Renaissance material within the purview of the
English tradition. And from now on we see a mixing of what
existed before and the high art of the Renaissance coming over
to Britain and England in order to curry its trade. We see a sort
of fusion of various European styles as the whole of the European civilization is beginning to wean itself away from the Middle
Ages, and it's beginning to look towards the creation of early
modern Europe. You have this sensibility which grows up during this century and the one to come after it which involves a
gradual de-Christianization, a return of the Classical in various
dimensions — this is the classicism of the ancient world — and a
slight mobility and a loosening of the rigid forms of Medieval
and post-Medieval art.

WOODEN SCREEN

Here we have another example of the High Renaissance. It's
the lightish spirit of Michelangelo come over to England,
hopped over, and in wood. It's from King's College Chapel in
Cambridge, forcing house and academic stamping ground of the
upper-class elite of the time, of course. Again, it's the belief in all
things Italian and Renaissance in spirit and style in stone, in

---

[11] Giovanni da Maiano (c. 1486–c. 1542), Terracotta Roundel of Julius Caesar, Hampton Court Palace, commissioned in the late 1510s.

[12] Bowden characterizes him as "the Roman Emperor and once
conqueror of Britain." Caesar was never Emperor. He beat the Brit-
tonic army but did not occupy Britain.

bronze, in wood, in jewelry, in literature, and elsewhere. So, we're taking during this period whole handfuls of Renaissance sensibility from the southern part of Europe and bringing it across and internalizing it as part of the national tradition.

Now, what's really happening here is two things: we're opening up to a humanism which is European; we're opening up to certain post-Christian sensibilities; and yet at the same time we're going back to certain of the conceits and styles of the ancient world. But we don't know entirely what they were, so we are stylizing what we imagine the ancient craftsmen did in bas relief, in two dimensions, in three dimensions, and we're bringing it forward several thousand years as Christianity begins to loosen its hold on the European imagination and we connect via Southern Europe and its cultural influences with the classical world.

THE WRIOTHESLEY MONUMENT[13]

Here we see a major sculpture from 1592 by Gerard Johnson the Elder. The tradition is well advanced now. This sculpture deals with death, of course, and an enormous amount of monumental masonry and three-dimensional sculpture deals with the relief of death both inside and outside Christianity. The power and solemnity of the tomb or mausoleum, the desire to incarnate oneself as a living corpse after death, the power of a provincial noble family to be seen for the entire community possibly for hundreds of years. This is the Southampton tomb at Titchfield. And yet it's also of a very important patron in the history of English art.

This is the Third Earl of Southampton, who was Shakespeare's patron.[14] The arts in all eras have to obtain money be-

---

[13] Gerard Johnson the Elder, formerly Gheerart Janssen, Dutch sculptor and mason who emigrated to England from Amsterdam (fl. 1568, d. 1611), The Wriothesley Monument, 1592, St. Peter's Church, Titchfield. This is the tomb effigy of Henry Wriothesley (1545–1581), Second Earl of Southampton, with that of his mother Jane Cheney (1509–1574). On the far side, unseen, is a third effigy of Thomas Wriothesley (1505–1550), his father, the First Earl of Southampton.

[14] Henry Wriothesley (1573–1624), the Third Earl of Southampton,

cause they can't finance themselves in a completely freestanding way. In this era, aristocrats and very rich individuals from the upper class would give money and be seen to give money to the arts as part of an organic tradition.

But they always had a certain element of self-interest, and they always wanted their family, such as through the vehicle of a tomb like this, to be the recipients of their largesse. So, the money is given. An enormous tomb of massive monumentality is built to a local dignitary. And you can sense the power in this church. Not only is it very big, very tall, very solid. There are these spear-like menhirs on the four corners of the tomb that make these stone corpses in state look like images from ancient Egypt almost. It's a sort of grandiloquence and power of an aristocracy that had life and death powers over the rest of society, brooked no word against them, and were totally in charge. It's also the sign of a ruling group that is completely self-confident in this world and what they presume will be the next.

GREAT FIRE OF LONDON MONUMENT[15]

This is another piece, a relief but yearning and striving in its stone-like quality for three-dimensionality. This is by a grave sculptor, Caius Gabriel Cibber, a Dane, who did an enormous amount of work during this Baroque, Augustin, and allegorical period. This is a truly sort of eighteenth-century version of a classical conceit as they attempt to realize it. Charles II pleads on behalf of art and science and the Muses to restore a damaged London which has been ravaged by fire and destruction. It's a sort of heroic, post-Renaissance painting in stone. Everyone's highly idealized; everyone's outward-looking; everyone's made to look as noble as possible.

Cibber, in turn, was an extraordinary sculptor, who's quite famous now for influencing some modernist sculptors, because

---

was indeed interred within this tomb, though there is no effigy of him. He appears as the kneeling figure on the right panel beneath his father.

[15] Caius Gabriel Cibber (1630–1700), sculpture on the west panel of the pedestal of the Great Fire of London Monument facing Fish Street Hill. The monument and sculpture were constructed from 1671–1677.

two of his most famous pieces are the grotesque and gibbering figures outside of what used to be Bedlam Hospital in South London. One's called *Melancholy* and the other is called *Raving Madness*. They're interesting grotesques that partly relate to Medieval art, and now are still there outside the entrance to the Imperial War Museum.[16]

THE CONVERSION OF ST. PAUL[17]

Here we have a relief, again very solid in its two-to-three-dimensionality, from St. Paul's Cathedral. It shows a biblical scene, the conversion of St. Paul or Saul who sees the divine light. On the road to Damascus he's thrown from his horse, and the persecutor of the Christians becomes the founder of Christ's church. And yet in a strange way, to my mind, the Baroque or post-Baroque and highly individualized sensibility of the piece doesn't have that much to do with Christianity. It's a typically post-Renaissance work whereby Christian discourse and narrative and heritage are used as the model on which you do a modern version of a classical sculpture. So, we've got the horsemen rearing up being thrown from their mounts, the divine sun coming down from the clouds, and all of these Israelites, as it were, are depicted like warriors from the ancient world who are mysteriously wearing armor and carrying weapons that are from the beginning of the eighteenth century. This dates from 1706, and it's by Francis Bird, who's a very famous sculptor of the period, who did an enormous amount of work in and around St. Paul's.

Probably the modern sensibility would find his version of the Duke of Newcastle in that cathedral to be the most interesting of his works. This is a savage and rather grotesque piece in the form of a large sculptural tomb in which two skeletons tear apart the bottom end of an oak tree.[18]

---

[16] They are now on permanent display at Bethlem Museum of the Mind, Bethlem Royal Hospital, Beckenham, Kent.

[17] Francis Bird (1667–1731), *Conversion of Saul*, 1706, St. Paul's Cathedral.

[18] Actually a memorial to Elizabeth Benson (d. 1710) at St. Leonard's in Shoreditch by Francis Bird. Although Bird did do the tomb effigy sculpture of the Duke of Newcastle, it is not what Bowden is

QUEEN VICTORIA AS A CHILD[19]

Here we move forward a little bit in time, but the vogue in the sensibility is still very much the same. This, believe it or not, is a bust of the then Princess and later Queen Victoria. It's from the collection at Windsor Castle and dates from 1829 by William Behnes. You notice the young Victoria is depicted much like the present queen's painting by Pietro Annigoni[20] as a sort of exultant and superbly modeled being, and she looks like the young daughter of a Roman senator. But this is very much the way in which the English and British nobility wished to be perceived at that time. A certain sort of yearning and sort of expectant and transcendent quality.

These busts were done for almost anyone of renown at the time, and they would have been done in her case by Royal commission and for such patronage. Although we've leapt from the beginning of the 1700s to the early section of the century that follows, you notice that this type of work is all of a piece, and there is a contiguous nature to English and British sculpture between the Restoration in 1660 and, say, the Great Reform Bill in 1867.

You can virtually say the sensibility that masters the sculpture of this period straddling over a century and a half is the same sensibility. It's pre-Romantic; it's Augustin; it's highly classical. And it's a light, stylized early Michelangelo-driven interpretation of what the sculpture of the ancient world would have been like. There are many, of course, falsities and discontinuities because ancient sculpture was highly decorative and painted. We see it without paint, because all the paint has rotted off. We see it as white stone or, on occasion, marble, but in actual fact when these images are recreated as they have been in the twentieth century by imagization techniques, particularly pioneered by the Victoria and Albert Museum, we get a totally different

---

thinking of or describing.

[19] William Behnes (1795–1864), *Queen Victoria, when Princess Victoria of Kent*, 1829.

[20] Pietro Annigoni (1910–1988), *Queen Elizabeth II*, 1955. Bowden is not referring to Annigoni's later portrait from 1969, which is significantly darker and more monumental.

idea of what ancient sculpture was. So, this is our idea of unpainted ancient sculpture thousands of years on in order to celebrate the then imperial British aristocracy.

THE COUNTESS OF BATH[21]

And here we have another piece of stylized and slightly Baroque classicism, although more stereotypically classical in its way. It's of an aristocrat, the Countess of Bath, and it's by Balthasar Burman. Again, it's this attempt to heroicize, through the revisualization of the ancient world, the aristocracy from the seventeenth, the eighteenth, and eventually the first half of the nineteenth century. So, you have this sensibility which you will see in churchyards and vicarages and churches in particular up and down the country whereby the nobility identifies themselves with the Christian tradition, with the classical tradition, the Greco-Roman and Hellenistic tradition, and wants to celebrate through patronage their power and solidity in stone.

SIR JOHN THORNYCROFT[22]

Here is another piece that relates to the style that I've just described. It, again, is of a provincial aristocrat or, at the very least, an august figure, Sir John Thornycroft. Whether he relates to Tory politicians with that name in the twentieth century, I've got no idea. This is by Andreas Carpentier. If you notice, the way in which this individual wants to be depicted, he looks as though he's a drunk associate of a poet like Catullus in ancient Rome, where he's lying on a bed or on the floor of a party making an allegedly witty remark, wearing a toga and an eighteenth-century wig! So, you see that people in vogue in their century wanted to be depicted as the heroes of the ancient world, particularly in literature and in the arts. So, it's partly a fantasy that these people had about themselves, but it's also part of the pow-

---

[21] Balthasar Burman (fl. 1674–1680), statue of Rachel Bourchier (1613–1680) The Countess of Bath, 1680, St. Peter's Church, Tawstock.

[22] Andrew Carpenter (Andries Carpentière or Charpentière) (1672–1737), Tomb of Sir John Thornycroft, St. Mary's Church, Bloxham, Oxfordshire.

er of the West.

In the middle of the twentieth century, a rather dissident American figure called Lawrence R. Brown, who was an engineer, wrote a book called *The Might of the West*,[23] and these people believed totally in the Western civilization and they believed in its domination and they believed in its civilizing mission. They believed it extended through from various incarnations in the ancient world. These were people who had no doubts about themselves, about their society, its extension imperially across the Earth, and the power of their own nationalities. They also saw themselves, Christian or otherwise, as the inheritors of the classical tradition. Full stop.

LADY FREDERICA STANHOPE[24]

In Augustin vogue, it's Lady Frederica Stanhope from Chevening in Kent, 1825. Slightly daring here, because she's actually feeding her young child, lying on her side in repose, although of course the sculpture is a tomb and is meant to imply death. But maternal expressions of any sentiments involving female sexuality would be permitted in this period. Don't forget we are slightly before what will become the high Victorian period. We have unnecessarily restrictive views about this time. We think this period was incredibly prudish and so on, when if you looked at its three-dimensional art you wouldn't actually draw that conclusion. The reason for this is the classicizing and Hellenistic tendencies which are so pronounced, so naked, almost literally so in this case. This sculpture is by Sir Francis Chantrey, and it, again, is part of this idealizing tendency in the aristocracy of the day to see themselves as the British equivalents of the leaders of the Roman Empire.

---

[23] Lawrence R. Brown, *The Might of the West* (New York: Ivan Obolensky Inc., 1963).

[24] Sir Francis Leggat Chantrey (1781–1841), Lady Frederica Stanhope, 1824, Stanhope Chantry at St. Botolph's, Chevening.

KING GEORGE III[25]

Here we have a bust, a sculpture from the same era. It's in Burlington House, which is in Piccadilly right in the center of London and which today is the center of the Royal Academy. Although technically private, you could regard the Academy as the leading state art institution, The National Gallery excepted, in Britain. The piece is of George III, dates from the 1770s, and is by an Italian artist and sculptor, Agostino Carlini. In the sort of somber magnificence of this truculent German who wants to be seen as a sort of Augustus really, a sort of modern Roman emperor. Wearing a toga, of course, which people in his era didn't really wear. Looking solemn, looking fierce, looking statesman-like if rather sober-minded and sort of lugubrious. No signs of the putative insanity which would have him leaving the coach in Windsor Great Park and engaging in excited conversation with the oak trees.

WILLIAM WILBERFORCE[26]

Yes, here we have a major monumental piece of sculpture. Life-size, very biographical, very characterful. The classicizing and heroicizing elements are downplayed, and we have a certain representational portraiture in stone and, of course, in three dimensions. This is in Westminster Abbey, and it's of the reformer and anti-slave trader William Wilberforce. Now, this piece, which is very characterful and you can sense the liberal-minded Whiggish sentiments and sensibility of this very upper-class gentleman of his era, influenced by humanism, Enlightenment, and post-Renaissance ideas as well as the dawning of the high liberalism of the middle Victorian period, as well as extremely Christian sensibilities. Nevertheless, there are different ways of looking at Wilberforce, because many slave-owners of the time wanted to introduce a mass class of black slaves beneath the white proletariat in Britain. So, paradoxically, and in a rather revisionist vogue, it is possible to see Wilberforce as a

---

[25] Agostino Carlini (1718–1790), *Bust of George III*, 1773.
[26] Samuel Joseph (1791–1850), William Wilberforce (1759–1833), 1838, Westminster Abbey.

man who may not have wanted this, but he did preempt the creation of explicit multiracialism in Britain by maybe one-hundred-twenty-odd years before it actually began to get underway in the middle of the twentieth century.

VENUS[27]

Here we have very much a classical image from the same period, the late 1700s: *Venus Reclining on a Sea Monster with Cupid and a Putto* by John Deare. An aristocrat would have commissioned this. We see her stroking the head of a horse, a rather serpentine-looking horse. Again, quite an erotic piece, a nude. You're a philistine if you're against it.

A very important point here: in nearly all Indo-European or Aryan art there's a strong concentration on the body and on the physicality of the body and the sexual delineation of the body— it has to be said—particularly in three dimensions. This is very much the pre-Christian tradition of the Hellenes and of the ancient world.

This corporeal element, this purely bodily and physical element, is at the core of Western art and Western sensibility in complete contravention to the Islamic civilization, for instance, which completely disprivileges the depiction of the face, the hands, the body and believes that all corporeal images, whether the three- or two-dimensional, are non-transcendental and erotic and therefore are forbidden. Extreme forms of Orthodox Judaism, which disprivilege art, are the same. You see in this tradition a very strong element of core Western art. Strong enough even to resist some of the critical and censorious blandishments of Protestant Christianity.

TWO SLEEPING DOGS[28]

Yes, this is a slightly sentimental piece in mock classical vogue. It's by a female sculptress, Anne Seymour Damer. It's of the dogs. It's very Victorian in sentiment, if you like. It's a senti-

---

[27] John Deare (1759–1798), *Venus Reclining on a Sea Monster with Cupid and a Putto*, 1787/1788–1790.

[28] Anne Seymour Damer (1748–1828), *Two Sleeping Dogs*, 1782.

mental piece about two dogs. There's nothing really much more to say about it than that.

It does relate to the sort of art that Sir Edwin Landseer[29] produced in the middle of the Victorian period, and in sculptural terms Landseer did the lions in Trafalgar Square that face away from the column with Bailey's form of Nelson triumphant and heroic at the top of the column. The whole thing originally conceived by the architect/sculptural designer William Railton.[30]

ADMIRAL HOWE[31]

Yes, here we have a monumental piece in St. Paul's Cathedral by the famous sculptor, John Flaxman, best remembered now in art history as a close friend to William Blake, who was then very obscure. It's a heroic image of a British marshal and naval hero, but again you notice the overwhelming desire to classicize. Britannia is behind him with the trident. Various heroic maidens and sort of nymphs reach out to him in stone. It's an absolutely enormous piece. Imperial lions exist to one side looking slightly sleepy. This is the Earl Howe. You notice in its solidity and in its power and its monumentalism and its neo-classicism extreme imperial strength and total certainty. This is increasingly the sculpture of the nation-state that believes it's born to dominate the planet.

NARCISSUS[32]

Here we have a piece of high classicism or neo-classicism. It's in Flaxman's spirit. It's just on the cusp of the Victorian era in the 1830s. It's Narcissus as he stares down at a mirror or water, of course, in love with himself. A naked male. Highly Hellenistic and late Roman imperial. It's part of what will become the quintessential sculpture of the Victorian period as chronicled by a historian called William Gaunt, in his two-volume history called

---

[29] Sir Edwin Landseer (1802–1873).

[30] William Railton (1800–1877).

[31] John Flaxman (1755–1826), Admiral Howe (1726–1799), 1813.

[32] John Gibson (1790-1866), *Narcissus*, 1838.

Victorian Olympus.[33] This was very much the tendency that the middle to high Victorian period wanted to exemplify, particularly in what might be called establishment or top-down art. It was the belief that we are the inheritors of the Roman imperial tradition, that we were the new and the greatest empire since Rome, that we were increasingly coming during this period to dominate at best a quarter of the planet. This was the art reaching back two thousand, two thousand five hundred years to the classical dawn of our civilization.

It's also interesting to raise two cultural points here. The first is that this tradition sees Britain as the inheritor of the classical world without any equivocation. The imperial or neo-imperial role of the United States in the twentieth century and official American art, particularly from the early part of the nineteenth century, is very much still in this vogue. The art of Washington, D.C. today is this type of art. It's effortlessly imperial, not particularly Christian, and it's essentially neo-classical in an extreme manner. The other interesting thing to point out is that in the twentieth century, from a liberal perspective, this is the sort of art, certainly after the era of the Great War between 1914–1918, that will become associated with what will be regarded as totalitarian regimes of Left and Right.

LORD BOTETOURT[34]

Here is the extension of this type of classicism to the New World, but it could be anywhere in England, Scotland, or Wales. This is from 1775. It's a colonial piece from the southern United States, from the state of Virginia. This would obviously be of the master and slave-owner of the period. It would be emblematic of the Southern ruling aristocracy that would only go down in the

---

[33] Actually the last volume of a trilogy covering Victorian art movements by William Gaunt: *The Pre-Raphaelite Tragedy* (London: Jonathan Cape, 1942), *The Aesthetic Adventure* (London: Jonathan Cape, 1945) and *Victorian Olympus* (London: Jonathan Cape, 1952).

[34] Richard Haywood (1725–1800), Lord Botetourt (c. 1717–1770), 1773, Sir Christopher Wren Building, the College of William and Mary, Williamsburg, Virginia. The original has since been moved and replaced with a bronze replica.

1860s, that part of the century later in the Civil War. So, we've got a sculptor here called Richard Haywood, and you can see the monumentalism of the piece. It's at least life-size as you can see from the people who are transfigured in the background of the photograph. It's raised—almost like a Donatello Renaissance sculpture from the middle of the second Christian millennium—on high. This was the Hellenistic pose of white rule in the 1700s on both sides of the Atlantic.

SOPHIA THOMPSON[35]

Here we have a mausoleum. It's from the Victorian period by Peter Hollins. It's of Mrs. Thompson who's probably an upper bourgeois as much as an aristocratic figure. Maybe died slightly early in life and therefore the family paid for this enormous tomb in the local priory underneath some stained glass. The sculpture would be at least life-sized, and she's depicted in a neo-classical vogue lying on a bed which is actually her tomb where her corpse is. So, you see in this art the desire for resurrection of the body in accordance with high Anglican and post-Catholic sensibility. You also see the power of local powerful families. We're seeing a situation where it's not just the monarchy; it's not just the aristocracy; it's not just imperial rulers who think of themselves in this way, but it's major provincial families within England in their own areas and localities, squires and so on, who want to see their corpses and their memories of themselves and their wives done up as if they were the consorts of Roman Emperors.

SIR JACOB GERARD[36]

It's again from the middle of the 1700s. It celebrates provincial strength and aristocratic license. It's of Sir Jacob Gerard. It's

[35] Peter Hollins (1800–1886), Tomb Effigy of Sophia Thompson (1800–1886), 1838, Great Malvern Priory Church.

[36] Christopher Horsnaile the Elder (c. 1658–1742), Tomb Effigies of Sir Nicholas Garrard, 3rd Baronet (c. 1655–1728) (recumbent), behind him stand his father Sir Thomas Garrard, 2nd Baronet (1627–c. 1690) and grandfather Sir Jacob Garrard, 1st Baronet (1586–c. 1666), 1727, St. Andrew's Church, Langford Church, Norfolk.

from Norfolk in the east of England. Here we've got a sculptor who gives a rather solid classical and three-dimensional representation to a provincial aristocratic family. One is reclining and lying, presumably in death. Others adopt a Roman imperial pose around the near corpse. It's again part of this transfiguring desire to see people in a Romanesque and imperial manner completely out of keeping with the society in which they're living, but it's this desire to see themselves as the repository of the Roman imperial and Hellenistic culture of well over two thousand years before.

WILLIAM BECKFORD[37]

Here we have another life-sized piece. Very much in a classical vogue, but more after the realistic delineation of an eighteenth-century gentleman. This is actually of the Gothic writer, William Beckford, who wrote *Vathek*, which is an extreme horror story in sort of high art terms of its period. Quite militant, atheistic, sort of amoral. And he was a bit of a so-and-so. He's captured here as he would have liked to have been seen by both himself and doubtless his favorable contemporaries. This is from Ironmongers' Hall, and it's by Moore. Again, the importance of these pieces is their monumentality. This is life-size in stone.

GEORGE N. HARDINGE[38]

Here we have another classical piece from St. Paul's. Very sort of neo-classical in feel. Idealized. A strong element of narratives creeping into sculpture at this time. This is from 1808, right at the beginning of the nineteenth century. It celebrates probably

---

[37] John Francis Moore (d. 1809), Alderman William Beckford (1709–1770), 1767, Ironmongers' Hall, London. The statue is of William Beckford, Senior but Bowden mistakes him for his son, also named William Beckford, an art collector and novelist (1760–1844). This is not the piece in Guildhall, the City of London, also by J. F. Moore. The one Bowden refers to shows Beckford with his hand on a scroll. It was originally commissioned for and placed in Beckford's Fonthill Estate.

[38] Charles Manning (c. 1776–1812/1813), Monument to George N. Hardinge (1781–1808), 1808, St. Paul's Cathedral.

the death of a man in combat, maybe in the Napoleonic and French Revolutionary Wars of the period. An angel has come down and weeps upon his tomb. A shroud is sort of been put on one side. The man, or the sort of transubstantiation of his corpse reanimated in accordance with the Christian doctrine of second birth, looks out into the distance. You see strongly elitist, hierarchical, and storytelling concerns three-dimensionally in stone in one of our major cathedrals.

ELIZABETH CULPEPER[39]

Here we have another piece which is almost a lying-in state, really, but it's of another aristocratic female lying side on, probably in a priory or vicarage in Kent. It's again this desire to depict people in death in terms of classical and Christian relief. There's a certain heaviness to the piece. It's very English, very stolid. There's always been the view, particularly on the continent and by certain art critics, that English classicism doesn't work too well, because their comparison is always the Southern European tradition when in actual fact it's the same type of art, but it is a different version of it. It's one in which some of the four-square and stolid values of English self-determination and three-dimensionality come through. From the very beginning of the sculpture that we've looked at in this short film, we can see certain abiding characteristics that pre-exist everything irrespective of style, time, and place.

THE DUKE OF QUEENSBERRY[40]

Here's the Duke of Queensberry from earlier in the period that we're looking at in terms of this particular type of classical sculpture. Sort of Restoration 1660 through to the middle and latter stages of the nineteenth century when the style doesn't change too much and is very much of a piece. This is by John

---

[39] Edward Marshall (1598–1675), Elizabeth Culpeper (or Colepeper, Lady of Leeds Castle) (1582–1638), 1638, Hollingbourne Church.

[40] John van Nost (d. 1729), Tomb of James Douglas, 2nd Duke of Queensberry (1662–1711) with his wife Mary, erected 1713, Durisdeer Parish Church, Dumfries and Galloway, Scotland.

van Nost. It's in Scotland. It's very ornate, and it's quite Baroque in spirit. He lies in death upon a bed or a divan sort of swooning and thinking great thoughts with several cherubs above him, and there's a plaque that lists his honorific titles and so on. There's a sort of Doric column next to him and an arch over. Don't forget this is life-size, extremely heavy, and the point is to indicate breeding, monumentalism, importance, and a link to the ancient world.

SIR JOHN CUTLER[41]

Here we have another classicizing piece, life-sized, from about 1685. So, quite a way back, but the style you'll notice from the Restoration in 1663 through to possibly the Great Reform Act in 1867 is very much of a piece. You could almost argue it could have been done, this particular relief done of somebody I think was called Sir John Cutler, at any time during that period.

ADMIRAL TYRRELL[42]

This is a very large and ornate piece by Nicholas Read in Westminster Abbey, 1770. Again in a style we've become conversant with during this phase of the film and this historical period with which it deals. It's a monument to Admiral Tyrrell. Behind him in relief, you can see his ship. You can see battle scenes. You can see a sort of angel or his guardian angel or the spirit of victory or his soul leaving his body in accordance with the doctrine of transubstantiation. You can see billowing sails overmastering the top of this angelic image and so on. It's a very big relief with three-dimensional elements. Probably would have taken several years to actually carve and produce.

---

[41] Arnold Quellin (Artus Quellinus) (1653–1686), Sir John Cutler, 1st Baronet (1603–1693). This is not the exact statue of Sir John Cutler to which Bowden refers but another life-sized sculpture of him made by the same artist. Cutler appears in similar pose and garb. This one is in Guildhall, London. The one to which Bowden refers was originally in Grocer's Hall but is since untraceable.

[42] Nicholas Read (c. 1733–1787), Admiral Richard Tyrrell, 1770, Westminster Abbey.

THE BOWLER[43]

Here is a piece from the early part of the nineteenth century, 1825. *The Bowler*, from *The Cricketer* and *The Bowler*, from Woburn Abbey in Bedfordshire by Henry Rossi. It's a somewhat more populist work, this one, dealing with sport. The bowler, of course, is anonymous. It's classical in its deportment and delineation, but of course he's clothed. And you see an encroachment of popular sensibility here as well as a narrative element. It relates, of course, much more to the period in which it was produced than to notions about the ancient world. So, you're beginning to see a sort of realism in certain elements even of classical sculpture.

RICHARD LADBROKE[44]

Here we see another large mausoleum. It's by Joseph Rose the Elder to commemorate an aristocratic or very upper-class family. It's in Reigate in Surrey. Dates from the early part of the eighteenth century. The figures are relatively small, or maybe the photograph is from a distance. They may be life-size, but an enormous, monumental edifice here. It's virtually like a sort of rock wall in neo-classical and heightened vogue dedicated to the power and magnificence of this provincial family, and it shows you the desire these people have to immortalize themselves as provincial imperial figures in their area to be watched by their own community, as they perceived it, forever and ever.

WILLIAM & ELIZABETH CROFTS[45]

Here's another of these increasingly Rococo pieces that we've been looking at. A sort of heightened Baroque classicism of an

---

[43] Henry Rossi (1791–1844), *The Bowler*, 1825, Woburn Abbey. Unfortunately, *The Bowler* has been damaged over time. The new documentary film of this speech shows the statue in its original and current state.

[44] Joseph Rose the Elder (fl. 1721–1735), Richard Ladbroke, 1730, St. Mary's Church, Reigate.

[45] Abraham Storey (d. c. 1696), Monument to William, 1st Baron Crofts (d. 1677) and his second wife, Elizabeth, 1678, Church of St. Nicholas, Little Saxham.

aristocratic couple gazing in an adoring way at each other, the female lying beneath the male. This is from Suffolk. The sculptor is Abraham Storey. Again, we're looking at the early part of this period, the Restoration through to the middle of the nineteenth century. This piece dates from 1678, and it shows, yet again, the ideals about themselves that the provincial English and British aristocracy had: a monumentalism, a heightened Baroque sensibility, a classicism, and a desire to glorify in family, nationality, and self.

WILLIAM HARCOURT[46]

Yes, here we have another rather classical, not particularly Baroque, piece. Quite heavy, solemn. A peer of the realm, a sort of imperial ermine. Again, this desire to present oneself as a Victorian gentleman, as a man of leisure, as a man of means, also as a leader, as a statesman, and something of a Roman senator in modernity. Again, this sculpture will be full size and will be there doubtless on a tomb or mausoleum to be admired by kith and kin in Oxfordshire.

SIR FRANCIS PAGE[47]

Here we have another slightly ornate piece. Again a tomb. Two life-sized vehicles, aristocratic husband and wife. Bewigged, in his case. Staring into the distance. Quite opulent. There's a slightly Baroque touch to it. There's a column that looks vaguely Doric to one side of them and an arch. Again, it's designed in a provincial setting. This is doubtless in a probably quite small church in Oxfordshire. It's designed to indicate power, local resource, and that one is part of a higher civilization that's solid, stolid, representational, and knows where it's going and what it represents.

---

[46] Robert William Siever (1794–1865), Field Marshal William Harcourt (1743–1830), 1830. Two were produced and stand in St. Michael's Parish Church in Stanton Harcourt and in St. George's Chapel, Windsor Castle.

[47] Henry Scheemakers (c. 1686–1748), memorial to Sir Francis Page (1661–1741) and his second wife, 1730, by in Steeple Aston Church, Oxfordshire.

THOMAS WHITAKER[48]

Right here we have another piece from Yorkshire: Reverend Thomas Whitaker. Possibly a local, sort of near-the-edge Anglican to non-conformist firebrand or Evangelical preacher of the time. Stares out serenely, but with a slightly Puritanical face at his would-be congregationists. Again, you see even extended out to probably a member of the gentry who happens to be in the clergy the same classicizing and heroic tendencies. A virtual full-size replication of self, continuation of one's bodily existence in stone after death, power, and permanence. A civilization that really was encyclopedic and thought that they could define everything, determine everything, knew what was what, and had the future in their hands.

ROBERT SOUTHEY[49]

Here we have a slightly new type of sculpture. Not in its form or delineation. Still classical, but you notice there's a Romantic feel coming in. It's quite naturalistic and realist, up to a point, given the classicizing tendency we've already mentioned. It's also biographical. It's actually of a person: Southey the poet. It also relates to a new movement and a new sensibility in the arts, what will become the dominant tendency of the whole of the nineteenth century, and this is the Romantic movement. You notice he's not wearing a wig. He stares directly at the sculptor's eye, if you like. Although it's in Westminster Abbey, and it dates from the 1840s, Southey, slightly forgotten early Romantic poet now who wrote a famous biography of the naval hero Nelson, looks out at you and is the dawn of a new sensibility: more representational, less idealized, and, in their own minds, a return to natural forms.

---

[48] Charles R. Smith (b. 1799), Vicar Thomas Whitaker (1759–1821), 1822, Parish Church of Saint Mary and All Saints, Whalley, Yorkshire.

[49] Henry Weekes (1807–1877), Robert Southey (1774–1843) Memorial, 1843, Westminster Abbey. Southey, an English poet of the Romantic school, is the originator of the story of "Goldilocks and the Three Bears."

CHARLES HOLMES[50]

Here we have another heroic and classicizing piece of a military figure, but he's also partly dressed in the military uniform of a Roman commander from the ancient world, even though he's got a cannon behind him and a coat of arms above. So, you've got this idea of modernity—cannon fire from the middle of the 1700s—and yet at the same time a Roman imperial statesman who in death looks out at the future and the past.

JONATHAN & ELIZABETH IVIE[51]

Here's an interesting relief, even though the skulls are slightly three-dimensional, from Exeter in the West Country, St. Petrock's Church, 1717, by a profound provincial sculptor called John Weston. It's of Jonathan and Elizabeth Ivie, and you notice that the background relief which is above the figures and is sort of transfigured or transubstantiated souls, some of them bewinged like angels, very much relates to artistic works that could be done by Donatello or Bellini.

With the skulls, you have a Gothic touch, even though this is very much prior to the Romantic movement. You have in this art, deep down, a form of tomb art really, an obsession with death and with decay, but also with finality.

Don't forget this was a world in which the next life was very close, was believed to be totally real, and the Christian way was to prepare for it. Therefore, the celebration of death in a manner which contemporary people would find very, very difficult to either stomach or understand was ever present. To put your skulls on the side of a tomb to celebrate your life would have been regarded as normalcy for a high bourgeois family from the provinces like this at the beginning of the eighteenth century.

---

[50] Joseph Wilton (1722–1803), Admiral Charles Holmes (1711–1761), 1761, Westminster Abbey.

[51] John Weston (fl. 1696–1733), Jonathan and Elizabeth Ivie, 1717, St. Petrock's Church, Exeter.

JAMES LENOX DUTTON[52]

This is a famous piece dating from the middle of the eighteenth century by Richard Westmacott the Elder. It's in Gloucestershire. The upper part of this powerful sculpture consists of a guardian angel seen in feminine form raising the top of a lid of a burial urn and sort of mausoleum. She looks down in a beneficent way upon the corpse who will now rise to ascension.

From the same image, we see the object upon which the female guardian, angel, or spirit looks from above to below and this is the skeleton of the departed who is now released from the burial urn and is looking up as a sort of fleshless monster at the angel who is freeing him from death, and he's about to rise in accordance with the high Christian doctrine of the Second Coming and the resurrection of the body and the Second and Final Judgment when, according to this particular theology, all will be redeemed or cursed and thrown down into darkness and hell, and those who will not will ascend into heaven and will in certain circumstances achieve again their own corporeal nature. So, you'll be reborn in life in death, even with flesh, but the bones survive and are being raised by this angel. There's a strongly Gothic element to this piece, but again you see the obsessionality with death and with the overcoming of death seen in terms of classical sculpture.

WILLIAM SHAKESPEARE[53]

Here with a high classical image from the 1740s by Peter Scheemakers. It's Shakespeare. You can see the beginning of the cult of the artistic personality in this work. You can see also the beginning of an almost cultic reverence for Shakespeare as a writer, which reaches a status of a secular god almost, in modernity, particular in anglophone culture. Occasionally regarded as rough and unhewn and Elizabethan and rather barbaric, Shakespeare comes in over stages and is gradually accepted despite

---

[52] Richard Westmacott the Elder (1747–1808), James Lenox Dutton (1712–1776) and his second wife Jane (1712–1776), 1791, St. Mary Magdalene's Church, Sherborne.

[53] Peter Scheemakers (1691–1781), William Shakespeare, 1740, Westminster Abbey.

certain Augustine and Victorian moral qualms with some of the
plays or their style. Shakespeare is depicted as a heroic creator
gazing upon the Muses, and this is the beginning of a classical
cultivation of artistic biography that will reach an apogee with
endless versions of Beethoven's face and upper body and torso
and bust and so on in the nineteenth century atop almost every
Victorian mantlepiece or piano. But this importance of the individual creative personality depicted physically becomes more
and more apparent, don't forget we're merging from a period
where priests, where warriors, where kings and queens were
put into this form. Now the artist himself becomes the subject of
his work.

THE DEATH OF GERMANICUS[54]

Here we have another piece of a military character, drawn
from classical myth and history, the Death of Germanicus by
Thomas Banks from the 1770s. The naked corpse; warriors
swoon around it, some of them peripheral figures, are almost in
relief, their three dimensionality is tapered and is moving back
into the stonework—but the key central characters (two of which
are youths or small children) are depicted almost three-
dimensionally. The background characters, again, merge more
into the stonework, so you've got this sort of relief tending to
radical representationality. It is an attempt in high eighteenth
century formulation, to recap what they believed the sculpture
of the ancient world to have been like and how it comes down to
us both from classical Greek sculptors like Praxiteles but also
from Hellenistic sculpture, dug up again, and made to bear witness in the imperial papacies of the higher Renaissance.

AUTO-ICON[55]

Here we have an extraordinary and interesting piece, which
almost goes outside sculpture and then steps back into it again.
This is of the utilitarian philosopher Jeremy Bentham, a key
founder of modern liberalism as it has come to be seen and prac-

---

[54] Thomas Banks (1735–1805), *The Death of Germanicus*, 1773–74.
[55] Jeremy Bentham (1748–1832), *Auto-Icon*, 1832, University College, London.

ticed. He wears a sort of Quakerish hat, and this is his corpse. This is an example of corpse art, almost the first in the West. It's called an *Auto-Icon*, and he believed that everyone should have themselves exhibited as a corpse, and as a sort of artwork/sculpture after death.

This extant form is still around. You can still see it in the precincts of University College London and Senate House in Bloomsbury. If you notice his sort of decapitated head/facial mask, or one version of it, is between his feet. Increasingly this sculpture is in very great disrepair. The head is believed to be full of maggoty blood and this sort of thing, because the non-cryogenic processes by which it was embalmed and created and frozen in time from the 1830s to today in the twenty-first century, has gradually destroyed it.

However, although this appears to many sensibilities to be ghoulish and freakish, this is part of a long Western tradition in its way. The death mask, the birth mask, the mask that's taken from your face in adulthood, this was done for Keats, it was done for Beethoven, it was done for Cromwell, it was done for Napoleon, it was done for Wellington, it was done for all sorts of figures, and was regarded as quite normal.

Also art, and anatomy have always gone together, since the ancient world, and many artists see themselves closer to surgeons in their coolness, coldness and objectivity than they do to necessarily emotionally-based artists. It's often a misconception of people who are never involved in the arts to think it's all about emotion and not about reason.

Bearing in mind that Western art is based upon the body, the cult of the body and of the body's decay in and towards death, is inevitably part of this. In anatomy, the tradition from Galen through Versalius and now through in the twentieth century to controversial practitioners of a sort of hybrid of the arts and the sciences such the German embalmer and contemporary anatomist Professor Gunther von Hagens are all part of this tradition that Bentham opened up with this piece.

What Bentham is really saying is here is my corpse, let my face and head be cut off and be used as something for people to look at, let my eyes be cut out and used as marbles by the children of tomorrow. It's a totally materialistic attitude towards death that believes there is nothing after. One is reminded of Danton the French revolutionary who went on the scaffold, turns to the executioner, and said, "Show my head to the people. It's worth looking at."

HYDE PARK FRIEZE[56]

Here we have again a very Grecian model, it's by John Henning, it's from 1828, it's of Hyde Park Corner, of course, millions of tourists and native inhabitants will have passed this, sometimes without seeing it at all day-on-day in the center of London. It's based upon the idea of the Parthenon and the Elgin marbles and what they meant when they were brought over from Greece, and it's yet another part of the heroicizing tendencies of early nineteenth century art. This idea that we were the new Greece, and the new Rome combined, and that in a rather Christianized way we could nevertheless bring the solidity of the ancient world to the modern, particularly in relation to memorials that dealt with war and sacrifice.

LORD TENNYSON[57]

Here we have a mid-nineteenth century bust and sculpture which depicts the artist as hero, for the very best artistic and yet heroic figure. It's of the poet laureate Tennyson, best known to sort-of middle twentieth century audiences by his poem to celebrate the defeat as it were of the Charge of the Light Brigade. He's depicted in a biographical, a representational, and a rather realist or naturalistic manner, and not bewigged, well out of the eighteenth century, a studied and sort of low-key heroic ombit to the piece, and yet it's the artist as hero who gazes out with a solemn and mature gaze. It's a sort of how they believed in the middle of the nineteenth century, the classical world would have

---

[56] By John Henning the Elder (1771–1851) as well as John Henning the Younger (1801–1857). Although it is based upon the Elgin Marbles, it is not a direct replica. The screen was completed in 1828.

[57] Thomas Woolner (1825–1892), Lord Tennyson (1809–1892), 1895, Westminster Abbey.

depicted a significant writer like Dio Cassius or Pliny or Catullus.

FRIEZE OF PARNASSUS[58]

Here in this sort of lineup, or column of figures seen from the
side, is a depiction in slight relief, but nonetheless three-
dimensionally, of a catalogue or chronology of British sculptors,
famous ones anyway. This is from the Albert memorial by Armstead and Philip, and many of the people that we've looked at in
terms of their works, earlier in this film, are depicted here. Of
course there's a certain element of artistic imagination and license going on, because how would the sculptors entirely have
known of the physiology of their forebears or predecessors, artistically speaking? But nonetheless we begin with Nicholas
Stone[59] who we looked at several centuries before in this chronology. Francis Bird[60] is there. John Bushnell,[61] whose eccentrici-
ties we mentioned at one moment, is also depicted, along with
Bernini and various people from the continent who infused the
solidity of the English style with a certain Renaissance lightness
of touch.

THE SLUGGARD[62]

Now moving from the middle of the Victorian period toward
its end, the Romantic movement has certainly infused sculpture.
It took a long time. Painting would be far more likely to suc-

---

[58] Henry Hugh Armstead (1828–1905) and John Birnie Philip
(1824–1875), *Frieze of Parnassus*, constructed 1864–1872 at the base of
the Albert Memorial.

[59] Nicholas Stone (1586/87–1647). Not mentioned up to this point,
he was a prolific baroque sculptor and architectural carver, and was
appointed master mason to the Crown in 1632.

[60] Previously mentioned in regard to the *The Conversion of St. Paul*
and other pieces.

[61] John Bushnell (1636–1701). Bushnell has not been mentioned up
to this point.

[62] Frederic Lord Leighton (1830–1896), *The Sluggard*, first exhibited
as a clay model in 1886 and subsequently cast in bronze.

cumb to Romantic treatment, in terms of Constable's.[63] We're looking at nature, Turner's[64] in pre-Impressionism, or the sort of Salvatore Rosa[65] view of nature seen in a gothic or troubled manner. Three dimensionally, it would be more difficult to bring in the Romantic idea, but here it is, in Lord Leighton's sculpture.

Now, one thing that you notice is because the idealizing tendencies of classicism are reduced, the sculpture is more naturalistic and therefore the nude will obviously be depicted more sexually, or at least psycho-sexually. This caused in the high Victorian period of course, quite a bit of consternation. But if you like, the nude is becoming more real, and one has this paradox about Victorian culture that in its era, which is regarded by modernity as very repressive and judgmental. Nevertheless, its three-dimensional art is increasingly erotic in terms of the nature of the classical tradition.

CLYTIE[66]

This tendency towards *eros* in stone can be seen even more in G. F. Watts' *Clytie*, which is a sort of naked back of a servant girl looking over her shoulder. You possibly realize that given the natural arta element of this sculpture, it couldn't be done from the front because otherwise it would be regarded as straightforwardly pornographic.

So, we're now seeing the naturalization of the classical urge as, of course, photography begins. And photography will affect all of the arts to the degree that Romanticism begins to come to an end towards the end of the nineteenth century and by the turn of the twentieth century is virtually over and is replaced in modernity by the sensibility which is now called modernism. But the engine for this change, amongst many, many other complicated factors, is photography.

In painting, it forces people not to reveal the nature around

---

[63] John Constable (1776–1837), English landscape painter.

[64] William Turner (1775–1851), English Romantic painter, printmaker, and watercolorist.

[65] Salvator Rosa (1615–1673), Italian Baroque painter.

[66] George Frederic Watts (1817–1904), *Clytie*, c. 1868–78.

them but to go inside the mind in relation to fantasy and dream and so forth as firstly still and then moving photography, namely cinema, the art of the twentieth century, takes over the realist and representational role in visual art.

Similarly, in sculpture, a turning away from the body and in towards a non-organic art of individual sensibility that doesn't relate to the society but purely the psychology of the artist, begins the trajectory which is called modernism.

What we now see is a splitting away of the classical dispensation. And radical regimes, Fascist and Communist, are the only currents in the twentieth century where the monumental and classicizing tendencies of the last couple of centuries within the West are to be found. Even that is complicated and possibly should be the subject matter for another film.

So, this finishes off our relatively quick résumé of English and British sculpture stretching over several thousand years. We've decided to end our film at the beginning of the twentieth century, end of the nineteenth, and I've ended it here because the modernist sensibility then takes over.

Personally, I believe you need another film about modernist sculpture, even modernist art, another two films maybe, because this sensibility is a total change and a revolutionary transformation in everything. So, the classical tendency, the Christian, humanist, and post-Christian tendency, the pre-Christian tendency, two, three, four thousand years of work really comes to an end at the end of the nineteenth century and the representation of the physical body perfect and imperfect then goes into film, into still photography, into moving photography, and then into mass cinema film as well as elitist forms of artistic photography. Obviously, if you stop many classical films and freeze the frame, you actually have both a representational painting, but also at times a certain three-dimensionality to the piece rather like Mantegna's Renaissance paintings which were a combination of sculpture and painting.

Now, if we look at the English and British tradition. You have examples like Behnes' bust of Queen Victoria idealized from before her reign really begins; you have William Anderson's version of the Scottish laureate or moral laureate Robert Burns from

1854; you have, as we depicted earlier in the film, the version of Robert Southey which exists in Bristol Cathedral and was completed by Bailey in 1845; and we have two famous sculptures which I would like to finish on, both for aesthetic and political reasons.

SIR HENRY HAVELOCK[67] & SIR CHARLES NAPIER[68]

These are the images of Sir Henry Havelock from 1861 and of General Sir Charles Napier in 1856. These were by sculptors such as George Adams. Now, both of these forms are very interesting, because Ken Livingstone, the present mayor of London, when he was elected, wanted to tear them down or at least remove them from Trafalgar Square where they sit at the front of the square often ignored in comparison to Nelson's Column designed by William Railton with Edward Hodges Baily's[69] sculpture at the top and Sir Edwin Landseer's lions equidistant from the pillar.

Now, many people, hundreds of thousands of people, will pass these sculptures of Havelock and Napier at the front of the square going down into Northumberland Avenue where the Ministry of Defence now is, and they will not know who these figures are. These figures are imperialists from the Indian *raj* in the nineteenth century. One of them is responsible for putting down the Indian Mutiny with quite considerable bloodshed.

And it's because Leftists like Mayor Livingstone know this that he wanted these figures removed. He couldn't get them removed, because his importance and alleged civic esteem as mayor doesn't extend to the appurtenances of Trafalgar Square. He's got no control over the statuary in the square. He can ban people feeding the pigeons in the square, but he can't remove sculpture.

So, what he did to get his own back was he had the empty

---

[67] William Behnes (1795–1864), *Major General Sir Henry Havelock* (1795–1857), 1861, Trafalgar Square.

[68] George Gammon Adams (1821–1898), *General Sir Charles James Napier* (1782–1853), 1856, Trafalgar Square.

[69] Edward Hodges Baily (1788–1867).

plinths at the far corner of the square, which is adjacent to the National Gallery behind it and looks across to the Canadian Embassy on the other side, and he used that for Turner Prize[70] exhibit art, deliberately to get back at the authorities who denied the fact that he could get rid of Napier and Havelock from the front of the square.

So, in this talk about aesthetics and politics we come full circle, because the high Victorian, classical impulse exists in the central square right at the heart of our post-imperial city, London, where we now have a sort of anti-British and unpatriotic mayor who wants to repudiate the imperial past, the imperial past which has in fact partly led, among other factors, to London's multiracial present status. Nevertheless, the thing he wants to remove from the square is the symbolism of the past, is the way in which it classed itself, is its classification of itself, i.e., its classicism.

So, to end this film, I would ask people when passing across the precincts of Trafalgar Square to have a look at these rather strong, slightly dour, stolid pieces of English sculpture at the front of the square depicting Havelock and Napier as imperial warriors and heroes in a subdued classical manner, the images and reliefs and bulk masses that Livingstone wished to remove to some obscure place in Sheffield or Bolton where you would never see them again.

---

[70] See Bowden's film *Against the Turner Prize* at the Jonathan Bowden Archive (https://jonathanbowden.org/) and transcript in Jonathan Bowden, *Reactionary Modernism*, ed. Greg Johnson (San Francisco: Counter-Currents, 2021).

H. P. LOVECRAFT*

This little talk is going to be on the horror and science fiction writer Howard Phillips Lovecraft, who has had many vicissitudes since his death—very early death—at forty-seven years of age in Butler Hospital[1] in Providence, Rhode Island. He was born in 1890 and during the course of the twentieth century has become almost a cultic figure, alternately despised—Edmund Wilson wrote an essay in the 1950s totally dismissing fantasy literature of every sort[2]—and yet now an enormous figure. He's been raised to iconic status. He's in the official American Library of Congress-related set of editions in black, embossed hardback books of great American writers like Poe, Hawthorne, Melville, Emily Dickinson, and so on, right through the eighteenth, nineteenth, twentieth centuries just gone.[3] Lovecraft is now included.

Lovecraft was an internet figure long before that was even invented, because he almost had his own media. At the beginning of the twentieth century often people used to have amateur press journals of their own which, if you like, are like a website or a blog now. And they would disseminate this material in certain cultural circles, particularly in the United States, where there's never been any state or public provision for the arts until the Kennedy era, and where private patronage went essentially towards paying forms, where the idea of, in a Protestant and frontiers manner, producing culture for oneself or doing things

* Transcript by Lee and Donna Hancock of Bowden's speech at the nineteenth New Right meeting in London on February 7, 2009, online at the Jonathan Bowden Archive (jonathanbowden.org). Also see Bowden's essay "H. P. Lovecraft: Aryan Mystic" in *Pulp Fascism*.

[1] Lovecraft did not die in Butler Hospital but Jane Brown Memorial Hospital. But both his parents died in Butler Hospital.

[2] Edmund Wilson, "Tales of the Marvellous and the Ridiculous" (1945), reprinted in *H. P. Lovecraft: Four Decades of Criticism*, ed. S. T. Joshi (Athens: Ohio University Press, 1980).

[3] The Library of America.

and disseminating them in the way Lovecraft did with his early volumes of poetry, was very much the vogue. And Lovecraft essentially published himself in small circles with others, and then, through a publication called *Weird Tales* in the 1920s and thirties.

One of the interesting things about Lovecraft is because fantasy and non-realistic literature, largely based on dreams and on phantasms and on nightmares — of course, in his case, both real and metaphoric — because that area was disprivileged, it was pushed down — down not just into popular culture or mass culture but even *lower* culture in a strange sort of way.

I want to talk just for a moment about the culture of displacement. Many cultural phenomena can never be destroyed. They can just be displaced. If you look at the cult of the heroic and you look at certain classical and realist ideas, if you look at certain pagan ideas, if you look at certain ultra-masculine cultural conceptions, they've become so implausible and so disacknowledged within the post-war liberal dispensation that they've been pushed not to the margins of culture but *down, down* into areas that critics don't even look at because they're beneath that trajectory. They're beneath that searchlight, if you like, to use that term. They're beneath that.

And if you look at a lot of comics or graphic novels and things that children and adolescents read — fantasy, adventure, escapist literature of all sorts — you see certain primordial elements peeping out at you, often without any ideological or philosophical baggage at all, because these are entertainment-based forms, let's face it. And yet it's quite clear that certain values are being disseminated by virtue of this type of phenomenon.

Lovecraft is famous today because he was once despised. He is famous today because he appeared in pulp magazines in the racks in drugstores and supermarkets next to the chewing-gum. Because teenagers would save their small amount of money to buy these magazines that were printed on paper that was so thin and so cheap that it was cheaper than newspaper print. He's famous/infamous now because he was in *Weird Tales*.

Most of the stuff in *Weird Tales* of course hasn't survived. Although it's interesting to notice that Robert E. Howard, who created a whole cycle of heroic, masculine figures, who engaged in sword and sorcery type dramaturgy on the page — *Conan the Barbarian* and that series of stories — is the most famous.[4] But there were many before that. He's widely known now and is a cultural brand in his own right. Clark Ashton Smith[5] is another one, and there are a few others — Donald Wandrei[6] — a few others who have survived the demise of the magazine that gave birth to them.

It's also true that modern capitalist or postmodern capitalist publishing likes a good seller and exists to make money, and, therefore, the science fiction and fantasy areas — what H. G. Wells when he created with Jules Verne the form called Scientific Romanticism in the nineteenth century — now fills . . . If you go into Waterstones or Borders or any of these other bookshops, whole walls are full of this stuff, because it is bought.

The interesting thing about Lovecraft is that it's quite clear that most of his horror literature is based upon the dream. He kept a dream book by his bed and wrote down just the skeletons, just the tropes — 'hand in lake, grabs child.' That's all it would be. It's a black fantasy if you like, and from that you embroider a short story of even a longish, multi-episode short story.

Horror and gothic fiction as the under-savage or blacker side of Romanticism as a cultural dispensation, is very suited to the short story form because it's intense, because it's plot-driven, because it focuses around a dénouement that reveals the reality of the tale and what has really been going on and proses it, and, therefore, in an American sense, gives closure. And also because it's concerned with externality, things that happen to people and things they fantasize about or configure before they occur. It's not given over to very long novel lengths, discursive treatments of the inner mind, how people felt when these things were going on, and so on.

Strangely, in horror fiction at the contemporary moment, you get these great triple-decker novels that are this thick and are

---

[4] Robert E. Howard (1906–1936). See also the five chapters on Howard in Bowden's *Pulp Fascism*.

[5] Clark Ashton Smith (1893–1961).

[6] Donald Wandrei (1908–1987).

written by James Herbert and Stephen King and these sorts of people. I've only ever read one Stephen King book. That's the one set in a hotel — *The Shining* — with the boy who has the second sight. And the thing that struck me instantly, about eighty pages in, is I realized that the hotel is alive, that it contains the psychic memory of all the people who've died there, committed suicide there, done something destructive there, that the building is sort of seething with a dark and negative energy, that it will take some of the characters over and destroy them, and that will be the result, and probably it will blow up at the end. I suddenly realized "I've got to page eighty," because actually it's four hundred sixty before you actually *get* to that moment.

And it came to my mind that what King is doing is extending a short story out across five hundred pages, because his editor has told him 'You've got to have a novel length, not a short story.' Because the horror form, the gothic form, from Walpole,[7] from novels like *Vathek,*[8] from early nineteenth-century literature, from Mary Shelley's *Frankenstein,* when the Byron circle all sat round and they all had to give a ghost story — remarkable set stories came out of that particular evening. Polidori's story came out of that.[9] Her story, although Shelley said he cleaned it up and improved it. And she later wrote another novel, I think *The Last Man* was one that survived and Oxford Classics still do.

But why is it that particularly our people find the gothic form, find the dark romantic form deeply attractive as many of our people do, subconsciously, as I do? I think it's because there's a *strength* to the capacity to dream. It seems quite obvious to me that people like Poe and people like Lovecraft and other similar writers, particularly short story writers — Oliver Onions[10] at the beginning of the twentieth century — Elizabeth Bowen,[11] the

---

[7] Horatio "Horace" Walpole (4th Earl of Orford, 1717–1797), Whig politician, art historian, and author of the first gothic novel *The Castle of Otranto* (1764).

[8] William Beckford (1760–1844), *Vathek* (1786).

[9] John William Polidori (1795–1821), *The Vampyre* (1819).

[10] George Oliver Onions (1873–1961), English writer of short stories and novels, best known for his ghost stories.

[11] Elizabeth Bowen (1899–1973), Irish novelist and short story

Irish writer who wrote some very crippled, gnarled, ferocious short stories. Perhaps the greatest short story writer of this sort is M. R. James[12] in the English tradition. He was a Master at Eton all of his adult life.

There seems to be, not just a desire to dream, but the desire to make the dream strong in the articulation of it. And strength in some ways means going artistically, if only for a moment, in a slightly sinister direction before you draw it back to have a resolution. It's the shadow that the tree casts, gives you a three-dimensional insight into the reality of the wood. It's almost as if it gives a visceral quality to that which could be softer and ethereal otherwise, and without that balance one can't find a center.

Certainly Lovecraft never wrote any of the stories for monetary gain, although he did do the odd bit of ghost-writing, some of which is now preserved. A book of the ghost-written material, the sort of touching up and the recasting of the story in his own imagination, has been published just recently.[13] Lovecraft is out of copyright, of course, now, which is why there's a great plethora of his material in the last year and year-and-a-half.

His career began in isolation and seclusion. He was an only child. His father died in Butler Hospital in 1898 in Providence, Rhode Island. Don't we hear in that name—Providence—the Protestant ancestry of New England? Salem, New Jerusalem, Providence—a people chosen by God, allegedly, leaving England to create a new world and a new dispensation. If you come from a town called Providence you sort of know that you're part of the chosen and there in a differentiated way. He never lost that New England element to him.

Lovecraft always regarded himself as a Briton, even as an American. He didn't like the American Republic—too modern, too new-fashioned, too new-fangled. Those people who didn't really care for Washington's revolution, some went to Canada;

---

writer.

[12] Montague Rhodes James (1862–1936), English medievalist and horror fiction writer.

[13] H. P. Lovecraft, *The Horror in the Museum & Other Revisions*, ed. S. T. Joshi, revised ed. (Sauk City, Wisconsin: Arkham House, 1989).

others called themselves loyalists or Tories, and they lived on in the United States, ultimately became a sort of gentlemanly cultural opposition to the nature of the American Republic, a looking back to the British past, a regarding that the United States was almost an extension of this country, that the theocrats who couldn't basically create a Protestant dictatorship that lasted after the Civil War had before left to create a new one on the other side of the world.

Parenthetically, of course, although we're talking about H. P. Lovecraft, I always use these talks to illustrate certain little things that are going on. We now we have the first decidedly non-European President of the United States of America, and it's interesting to notice that apart from maybe Patrick J. Buchanan there's not one contemporary American politician who's seen this event for what it is, and this event is a defeat, at least a defeat for one definition of America, for a definition of America that's grounded in a post-European experience, for an America that is an expression of Nation Europa, for an America that is a vision demographically and, more importantly, culturally, of what David Duke calls European Americans. His victory is a symbol not only of what has occurred over the last forty to fifty years, but also what the future holds.

In most American cities, put rather bluntly, white Americans are in the minority now or, if they're not, feel that they are. Therefore, his election on Latino, liberal white, black, and other votes is symptomatic of the way in which America has changed. Since the all-white immigration policy was done away with in the late 1960s — and it had lasted from the early twenties, of course — seventy million persons of color have entered the United States and changed it out of all recognition.

Now, Lovecraft's America was white to a degree that many Americans now couldn't even envisage. And yet he regarded it as *appallingly decayed* and *decadent* and *miscegenated* and utterly in racial chaos. And that was in 1908, so what he would have made of 2008, 2009 is quite unbelievable. On his first trip to New York he said he was almost maddened by the *seething whirlpool of the races* and *the destructive intensity of a world clashing upon the city*. Because he was seeing it as someone who was very provincial—from Providence—transported to New York, the *seething masses* of New York, the field of energy as they come in from Europe off the boat, and he sensed all that energy for both creation and destruction and, like all artists, would be appalled and yet also excited—because energy always excites.

The interesting thing is that if you look at his Wikipedia entry—don't we all love Wikipedia, eh?—it testifies, 'Lovecraft had certain views of a racial character,' and that is true. He was influenced not just by Spengler's cosmology, of the undulation of cultures, of their decline, of their relationships to theories of plants, theories of growth, theories of decay. If that has any truth to it, that book that came out called *The Decline of the West* at the end of the Great War, we are truly in an autumnal period. But, as my edition of *Chambers Biographical Dictionary* tells me, Spengler's views are only a theory. So there we are.

But Lovecraft was strongly influenced by him, strongly influenced by certain racialist writers like Günther[14] and so on, but also by the nature and temperament of his Protestant hierarchical and culturally elitist experience.

As his major American/Asian explicator, S. T. Joshi, says, Lovecraft was typical of his era, and yet more typical than many, because it's quite clear he had an ideological commitment to these ideas of decline and degeneration from which there could come new fulfilment and growth by virtue of reverse eugenisis or cosmological change or moral change or social transformation, whatever words and theories you wish to place upon it.

Always an eccentric, living at night like a sort of psychic vampire, writing gothic stories, living on a pittance, almost refusing to work because work was sort of slave morality, attitudinizing about the old aristocratic past which his family had never really lived through. But, of course, the man is a writer of fantasy.

His father died of nervous exhaustion, but he actually died of tertiary syphilis in 1898. His mother died in 1921, possibly of an

---

[14] Probably Hans Friedrich Karl Günther (1891–1968), German scientific racist and eugenicist.

infection of that sort. There just seems to be little congenital disturbance in Lovecraft. However, the family had died around
him, and, as a child, they'd moved [him] from quite august, large
quarters to a very small cramped flat. This had a real impact
upon the infant Lovecraft.

Lovecraft didn't really go to school and educated himself, primarily, in science. One of the interesting things about Lovecraft
is it would be easy to look at him as an eccentric artist and a
writer of Wildean, Swinburnian, Edgar Allen Poe-like short stories, a sort of New England gothic, as it could be described. But
Lovecraft really was as much influenced by science as by the
pedigree of artistic literature whether they related to the gothic
area he made his own or not.

One of the other interesting things about Lovecraft is he
wrote an enormous number of letters. Rather like the compul-
sive e-mailer of today he would write seven, ten, twenty letters
a day. His biographer in the 1970s—a science-fiction writer
called L. Sprague de Camp[15] (what a marvelous name, eh?)—
was a French American. He wrote over one hundred books including some of the Conan cycle that he finished after Howard
shot himself. Howard knew Lovecraft, of course. Howard was,
again, an obsessive writer from Cross Plains in Texas. His
mother died one day so he took a shotgun[16] and blew the top of
his head off, the same day, when he was thirty. And yet he wrote
before thirty years of age what many writers struggle to write in
half a lifetime, and all of this stuff was being published during
the course of the twentieth century.

But to return to Lovecraft, Lovecraft wrote over 100,000 letters according to de Camp. According to Joshi's biography that
appeared in the mid-nineties, he wrote about 85,000 letters. But
in any respect he wrote an enormous amount, and many of these
letters—because they're often to quite famous writers he influenced, and the letters went back and forth—are being published

---

[15] Lyon Sprague de Camp (1907–2000), American science fiction and
fantasy writer, wrote *Lovecraft: A Biography* (New York: Doubleday,
1975).

[16] Howard actually committed suicide with a pistol.

over time. He also wrote five volumes of essays which have now been published and are now available via Amazon and so on.[17]

A cartoonist did an image of Lovecraft from earlier in his life dressed like Poe but further back, dressed like Poe as Dryden as Poe, with a wig, writing with a quill pen—because modern pens were just too modern—with bats and various things in the background, an image that appeals to his antiquarian bias, his eighteenth-century bias, his gothic bias, his image of himself and so on.

These essays are gathered together in the five volumes as I say. One is on science, one is on art and literature, one is the amateur press journalism, which is like this contemporaneous material, one is on politics.

He began with a short journal of his own called *The Conservative*. Rest assured that was indeed a conservative journal in 1909–1910. In America, of course, the word "conservative" has totally different connotations as it does in the European continent. Because we're so used to the center-Right liberal party being called Conservative, we actually have a slightly sort of Anglocentric view of it. In France "conservative" largely means someone who philosophically rejects the tenets not just of the Enlightenment but of the politics of the French Revolution which is itself a radical or revolutionary position in relation to the last two hundred years of French history. So the word "conservative" has quite a different connotation. In certain other cultures it can be considered to be the thing you call a party for people who've got a little bit of money.

Lovecraft wrote about thirty stories—thirty-two, thirty-five—including some juvenilia—three of them are long enough to be novels of a shortish compass. Many critics divide them into three [periods]—the period when he's very much under the influence of Poe and Lord Dunsany[18] and the Celtic, national-Romantic traditions, slightly darker. It's almost like the equivalent

---

[17] *Collected Essays of H. P. Lovecraft*, 5 vols., ed. S. T. Joshi (New York: Hippocampus Press, 2004–2006).

[18] Lord Dunsany (Edward John Moreton Drax Plunkett, 18th Baron of Dunsany, 1878–1957) was an Anglo-Irish writer.

of somebody like Arnold Bax[19] in prose. This is his early phase, more derivative in a way. The second phase is largely when the material becomes stronger, less prolix, less baroque, more visceral, and darker in tone. The third phase — the so-called cosmic phase — is when he introduces many of his scientific ideas into horror literature and when he develops a new vibration, a new discourse, a new way of methodologically capturing that era of fiction.

Traditionally it dealt with dreams; it dealt with interpretations of reality that come out of the Christian cultural legacy very explicitly; it dealt with diabolical possession, or it dealt with demonic forces, or it dealt with ghosts, or it dealt with the concept of guilt, or it dealt with the ambience or auric manifestations of a place. Place, position, topography: very important in this type of genre literature, because you're dealing less with fully wrought out Iris Murdoch-like presentations of personality, much more with mood and with atmosphere — mood within an individual and within the environment that they shape and are shaped by. That's why a lot of horror literature consists in a sense of building up an atmosphere of threat or plausibility or suspension of disbelief, and so on, particularly if it's got any pretensions towards literature.

Now, Lovecraft at one level could be considered as religious in the sense that his work is so fantasy-laden, so imaginative, that it transports people into other realms. That's why it's remained extraordinarily popular with adolescents. Adolescents often want primal answers particularly about death, and about humans or the morphic, about decay, about radical things that people of slightly more mature years don't wish to talk about quite so blatantly. They also love escape, and they also love adventure, and the idea of violence — action, if you like — appeals to them. I remember Evelyn Waugh once was asked 'What was your favorite book when you were nine?' He said, '*Captain Blood*, because that's what you want when you're nine.' But not maybe when you're twenty-nine.

Lovecraft, although he dealt in fantasy, was rhetorically and

---

[19] Sir Arnold Bax (1883–1953), English composer in a Celtic idiom.

intellectually an atheist. He believed the imagination was our way to freedom by virtue of the fact that we were imprisoned within normative worlds of materialism, of mechanism, but also of chaos. Quite early on he devised an idea that the Modernist movement was to exemplify in many ways that has become rather a cliché now, as that order is ordered and yet seething and pulsating, as advanced physics allegedly tells us with the prospect of dissidence and decay. The point of the artist in this particular rendition is to hold as much order as they can together amidst the seething, indeterminate nature of the universe.

Now if we're the prisoner of our genes, allegedly, if things are biological and morphic, if genetics (a term that wouldn't have been used in Lovecraft's intellectually formative era, of course, except by specialists) dominates everything, how can man be free in his own mind? How can he obscure the threatening nature of the universe? When Pascal looked out upon the universe in these great interstellar depths and chasms, he felt a strange alienation. He felt a cosmic coldness there and partly admitted, at least to himself as an internal reference point, that religiosity was not a way of dealing with that, as John Updike who died recently said, but certainly was a way through to dealing with that.

Few of us really can configure that if our universe is one speck of sand in the Sahara, as certain cosmologists say — if that's what this universe is, and there are universes upon universes upon universes allegedly clustered together in various ways — if the human mind really only at the edges of consciousness can completely conceptualize this, even if most of these are theories that may be mathematically true, but we don't know if they're physically true or not. Science in the future may determine that, may not.

But Lovecraft's way of dealing with this, a very modern way in actual fact, was to throw out the imagination, was to throw out the element of fantasy in the mind, that which often in the child is permitted for a moment and yet is discouraged. The child wants to draw. The child wants to paint. The child wants to drink. 'Don't do that. Don't do *that.*' You have to stop all that and get real and go into adult life and earn a living and that sort of thing at a certain time.

Lovecraft wanted to keep alive that facility of dreams, to go onwards, and to *mature* and deepen the nature of those dreams both positively and negatively. Indeed, in a way he's only arguing for what many artistic types really do naturally anyway. Writing itself, in some ways, often for many people who write about the nature of writing, particularly fictional writing, whatever genre or area they're involved in, talk about the resistance to doing it before you start, then talk about slightly disengaging from the most conscious part of the mind and allowing certain other things to come out. But this isn't stream of consciousness necessarily at all, because it's deeply structured, deeply ordered in dealing with different types of memory and different types of the re-interpretation of things which you've experienced and made up even as you experience them. So quite complicated things are going on.

The nearest parallelism I can give to such processes is when you're in an exam and you want a fact, if you screw your mind up and think, "I must have this fact. I must have this name, date, and so on," you won't remember it. But if you allow the mind to relax — which of course is difficult when people are under pressure — but if you allow that moment to occur, suddenly it comes back to you, just like that, just as if a prayer has been answered, because you didn't force it, because you used a different part of your mind.

And in many ways, I think this type of literature, which is in part about death . . . I think a lot of literature is about death, and about how you place yourself before it and how you deal with it imaginatively. Let's face it, the one human experience which you can never write about afterwards is death. So, how do we pre-configure it in the mind in an advance way? And isn't it also extraordinarily human to configure this ultimate topic as a form of *play*, as a form of entertainment? The people who like horror and genre and monster material and so on more than anybody else are adolescents, aren't they? And young people. So right at the start you like the goriest type of material which you conceive almost as a joke to yourself, partly possibly to hide the seriousness of some of the depths it can bring up. So some very interesting things are going on here.

I'd also like to mention that in relation to the culture of the far Right there's a strong influence, strongly gothic in many ways, particularly in contemporary culture. In a post-Christian society, which is morally dualist and where the values, in a very humanistic way, of Christianity have been secularized by liberals — as Iris Murdoch once said, we've kept the soft element of the Christian values and dumped the religion. And she's saying the truth in relation to the mainstream culture that we're in and its supervision by something like the British Broadcasting Corporation, for example. Now, in relation to that liberal culture, the radical Right, and certainly the forms of Rightism that are to the Right of accepted Conservatism, have been demonized, have been demonized in a way that you would almost demonize a rival religious tendency of opinion, since the second World War. And demonization works as a strategy. That's why it's adopted. It works, in a way.

But it also creates an enormous area of disfigurement, doesn't it, and fantasy and illusion? Because people are attracted to the darker side even as they're appalled by it. So as you actually demonize something you actually make it stronger at certain levels of psychological resistance.

It's noticeable that in this society there are two tendencies of opinion that can't be integrated. There's a Left-leaning form of modernism called Surrealism. We had a talk about Futurism earlier, which was of course Italian, and Vorticism that was British. Surrealism's French and had no connections with the Right at all because André Breton aligned it to the French Communist Party of Maurice Thorez very early on. But Surrealism broke apart as its leading gurus died after the war, such as Breton. Situationism, as this minor shard, emerged, and this was the idea that all these tendencies were tied together, that everything's the same, that everything can be made a joke of.

You go to the Eastern bloc, and people are selling you stuff out of the back of vans and cars and thought this was petty capitalism. There are youth gangs around. Anthony Burgess went to Moscow and was appalled at the social disorder even under

Brezhnev, and he based *A Clockwork Orange*[20] and the gang culture not on the ghettoes of Los Angeles, but on the ghettoes of Soviet cities where they developed this language of their own to exclude adults and exclude the police and this sort of thing. Burgess was a lecturer in linguistics and so was incredibly interested in this.

Now, Situationism has the idea that everything's mixed together. There's a bar that used to exist in Maidenhead called the Soviet Bar. This is after the Soviet Union has fallen. You can go into the Soviet Bar, and you can have a Dzerzhinsky. You can have a drink called a Dzerzhinsky. How many people in Berkshire know that he was the founder of the Cheka, one of the major mass-murdering organizations of the twentieth century? But you can buy a drink named after him in Berkshire! That's because nobody knows, and they've not got Google in front of them, so they can't Google it before they drink it, to be offended. Do you know what I mean? But it's the idea that something can be celebrated. The Red Bar — go in and have a Red! There's a slogan above the bar that says, 'Drink as much as you want,' and there's a red flag next to it that says 'Drink, and be with the masses. Be with the people.' They're making a joke of Socialist Realism and *Proletkult*, because they're spitting on it after it's fallen. It's been integrated.

But there are two tendencies that can't be integrated into Western life, that's where Guy Debord's idea of the spectacle falls down. And they're the far Right and what's called religious fundamentalism. They're the two areas that can't be drawn in. That's why this audience will consist of far Rightists and some people who may or may not be considered by liberals to be metaphysical objectivists, which is the correct word for religious fundamentalists. That's because these visions of reality can't be integrated into the contemporary pea soup.

So the radical demonization of tendencies of opposition and the fact that with the British National Party, say, at one end and

---

[20] See Bowden's "Mechanical Fruit: The Strange Case of Anthony Burgess' *A Clockwork Orange*" in *Pulp Fascism*.

Hizb ut-Tahrir[21] at the other end, liberals know that they can't be integrated. They break their teeth on those. They can't be drawn in. Almost everything else — including the old far Left of the past — can.

This creates an odd energy, because people are attracted towards that which is hated, particularly by power. But they're also revolted as well. So there's this division even in the nature of the attraction. People who've been involved in far-Right groups for a very long time are aware of the psychology of certain of the haters, certain of the people who are most manifestly against, who are *seething* with anger whenever anything that could be attributed to the tendency that used to be called fascism comes up. There's a sort of Pavlovian moment of *hatred* and *fear* and *loathing*. And yet often that's hiding and masking a degree of quite subconscious attraction, which is not a foolish statement psychologically, otherwise that superficial reaction wouldn't be as extreme. You don't burn and rage against something about which you're indifferent. So demonization has all sorts of positively negative — queasy, but also genuinely negative — formulations.

It's also quite true that what's called the Hollywood Nazi element has done no one any favors at all, because you don't have to be involved in the radical Right for too long before to realize that there is a small number of people of psychopathological tendencies and all the rest of it who are attracted *because* it's hated, *because* it's regarded as evil.

I know when Winnie Mandela was demonized by the apartheid state she used to drive around Soweto in a limousine — the new black elite and their limousines — and she had 666 painted on the bonnet because she exalted in being a demon, because she committed many murders of rivals in the ANC, and so on. She had a crew of her own called the Mandela Football Team who used to do it for her: 'A necklace a day keeps Winnie at bay.' And how right they were! And she's even been excluded by all the people who came in after apartheid, in a strange sort of way.

---

[21] A pan-Islamic fundamentalist organization.

But demonization doesn't do people any favors at all. It's certainly true that it terrifies many people in the middle, or of no views at all, which is the majority of people in a Western society.

I have gone slightly off the track in relation to Lovecraft. But the idea of that which is demonic, that which is "other," that which is incredibly powerful, that can't be mentioned, that can't be named becomes a real force in Western society, and the literature of the Satanic, the pseudo-Satanic, and so on—outside of all religious constituted architecture—becomes very, very powerful culturally, and that's what's happened.

In actual fact, of course, the far Right is, of course, one of the three views, if you like, about how the West should be organized: the radical Left-wing view, the centrist view tending to the Left which in a complicated way we all live under, and the tendency of opinion that was defeated in 1945, although it's had other movements and so on subsequently. So the demonic and the use of it in a dualist, very moral dualist culture, is very powerful.

When Nietzsche wrote *Thus Spake Zarathustra* he brought back a Persian sage who institutionalized morally the idea that there was an absolute for evil and an absolute for good, and they warred forever—a Manichean viewpoint, a heresy in Christian terms, the basis of Pauline Christian morality really. They needed a morality for this new post-Jewish faith, so they found one. When Nietzsche wrote that book he wanted this man from the mountains, if you like, to come back—this figure with the white beard and staff, maybe a hat as well, an iconic figure in all cultures. He wanted him to come back and advocate non-dualism, the overcoming of the positive and the negative force and their institutionalization into one area.

And, in a way, gothic fiction, you could argue, is in some ways a recreational, entertainment-oriented version of that type of philosophizing. Because in many of Lovecraft's stories, in many of Poe's, in many of Hawthorne's, it's very difficult to see who's the hero and who's the villain. The villain is often circumstances of God, if you like, or it's something from the outside, or it's something that's very arcane.

Even in relation to literature that's very much more of an explicitly Christian period, the idea that the destructive or the diabolical comes from *outside* is very powerful. But, then again, if it's to come from the outside and into the inside of the human mind and purpose there's got to be an entry point, hasn't there? There's got to be an asking of the force to come in.

I remember at the beginning of *Dracula* by Bram Stoker, Jonathan Harker goes to the castle. You know that magnificent scene in Transylvania, and he's there, and the Count appears, and the Count can't ask him in. He's got to *ask* for the door to open to all that will follow and *admit* the force, which, of course, is a religious idea, completely so. But in another way the force of destruction is willed. There's a volitional element. It's come inside.

I'm very struck whenever I think of the gothic tradition in our own culture by the great Scottish novel *Confessions of a Justified Sinner* by James Hogg,[22] where at the end, after having built up the entire demonic character of this extreme Calvinist of a particular type in Scottish history, the Devil appears; the Devil makes a physical [appearance], or sort of is construed in the narrative to have appeared. But if he's there, he's *there*, sort of steaming and so on. But you can read the entire novel, that was brought back into modernity — partly by the example of André Gide, who was fascinated by this novel — because it's psychologically plausible to the modern mind and ear and eye and insight and so on, before you have this *return* to that which is otherworldly, that which is physically diabolical as the explanation for it all.

For those who don't know this novel it's about an extremist form of Protestantism, antinomianism, which is a sort of power-moral Calvinism, a pre-Stirnerite, pre-Nietzchean form of power morality. Don't forget, extremist Protestant ideas are very close to Jewish forms of theology, the belief that we are perfect, that we are the chosen. But if you say in a very ultra-Calvinist way, "I'm predestined. I'm chosen. I'm the elect," can't you step out of dualist Christian morality? "Morality's for the others, for the

---

[22] James Hogg (1770–1835), *The Private Memoirs & Confessions of a Justified Sinner: Written by Himself: With a detail of curious traditionary facts & other evidence by the editor* (1824).

sheep. I'm of *the elect*! I'm of *the glory*!" As this chap in the novel says, 'My brother-in-law's got a bit more money. I need to dis-possess him of that money because I'm of *the chosen*. I'm of the Zion. We stride over the others.'

My mother was a Presbyterian, and I once entered a Protestant chapel, and they were all chanting, 'We are Zion. We are Zion. We are Zion.' Now you know why Americans in the Deep South support the Israeli gunboats and planes as they bomb the Gaza Strip, because in their own minds they think of *themselves* as Zion. They think of *themselves* as elite, because that wing of the Protestant religion believes those sorts of things.

Now, Lovecraft came out of that tradition and was formed by it, even though he had a sort of cynical, an edge of the corner, knowing, and artistic attitude towards it, because of course art-ists make play of, as well as celebrating, the traditions out of which they come.

Conceptually now in the West people who create say they be-lieve in nothing. They're just interested in everything but believe in nothing. This is the new line. This is the mantra. When of course without any beliefs there's no creation, because there's nothing even to rebel against. There's nothing *there* before this creation. So when people say they create out of Western culture but don't really know what it is, it means they're just stirring the top of a heap of dirt, because they don't *know* where they have come from. And the interesting things in the view of Obama's election in the recent weeks is that people like Lovecraft repre-sented an America that was a minority, even a minority/minor-ity experience to the lives of most Americans.

But there is another America. America is not necessarily Pepsi Cola signs everywhere and trash everywhere and so on. There is the tradition of Pound and of Eliot and the first American dic-tionary by Mencken,[23] and of the great literature that they could

---

[23] H. L. Mencken, *The American Language: An Inquiry into the Develop-ment of English in the United States* (New York: Alfred A. Knopf, 1919) is not a dictionary but an investigation into American idioms, spelling, and grammar.

create as an extension of the European civilization and its mission. It's not the America of MTV. But MTV's controlled by a different ethnic group to these Americans and what they did in relation to their past and any future they may have in that particular union. I personally — although it's a long shot, a long punt, and we're talking decades ahead — I don't think white people have much of a future in the United States, particularly. They'll be in a minority by the middle of this century. They may be armed to the teeth, they may have their condominiums, they may be able to move, and all the rest of it.

I was in Houston a couple of years ago, and you can fit England into Texas twelve times, and you can fit Britain eight times, and you get a publication, and it'll talk about 'foreign news.' *Foreign news!* The foreign news was what was happening in Oklahoma! Texas is so big that the rest of the world is nowhere.

Henry Miller wrote an extraordinary book about the United States. It's very odd to talk about Miller, the great sexologist, but he wrote this book called *The Air-Conditioned Nightmare*,[24] which is an *extraordinary* book of an old European sensibility about the United States. He said, 'When you return from Paris to the United States, you know where you are because at the first gas station a Joe, a chap, will tell you, "Isn't it great to be back in the world, buddy?"'

'*Back in the world.*' Because America is so big that, to many people inside it, it is the world. They talk about themselves as the world. The 'rest of the world' is nowhere! America's where it's at; you'd better believe it. Although when you're that big, when you're putatively an actuary that powerful, those are the sorts of beliefs that you will have, any group would have, if they'd amassed that degree of strength. The irony is that the intellectual brilliance of some Americans has been completely disprivileged, and a mass, low-level lumpen capitalist metaphysic has been translated as what America is all over the world.

The best thing that could ever happen to America in many ways is for all of their post-imperial power to collapse and for

---

[24] Henry Miller, *The Air-Conditioned Nightmare* (New York: New Directions, 1945).

them to go back to being the United States, to go back to being what they always wanted their country to be, which is a country of people who'd come from Europe to get away from all of the fratricidal wars to build a new line.

That's why the most patriotic people in the United States advocate maximum isolation from the rest of the world. That's why when Gordon Brown gets on the box he says isolationism's a great peril, a great danger. These protectionist people, these 'British jobs for British workers' (his own slogan, of course!), these terrible people who want these sorts of things: American isolationists have always wanted it. The radical Right has always wanted it inside the United States, whatever it's been called. Black America has always, until now, loathed the dispensation of the American state internally, has always wanted never to be involved in any foreign conflicts at all. America's last war that they meaningfully fought would be the one over Cuba at the turn of the twentieth century. After that, American isolationists would have kept out of almost *any* other war that didn't relate to the Monroe Doctrine and to what they were hemispherically.

Now, to return to Lovecraft! Lovecraft began as an Aryanist and as an American first and up to a point, but didn't like Theodore Roosevelt because he wanted to go abroad. He wanted to manifest the American power externally, because by the beginning of the twentieth century America was getting very twitchy and would increasingly interfere not just in the Caribbean or Central and Latin America but all over the world. They tried one great attempt to intervene of course at the end of the First World War when Woodrow Wilson adopted a liberal mantra for American global hegemony, and then there was a resigning from that, there was a retreat. Nothing is forever. America retreated from globalism once.

One of the most famous history books written in post-Second World War America is *Rise to Globalism* by Stephen E. Ambrose.[25] It's totally mainstream. All of its views are utterly Harvard and CIA-appropriate and so on. It's interesting because it's

---

[25] Stephen E. Ambrose, *Rise to Globalism: American Foreign Policy Since 1938* (New York: Penguin, 1971).

such an insider's view. And the idea that our empire declines, of course. We once ruled quarter of the world in 1908. Look at us now. And our power was pretty straightforwardly taken from us by the United States, who've ruled in a neo-imperial way since.

This is why American cultural figures — post-European figures in the United States — are so culturally important. Because whether they're obscure or whether they're mainstream, if they become mainstream, their culture is ventilated all around the world. His books are in every bookshop in the world.

He died when he was forty-seven, almost of semi-malnutrition, because Lovecraft was so poor at the end he was living on baked beans, uncooked. Pretty bad. Pretty bad. If I was there, I'd have said, "Look, Howard, if you are starving to death, but couldn't you think of anything better than cold baked beans? Even a candle can heat it! Even that can heat it. Put a tin there, boy." Cheese and bits of old bread, that's what he was living on.

So in a strange way it's how the aristocratic sensibilities declined in the United States, because you can have an extraordinarily lopsided, gifted individual who can write great big thick books of no commercial value whatsoever, who's not an academic, who can't make money, and whose family inheritance has gone in a world where, if you can't make money, you're nothing in the United States, and where the only class they had of a higher sort, the slave-owning, Southern aristocratic class, was gone down in the 1860s, had been completely destroyed in the war to end war within the States.

When I was in Texas, you realize pretty quickly that people from the South don't call the American Civil War "the Civil War." You say the Civil War, and they say, 'What's that?' 'You know, the Civil War.' They say, 'No, the War between the States; the War of Northern Aggression, against us!' So it's very important for tribalism. America's not one country but many countries. Every tendency, every race, every culture, every religion is there now. So the America that Lovecraft addressed was *largely* a sort of organic culture — Inca with the blacks excepted — in comparison to what it is now.

Now, Lovecraft's later phase, which is called cosmicism, is

when he thinks of enemies of the human coming from the outside. This has led certain people to compare some of his work to some of Evola's theories. It's always said, and I remember well in a book . . . A female academic in Northern England—a Jewish woman named Gill Seidel—wrote a book called *Holocaust Denial*.[26] It's published by a very obscure press about fifteen years ago. And she said something very interesting in that book. She said, 'All Right-wing discourse is an attempt to build hierarchy and is an attempt to justify inequality and is an attempt to exclude, by virtue of its hierarchical ordination.' And that is a totally truthful statement. It's one of those moments when the outsider sees from the outside the truth of the discourse.

Why do Right-wing sensibilities do that? Because they want to create order. There are then definitional debates about where the order comes from, and, of course, there's two great views. One is the order is prior and is metaphysically objective; in other words, there are outstanding truths, outside time, outside history, outside Man, outside his circumstances, that they are divine. But humans don't maybe necessarily need to intelligently know everything that pertains to the truth of that, but they are prior to man. That's one of the views upon which you base the idea of a civilization. Not, 'It's all made up. I just thought of having it today.' That's called heuristic thinking; you make it up as you go along.

The other great sort of polarity, which is the more modern one, is people in a sense who can't accept the religious verities of the past. Don't forget, almost everyone in a Western society has grown up in a society where the religion has crashed down around. It just doesn't exist. I was born in 1962. The Christian religion, even if I had any partiality in that direction there anyway, was dead. It had been really dying for at least a century in my mind, in the mind of many young [people].[27]

Now, in this situation, the one we're in now, people of a

---

[26] Gill Seidel, *Holocaust Denial: Antisemitism, Racism & the New Right* (Leeds: Beyond the Pale Collective, 1986).

[27] Break in audio.

Rightist bias, if you like, in the last two hundred years — someone like Charles Maurras,[28] someone who actually founded Action Française thought, 'I may not know what the absolute truth
outside of this life that I experience is, but I can still support order, and I can still support that which is given, and I can still
support prior structures that lead to hierarchical inequality.
Why? Why? Because they give meaning, because they lead to
transcendence or the idea of transcendence which is the metaphoricization of hierarchy as you go up.'

Why do you want that? Your liberal would say, 'Why do you
want all that?' You want it because it makes life deeper. It makes
life more three-dimensional. It makes life more real. It makes the
prospect of death more real. 'Why do you want that?' You want
that so you can be more alive. Then they stop saying, 'Why do
you want that?' because it's become rather obvious. But he[29]
said, 'Oh, but that would lead to a tragic view of life or to a more
profound view of life.' And one of the modern conceits is to have
things of such a low temperature, to have everything so boring,
so nice, so compartmentalized you're feeling depressed for it.
That's what life's about now in the West.

The irony is many people from cultures outside the West look
on at us from the outside and think we're all ninnies, and we've
all bought what goes on here. And the truth, of course, is that
the bulk of people have accepted liberalism because their prior
religious tradition has collapsed for many of them. And they're
lazy, and they're enmeshed in materialism, and they're enmeshed in materialistic lives. If their credit cards were taken off
them, they'd be crying. Our Marines are crying when the Revolutionary Guards take their iPods away. I said if I was running
this country the men who *train* those Marines would be crying.

But there is a degree to which, if you like, a constructive non-
religious-based view of Right-wing thought is also valid in this
sense, because if a prior hegemonic religious viewpoint has col-

---

[28] See Bowden's speech on Maurras in his *Extremists: Studies in Metapolitics*, ed. Greg Johnson (San Francisco: Counter-Currents, 2017).

[29] The hypothetical liberal.

lapsed many Left liberals would argue 'Just plump for what exists now.' Safe, utilitarian, global, market-based, we're all the same, we all want the same things, allegedly. We all want to shop. We all have the same desires, an Asda in every street. This sort of thing. But in actual fact we're not all the same, and we don't want all the same things, and we don't have the same dreams or desires. And so Lovecraft's literature is about some of those dreams and some of those desires.

In closing, particularly for people who've never read him at all, I'd like to look at one story in particular called "The Dunwich Horror,"[30] which is very interesting. It's about sixty pages long, and Lovecraft builds atmosphere amazingly in these long, archaic, and baroque sentences that seem to go on for almost too long.

The story is about an eccentric backwoodsman who's a black magician and who has a sort of Sabbat or circle up by these stones in the heath. Because he has such a sort of Salvator Rosa imagination, Lovecraft could see a nice wood in sunlight, and what he *sees* is gothic gnarled trunks and the prospect of human sacrifice in the woods. That's what he *sees*, when in actual fact it's a nice sort of Woolworth's postcard as De Sade, in his imagination. Because he sees things in this dark sort of a way.

And the story involves, always with Lovecraft, even about his fellow Americans, conceptual elitism. Because there's this attraction to the barbaric, the instinctualism of the lower orders, and also this moral revulsion as well. And also *they're* the ones who will allow in the forces from without.

And there's this decayed family—decayed genealogical line—called the Whateleys. And it's quite clear that this sort of malformed woman in the family allegedly has some sort of congress with a being of nethermost essence from without, and she has two children. And the uncle who's left creates a dwelling inside the house where he locks all the windows, and he closes them down, and he builds a wooden structure on top of the house—the idea of an extended padded cell, if you like.

This is very much a staple of gothic literature. It was always

---

[30] Written in 1928, first published in *Weird Tales*, April 1929.

said of the old British aristocracy, the big family chain, you'd have one who was mad — one who was *utterly insane*. But you wouldn't have him in the black wagon dragged off to the local asylum. You'd build a padded cell in your mansion for him. 'Is that Jeffrey screaming?' And he'd be there. 'He wants feeding again.' And approached with a long pole, in that English sort of British way. In a way, this sort of literature is like the fulminations from that room, at a distance.

And so he builds this structure onto the back of this barn, and there's two brothers that have come from this illicit congress with this thing from without. One can be seen, and he speaks this sort of New England hick dialect: 'Now I'm goin' out in ma buggy.' And he's always very tightly dressed, *tightly dressed*, the idea being that there's bits of him that could slip out that you wouldn't want to see, bits that aren't human, particularly from beneath the waist. The old idea of the hooves and what is above them.

And every time he winds down into town to have a chat, to have a jaw, at the local drugstore with a few of the characters who prop up these stores, he's very careful about his diction, about his way of behaving, about holding his trousers up, as of course you would be if you were half-demonic nether-essence and going down to the local store to attain provisions. Put yourself in the chap's place. Then he gets in his buggy and drives back up to the family farm. All the time there's incessant tapping and knocking from the creature inside the extended wooden balustrade that's wanting to get out.

And, of course, there's always a professor in Lovecraft's stories from Miskatonic University or the University of Arkham or something like this, and he will say,

> 'I'm very troubled by these stirrings amongst the peasantry out in New England, Arkham town. There are some very primitive, underformed types out there who engage in some very strange rituals after dark. I've heard tell of some strange mongrelization by things from without and things that can't even be discussed. There are strange tappings at night and wooden promontories on the extensions of these clapperboard dwellings. I tell these to my

colleagues but they think I'm maaaaad. They think I'm totally insaaaaane! But I mean to quest out these provincial outposts and rec 'em in.'

It's always Lovecraft's personality as the academic bachelor of means who wants to go out and see what the dark side of New England peasantry's up to.

So, of course, things take a pretty turn when one of the brothers who's a sort of half morphic and a shape-shifter and semi-diabolical and a bit of a goat dressed up like the Black and White Minstrels, breaks into the Miskatonic University to look at a forbidden volume. Lovecraft loved, like all bibliophiles, what post-structural critics call "intertextuality," the fact that one book leads to another book leads to another book that leads to a reference in a footnote that leads to a footnote that leads you back to another book, so you become completely imprisoned — a glorious imprisonment — in the world of books.

There's, in some ways, a sort of anti-fascistic novel called *Auto-da-Fé* written by Elias Canetti[31] about a crazed bibliophile who lives increasingly surrounded by books, and the books get closer and closer, so that they're toppling over him. They're almost sort of animate things that are about to destroy him, and he needs his crude housekeeper to keep the knowledge *at bay*. It's a satire on the mind/body split in Western civilization where intellectuals become so lop-sided they almost topple over because the physical bit gets this small in comparison to the brain, metaphorically.

But with the Whateleys, this demonic family: he breaks into the University to consult the *Necronomicon*, this book that Lovecraft made up of forbidden lore written by a mad Arab — can you imagine it? — and the ink is the sort of inner blood of a tarantula and so on. And the mad Arab is writing these sayings that the nether-gods are telling him in a spidery hand. It's marvelous stuff. And Whateley breaks into the library, because 'I've just gotta git what that crazy ol' Arab was into. 'Cos I feel somethin's

---

[31] Elias Canetti, *Auto-da-Fé*, trans. C. V. Wedgwood (London: Jonathan Cape, 1946).

a-comin. Somethin's a-comin,' and I gotta see this book.'

And he's caught in the University library, transgression. He's caught trying to get this volume, translated in Lovecraft's field by John Dee who was a famous magician and famous writer in that era of pre-science where magic and classical lore and extreme learning and arcana and madness all sort of gel around in one sort of area. How a backwoods peasant who's got goat's hooves could read Latin written by a mad Arab is not dwelt upon, because of course in this literature you don't do details! That's for the critics. That's for the Edmund Wilsons of this world, not the adolescents reading this sort of stuff.

And he's written it all down, 'Yeesss!' He has all these sorts of sigils and strange terms that when he speaks to his father, the Old Ones — the ones out there — at the Sabbat, he's going to 'Bring down! Oh the glee!'

[. . .][32] It's the simple ones left at the turning with the car who see it as the sort of half-brother morphic form, the other thing that was mated at the Sabbat hidden in the farmhouse by the wooden extension that then burns down. They're the ones who see it, not the intellectuals. And they come back. And the New England rural citizens are on the ground rolling around saying, 'Oh my God, I saw it. I saw it. Now I can no longer see.' It's like the blinding in *Lear* in reverse.

And the professor's asked them to recount in their own words — which gives Lovecraft the chance to do the sort of hick dialogue that he loves — about what they've seen. And one of them, a couple of whiskeys down the throat and the tie released, says:

> 'I saw it, man, I saw it! It came out of the farmhouse, big *like a cloud*, but it was brown, and it wasn't human, you understand? It weren't human at all! It was writhing snakes — snakes afresh! — and they were grey, going on pink. And each hosepipe, each thing had a sucker like a mouth at the end of it. Some of it was green, and some of it was violet, and some of it was brown, and some of it was

---

[32] Break in audio.

some kind of color you don't even want to think of, and on top of it was this great sort of a disc.'

'A disc? Was it a metal disc?' You know, the sort of obtuseness of the academic mind that when they're being told about an enormous monster coming out of a farmhouse they want to get it down what sort of disc it was on top. Yes, of course.

'I don't know, professor, some sort of a disc, you get me? And it was coming out of the farmhouse like this! But that wasn't the worst.'

The academic's going, 'Not the worst boy, not the worst!'

'No!' he said. 'On top of this disc-like mongrel entity of flesh and suckers there was a face!'

'Uarghh! It was a face?'

'Yeah, it was even worse than a face!'

'God damn, what's worse than a face?'

'On top of a critter like that, boy, what's worse than a face? It's *half* a face.' Because it's got half the face of its brother on top of this great seething mass, as it goes up.

And then the professor ends his tale by saying,

'I know my fellow academics will not believe this occurred. I know it's the testimony of simple backwoodsmen. I know that for many you sitting in your hearths and booths stories of farmhouses exploding unleashing demonic taint with half-faces on top of hosepipes blancmange is not your cup of tea. But I am saying, as Jesus is my witness, I saw it. Well I didn't see actually every moment, but it was recounted to me by a man who knew, and he saw, because there are evil people out there like the Whateleys, and they want to bring in these things from the outside, and it ain't permitted, you understand, to bring them in without a by-your-leave. We came here to New England to build a new world. To build a new world! And these low-grade peasant types with their primitive folk religions are bringing in these creatures from the outside, but I tell you, the professors of Miskatonic will stand against it!'

Well, that's alright then, isn't it? The idea that they will stand against nether forces of the dark that are always brought in by those who are more primal, and then the story ends.

The Dunwich horror, which is the horror of the thing at the end, of the half-brother who isn't quite human and breaking into the museum to get the sacred/blasphemous book that will release in more of those things and this sort of thing.

There's a great moment at the local store when the uncle who's helped give birth to these monstrosities comes in and chats at the local store and says, 'I've got some people in ma family the likes of which you wouldn't believe. They're not even human. Indeed they're better than human, and worse!'

Yes, and people extrapolate. Marxian, deconstructive thinkers think, 'Is Lovecraft really talking about some of the people he met in New York and that he didn't like very much?' 'Or is he talking about civilization and decay?' 'Or is it a complete fantasy where it's just a dream/nightmare and has no reading beyond the text? It has no reality beyond itself. Who knows?'

What we do know is that Lovecraft died penniless in 1937, and yet a publisher and people who admired him — many of the people he'd sent the emails of his era to, thousands and thousands of times, all his correspondents — clubbed together to create a publisher called Arkham House who brought him out over the last twenty to thirty years. And then he gradually became a more and more significant figure.

Even the great sort of popular novels . . . I knew somebody who actually printed Stephen King's *It*. Six million were printed in Britain alone. *Six million!* They ran the presses at one of the very big printing firms in Britain for twenty-four hours. It never stopped. Six million. I always think to myself whenever I hear that figure . . . It's so amazing. That figure always recurs. It's come back like a tic, in the most inappropriate of places, like a tic. But King has said of Lovecraft, 'Lovecraft is the greatest writer of the baroque and highly wrought literary horror fiction in the twentieth century,' and, in a way it's true, because he creates his own world, you go into it, you sort of know what you're going to get.

Other stories are very Poe-esque. There's an early one called

"The Outsider"[33] where a man sort of meets himself in the mirror and has dénouement thereby, a self-reflective moment. It's a very old classic sort of gothic fare.

There's a few extraordinary ones, which I'll close with. One is "The Colour Out of Space,"[34] where this force comes from without like radiation and infects this farm, and they all decay. And there's great lines in it like, 'As Uncle Wilbur sat by the fire with a little pipe, suddenly part of his body falls off.' And one of his relatives goes, 'Wilbur! What's happened to your arm?' And he goes, 'Aw, shucks, it's gone and fallen off.'[35] And it's there! Because they're all turning to dust under the radiation, this color that comes from without. The interesting thing about Lovecraft is the monstrosities are sort of pseudo-scientific. They're like radiation.

Remember the scientists who developed the American atomic bomb? They used to chuck bits of the inner machinery to their children, because they knew very little about the concept of radiation. They all died of cancers about ten years later. There are pictures of them from the Manhattan Project. There's one famous picture of one of them holding up an inner component from the bomb. He's holding it on his aunt's head, thinking, 'Gee, look at that. Smile! You're on Kodak!' She'll be dead in a couple of years. Because they didn't know! And therefore to write a story like "The Colour Out of Space," which deals with the fear of radiation before that was even mentally known, is extraordinarily prescient really, isn't it really?

And that's why I say, that in a way, people like Lovecraft and the tradition that he represents are dreamers. There's the old theory that Colin Wilson once put in one of his books. It's a theory that sometimes works, although there's no scientific basis for it. If you have a face before you photographically and look at the left eye, it's said that that indicates the inner personality. It's not

---

[33] Written between March and August 1921, first published in *Weird Tales*, April 1926.

[34] Written in March 1927, first published in *Amazing Stories*, September 1927.

[35] Nothing like this happens in the story.

scientific, but policemen still use it. It's very interesting. You look at the right eye, and that is allegedly the personality as it's configured for presentation, for the world. It's the mask, as they call it in Eastern cultures. It's that which you wear. The left eye indicates the inner personality. It's very odd. If you look at many poets, there's an enormous development of this eye. It's just a way of looking at it, even an artistic way of looking at it, or an intuitive way of looking at these things.

But Lovecraft's eye is that of somebody who's not entirely on this world, as mentally he wasn't. He was a dreamer, a visionary, partly mad, partly sort of glorious, but very much part of *our* tradition, I think, this capacity for transcendence and a capacity for a sort of Saturnalian and darker element, to the notion of that transcendence. I think it's visionary power in art. I think it's the greatest things we've achieved — tragedy is usually — the greatest things that we've culturally achieved.[36] The Elizabethans, the Greeks: they *deal* with this sensibility and its power.

And I think that when one sees an advertisement for a mobile phone or one sees some egregious Americana that one doesn't like the look of, you must always remember these other figures, people like Lovecraft, like Poe, like Pound, like Lewis (though he was Canadian by birth), like Eliot[37] — often ultra-European figures with their dicky-bow ties and all the rest of it, from the early part of the twentieth century, and we understand that there are many Americas, and that we feel spiritually closer to the one that they represent than the one that Obama represents.

Thank you very much!

Counter-Currents, November 7, 2014

---

[36] On tragedy, horror, and transcendence in Western art, see Bowden's "Western Civilization: A Bullet Through Steel," in *Western Civilization Bites Back*, ed. Greg Johnson (San Francisco: Counter-Currents, 2014).

[37] Bowden's speeches and writings on Pound, Eliot, and Wyndham Lewis are collected in his *Reactionary Modernism*.

ROBINSON JEFFERS:
MISANTHROPE EXTRAORDINAIRE*

I've always wanted to talk about Robinson Jeffers for various reasons, partly because he is American, partly because there was an enormous cult in literature of him in the 1930s and forties, as big in our literature — in the literature of English-speaking peoples — as that of D. H. Lawrence. And yet Jeffers has dropped through a memory hole just like that. Stanford University in the 1980s produced a four-volume version of his poetry from the 1920s, and that's sort of archival, and it's basically of purely academic interest. He's important for certain developments in restorationist English-speaking poetry in the twentieth century.

Jeffers represents in one crucial way an alternative America and an alternative discourse within America that has got completely lost. We heard earlier from other speakers references to McDonald's, references to Coca-Cola, references to American cultural imperialism, as the French New Right would call it, and all of these are true. But it's important to realize that there is another strand in American life, in their literature, in their art, in their films from early in the twentieth century.

The founder of Hollywood cinema in some ways, cinematographically, is a man called D. W. Griffith, who did a film called *Birth of a Nation* in two parts. And there was a prize of the Director's Guild of America well into the 1990s called the D. W. Griffith Award. And then somebody remembered some of the films that he had been responsible for. Not *Intolerance*, not the founding of United Artists with Charlie Chaplin and various other people, but a film called *Birth of a Nation*. And quietly and slightly guiltily Hollywood and its bureaucracy gave up on a man

---

* Transcript by V.S. of Jonathan Bowden's lecture "Robinson Jeffers: Misanthrope Extraordinaire" at the ninth New Right Meeting in London on January 13, 2007, online at the Jonathan Bowden Archive (jonathanbowden.org).

who actually, in some ways—as a Southerner and as a proud white American—founded that industry, culturally and artistically.

He is just one example of another strand in American discourse, which theoretically involves people like Harry Elmer Barnes[1] writing about the First World War and American involvement in it; involves Francis Parker Yockey[2] after the Second World War; involves a professor of classics and Indo-Aryan languages called Professor Revilo P. Oliver[3] that straddles these two particular individuals, that goes to one side and links to the theory of writing of Lothrop Stoddard, who wrote quite a large number of books in the first three to four decades of the twentieth century, such as *The Rising Tide of Color* or *Racial Realities in Europe* or *The French Revolution in San Domingo*.[4] The prominent black Marxist intellectual C. L. R. James wrote a book, which is part of Black History Month and is on the official book list for all schools in Hackney, where there is a library named after him, called *The Black Jacobin*,[5] so he's actually responding to Lothrop Stoddard who got in first, and so on.

There is also within American art and letters a strand of extreme white racialism and self-affirming ethnicity and a strand of Eurocentrism as it would be called today. This is perhaps best explicated by Jack London. Even in writers who are Communist

---

[1] Harry Elmer Barnes (1889–1968), American historian and holocaust revisionist.

[2] Francis Parker Yockey (1917–1960), American Spenglerian political theorist and organizer.

[3] Revilo Pendleton Oliver (1908–1994), American classicist and political commentator.

[4] Theodore Lothrop Stoddard (1883–1950), American historian, political scientist, white racial activist, and author of eighteen books, including *The French Revolution in San Domingo* (New York: Houghton Mifflin, 1914), *The Rising Tide of Color Against White World-Supremacy* (New York: Charles Scribner's Sons, 1921), and *Racial Realities in Europe* (New York: Charles Scribner's Sons, 1924).

[5] Cyril Lionel Robert James (1901–1989), black Trinidadian-born Marxist historian, author of *The Black Jacobins: Toussaint L'Ouverture & the San Domingo Revolution* (London: Secker & Warburg, 1938).

leaning, like Theodore Dreiser,[6] an irreducibly European and partly WASP and white and Anglo-oriented — irrespective of the European ethnicity of these particular Americans — comes over in their work.

You get a whiff of it when you listen to somebody like Patrick J. Buchanan, for example, in the contemporary American media. A man who doesn't stumble over his words, a man who doesn't need an Autocue, a man who doesn't need everything written for him, a man who wrote Reagan's speeches in the first term and so on, a man who goes around in the studios with a dicky bow-tie, a man who quotes ancient Greek and Latin literature when he's talking to trash American channels. You just get a whiff of another America, of a European inheritance in that society which is *gone*, basically, from most mainstream discourse, just as this poet and his work have gone down the memory hole.

Now, he's part of a tradition, part of a gothic tradition in some ways, in terms of his temperament, which is very quintessentially English in certain respects, even though he was of Ulster Scots ancestry himself. When one thinks of the dark, macabre stories of Poe, their replication in the twentieth century by a sort of Aryan mystic and ultra-conservative like H. P. Lovecraft, whose work was misunderstood for many years, you begin to realize that there is a whole hinterland out there of another America.

In the southern states of the United States, which Jeffers had no particular connection with, there is a different doctrine to the one that prevails in the larger society. If you talk to a Southerner about the American Civil War, those who are self-identifying don't call it the Civil War. They call it, slightly more meatily and controversially, the War between the States or, even more radically, they talk about the War of Northern Aggression. Because there are different versions of America. Just for a moment consider what would have happened to the history of the world in the twentieth century if the South had won that war. If the South had won that war everything in human

---

[6] Theodore Dreiser (1871–1945), American novelist and journalist.

history in the twentieth century would be distinct and would be different.

In the 1920s, an immigration act was passed thanks to the machinations of an *enormous* organization called the Ku Klux Klan, that had four million members who marched on Washington, District of Columbia, in the 1920s to basically get an aliens act imposed. When the Kennedys and Johnson after them came in the 1960s—forget the stories of drug taking and bonking with Marilyn Monroe and all this sort of dark side of Camelot nonsense—the destructivity of the Kennedys was the undoing of this deep European tradition in the United States.

Since the winding down and the closing off of the immigration act which dates from the 1920s, seventy million persons of color have entered the United States, since the late 1960s, and have totally transformed the nature of that society. Not entirely in its clerisy, but in its demography. You walk around American cities now, and they have changed out of *all recognition*, just as many Western European cities have during the same period. Indeed, there is a replication the one of and against the other.

But there's always been a contrary discourse, culturally, within the United States. Usually it's mentioned in inverted commas today and is sneered at and is regarded as somehow unwholesome or even slightly morally unclean. But the word is quite neutral and is called "isolationism." This was the idea that America did not want to be an empire, but wished to be a republic—to adapt one of Buchanan's slogans, 'republic not empire'—and this tradition of white European people, with the small aboriginal groups that existed on the North American plains before them, forming a society to one side of the rest of Europe and not, maybe with the exception of Central and Latin America and the Caribbean basin, wishing to intrude into the rest of the world, which many of them had gone from.

Imagine for a moment a United States that kept out of the First World War. It went isolationist after the First World War, of course, and then veered again towards militant policies of what has become, transparently, a form of world imperialism since then. The whole of the post-war era delineates that fact in every country on Earth, because almost every society on Earth, almost every race on Earth is reacting to elements of global Americana. Through resistance you react. Through absorption and acceptance you react. Through a half-way house position you react. Even the European New Right is in some ways a reaction to what the Croatian thinker of partial American extraction—in the sense that he lived there and became a university professor there—Tomislav Sunić calls *Homo Americanus*, American Man, the alleged American Century and the alleged American Man.

Often you do find, particularly amongst Europeanists and people who are very hostile to modern America, a sort of gut reaction which forgets the dignity of white Americans, forgets that many white Americans are *not responsible* for what their government does in many parts of the world, that an ordinary white American living in Missouri or something has as much control over Bush and his clique as we have over Blair and Brown and theirs. But there are Americans who've always delineated a separate and a dignified and actually what is an American nationalist course *for them* in the situation that *they* have found themselves in.

I want to look at this man, Robinson Jeffers. Now, he's an extraordinarily gifted man who went to university when he was fifteen, because he was so intellectually superior they just let him in, basically. He could speak Hebrew; he could speak Latin; he could read ancient Greek. Like Enoch Powell, he was a great linguist. He was educated by his father. He came of pioneer stock. And like a large number of the original founders of the country and the framers of the American constitution, he was Ulster Scottish in ultimate derivation. That's an important identity within some of the deeply white sub-groups that founded this republic as it became.

Jeffers in the title of this talk is called a misanthrope extraordinaire, and his reputation in the 1920s and the 1930s was as a hater of humanity, or a man who goes into a cave like Zarathustra and casts anathemas upon the world. But what he was rejecting was what America has become: crassly and vulgarly materialist, grotesquely swinish in its attitudes towards all questions of moral worth and dignity and hierarchy. He represented, if you like, a pure spirit that wished to live on the frontier, that wished to be isolated in relation to nature. He wanted a smaller America, a more ecologically sufficient America, a more natural America, and a more pagan America.

He was brought up in the tradition of Calvinist radicalism and extreme individualism, which of course is part of the metaphysic of American life. It's the belief that you don't call in the state, but you deal with things on your own in the woods with a gun. Because all these people in their own ideology and as fact are born gun in hand. And they have a different attitude towards the nature of what it is to be human and post-European in an *enormous* environment, an environment of space and the dimensions of air and, in California, of light of a sort that shocks Europeans when they first see it, because it is a New World, quite genuinely.

The white artistic response from the late eighteenth century on to this new experience, this post-European experience, is actually an extension of *our* experience. But we've lost it today because the America that we think of is that which *click!* MTV appears on the screen. While the logic that has led to that, this man and people like him were the inversion of that.

Now, it's interesting that this man rejected Christianity. 'I rejected the Christ,' Jeffers said, 'when I was fifteen!' Which is quite early. And he rejected it in a fundamentalist American society, far more so than even now, because even the fundamentalism that exists now is this synthetic, psycho-babble fundamentalism where people are "born again" every thirty seconds. He came from a deeply Presbyterian Ulster Scottish tradition that believed in that sort of rhetoric, but actually also created Kierkegaard and Nietzsche and many other thinkers with whom Jeffers has a correlation.

In an earlier talk, I talked about Nietzsche,[7] and there's an element to which this extreme Protestantism — which is part of our tradition in these islands, let's face it, which is still manifest in places like Ulster — does have important lessons which can be used for our future. Technically, in philosophical terms and

---

[7] See "Credo: A Nietzschean Testament," in *Western Civilization Bites Back.*

theological terms, I suppose Jeffers would be described as an antinomian. This is somebody who takes a particular Calvinist heresy of strength and of glory and of pride and of power and of masculinity and of the ruthlessness of nature and wrenches it out of Christianity. In extreme Protestantism, there are certain discourses, which if you push them a bit further, cease to be Christian at all. They go outside.

There's an extraordinary novel, which is one of the great novels of our tradition and one of the great novels of Scottish literature, by a man named James Hogg, called *The Confessions of a Justified Sinner,* and which was partly rescued, in other words, brought back to textual attention, in the twentieth century by André Gide, who was influenced himself strongly by Nietzsche.

Now, this novel is about this particular Calvinist sect in Scotland. Don't forget, the Church of Scotland is not Anglican, is not a mild Evangelical, middling, and Catholic hybrid, but is a really Protestant dispensation, collapsing and dying now as most of these Christian dispensations are throughout the British Isles. But they were powerful once, and they led to powerful traditions and forms of European identity once.

The interesting thing is that Jeffers takes these ideas of election. In extreme Calvinism, whatever you do in this life doesn't determine what will allegedly happen to you in the afterlife because destiny, God has decided. The elect may know or may not know themselves, but the elect are set above. And if you have an idea of an elect which is sovereign and irrefragable, they step outside the remit of Christian morality, which is why this became a rather dangerous heresy rather quickly. Because you're actually talking about people who are so superior in their post-Christianity they can actually dispense with quite a lot of its ethical system.

But Jeffers went a little bit beyond this and embraced a type of radical and non-humanist paganism which has rarely been seen in the twentieth century. The critic, Colin Falck, who does the introduction to this short version of Jeffers' shorter verse published by Carcanet, which is a Manchester-based firm that gets Arts Council money.[8] As always with these things, the arts state spreads its largesse in all sorts of ways, and yet they often don't realize the sort of people that they're explicating, because the truth of the matter is that the spirit of this man and his revulsion against modern Western societies is almost, *almost* morally terroristic.

Jeffers is a fanatic and an outsider and a deep pagan and an extreme anti-materialist. He believed that human nature has never really changed, that we're essentially primordial. All of his work is a revolt against dualism. In liberalism and in Christianity—if you consider liberalism in part, for many people, to be a secularization of elements of Christian ethics—you have the idea that there's a force of evil and a force of good, and the two war with each other. It's a Persian concept in some ways. It's a Zoroastrian concept.

Jeffers cuts completely through that. Like many of the things I've just mentioned in relation to him. To him, life is a totality, and when an eagle comes down and tears its prey to pieces in the stump of a tree, there's no talk of good or evil, but of *life* and of *glory*. Imagine he's seen these things in a Californian sun, this pellucid light, this land that was virginal, certainly in 1900, 1910, 1920. Almost unsettled some of these areas where he chose to live deep on the Californian coast. These were sort of *primal*, aboriginal lands conquered—at least mentally as well as physically—by white people.

Now large parts of Hispanic America have come up to take California. Californian whites are now a minority in their own state. Don't forget California is the twelfth most powerful economy on Earth, considered as a state. They just elected a body-building actor to be their governor, of course. But it's all a bit too late. He may hang a few gangsters from Los Angeles, may put the syringe in their arm and that sort of thing. He may terminate a few of them. But I'm afraid that's all over.

But a man like Jeffers warned against what America has become. Half of Texas is non-white. All of these societies are

---

[8] Robinson Jeffers, *Selected Poems*, ed. Colin Falck (Manchester: Carcarnet, 1996).

changing. But when he wrote, these lands were virginal and were open and were a sort of Alsatia for European experience in the New World and in a new era.

But the interesting thing is, like all artists that seek out the primal, Jeffers wanted to base identity and art on things that were deeper than reason and which were instinctual and which were ultimately biological. So, in a sense, he's a *primal* artist, and primal artists are dangerous now and are rather tidied away, because they inevitably bring up ideas that our civilization isn't about to the right to shop, that such things as the heroic and the glorious exist and are just waiting in certain circumstances to be brought back. These are dangerous ideas.

Jeffers doesn't believe in human equality. He doesn't believe in democracy. He doesn't believe that men and women are the same and should be treated the same. He doesn't believe in peace. He doesn't believe in anti-slavery. He doesn't believe in intervening in the rest of the world. In other words, he's a bit of a *monster*! He's a bit of a *rogue*! He's a bit of a Jesse James.

And there's an irony about many of these outlaw figures. Because many of these figures about whom country and western artistes strum and so on, many of them are actually white paramilitaries, because many of these people were irregular, post-Confederate people who fought against the Republican carpet-bagging restorationist regime—Reconstruction it was called—in the southern states of the United States of America. They were actually guerrillas essentially, and they entered into folk music with a Confederate flag, which of course is the Scottish flag, behind them representing their particular dispensation in the United States.

Now, Jeffers wasn't a southerner. He has no absolute connection with Allen Tate[9] and those who mourned the Confederate dead. He has no particular connection with the movement in arts and letters known as the Southern Agrarians that begins in the twentieth century to put forth a revisionist thesis

---

[9] John Orley Allen Tate (1899–1979) was an American Southern Agrarian poet, critic, and social commentator. He was US Poet Laureate from 1943 to 1944.

about the United States. Because there is a revisionism, not outside in the rest of the world, but *inside* America.

You have to understand given the size of this enormous federation, many Americans think of themselves as the world. I know an American who went back to America recently and a chap said to him in a gas station, 'Hey buddy, isn't it good to be back in *the world*?' He obviously meant *America!* It's all here! Never mind the others! But when you realize that England can fit into Texas twelve times and Britain eight times, when you realize the dimensions of this society, foreign news is Oregon. Foreign news is what's happening in New York.

I know a chap who went to a rodeo in the United States recently, and the chap said, 'Is there anyone from New York here? Anyone from New York here?' And one bloke with the ubiquitous baseball cap shyly put his hand up and he said, 'Buddy, welcome to America!' And that is their sort of attitude, their sort of redneck attitude. And Jeffers represents, in some ways, the way Enoch Powell in a way did and a way the British masses understood that he did, the extreme intellectualization of *primal emotions* that almost everybody feels.

All sorts of youths and soccer fans and so on in the late 1960s on terraces used to chant "Enoch! Enoch!" This is a man who, superficially, they had little connection with, a man who used to write ancient Greek poetry for his own amusement when he was twelve. But there is a degree to which this man — who like Nietzsche was given a professorship when he was twenty-four, at the University of Sydney — this man, the masses understood that he incarnated what they *feel*, and what most intellectuals in the twentieth century have singularly failed to do, because they are beholden to and philosophize about ideas which are separated from *life* and which are separated from *vigor* and *identity*: sexual identity, racial identity, power, and violence.

Art is always primal at base. Our art began with tragedy, split into comedy, and its power always to move our people, and *any* people is primal. All art begins with a folk. It begins with a people, and you go up from that, depending upon the intellectual level that you want to ascend to and lead in accordance with your aptitude, your mind, your circumstances, and your desire to be ennobled.

This is why poetry, of course, has an oracular power—with music, and poetry aligned to music is in some respects even more powerful—that many other arts don't have. It's a bardic tradition. It's a tradition that's almost before all other traditions. In the Homeric tradition, in the tradition that leads to the explication of *Beowulf* in our culture, you have a man who is a skald, who has a musical instrument with him or an accompaniment of same. He improvises. Modern theoreticians like to call it the white form of jazz.

But it is actually something else. You have an idea, but you don't know where you're going. You know the story of Beowulf, you know Grendel comes, you know Grendel's mum comes, but you partly live it again in the performance. Because the performance is dynamic. And the audience is part of the performance. That's why it'd be rather strange doing it on your own. They are part of it. They are necessary. They are a character within it. Because they are your echo and beyond that.

This sort of bardic element in poetry in the twentieth century has been completely lost sight of. Poetry's about itself. Poetry is about language. Poetry is about the navel-gazing of the poet. Poetry is about what other poets say about you.

Kingsley Amis once wrote a poem saying that poetry should no longer connect mythically with the Western tradition, because we've got rid of all that. Well, there's a degree to which even this other week a not uninteresting poet called John Heath-Stubbs died.[10] Not that widely known, but John Heath-Stubbs, who was blind, represented that sort of bardic and oracular tradition. Of course, one doesn't need to mention Milton or Homer, but there is a degree to which in oral traditions if one loses a sense and is blind, of course, words become immensely powerful, because it's a compensation for the sight that you've lost, and therefore it's a redirection of energy.

Now, Jeffers believed that life would go on much as it had

---

[10] John Francis Alexander Heath-Stubbs (1918–2006), English poet and translator.

done for ever and ever, without change. He was an anti-progressive. He didn't believe in the Enlightenment, which is the theories which dominate the minds of most of our professors. When you go to the university these days, and you express an illiberal opinion, when they say, 'You're a monster! You're one of these far-Right fanatics! You're one of these outsiders' what they're actually saying is that you don't agree with certain ideas that philosophically entered our civilization, in stages, but in their core way in the late eighteenth century. And Jeffers rejects the Enlightenment. Even the term "Enlightenment," of course, is a slogan. It's a piece of propaganda. Why so? Because if you're not enlightened, you're unenlightened, aren't you? You're a barbarian. That's what they're saying. 'We are enlightened. We are progressive. You are a reactionary. You're an outsider. You're *uncivilized*.'

If you've ever been into liberal studios to debate about politics, and you have a view which is to the Right of the UKIP, you will soon know that liberals actually have, in part, not a physical fear of you, but a *moral* fear. Oh yes, they do! Because they think you actually represent *evil*. They do think that, because it's a system of ideas that most of our most clever people are loyal to, which is why it surrounds us, why it's in the ether at the popular level, at the middle level, at the elite level. It's everywhere! And it's everywhere because most of our elite minds have only been trained to think in this way.

Those who are outside, even the professors who are metaphysical conservatives—that means they're *illiberal* conservatives—people like Professor Roger Scruton, for example, people like the late Professor Maurice Cowling,[11] who I knew, these sorts of people, *they're* almost demonic. They are treading on the edge of the pit . . . and they are! I once said to Cowling, "Did you know that a group called National Alliance sells one of your books?" And he said, 'I don't want to know!' And they sold that book because Dr. William Pierce recognized in Cowling's book on the diplomatic response to Hitler—which is

---

[11] Maurice John Cowling (1926–2005), British historian. See Bowden's "Maurice Cowling," in *Extremists*.

probably his major academic book[12] — a sensibility which was untainted by liberalism, a sensibility that fought for itself outside of the correct moral compass.

Professor George Steiner,[13] who was comparative professor of culture at Cambridge at the same time as Cowling, was once asked about Cowling. Somebody said, 'What do you think of Cowling?' And he said, 'Oh, a brilliant man, but he represents unregenerate evil.' *Unregenerate evil.* Unregenerate evil! This is a man who had non-humanist and contradictory views in relation to liberalism, and he's really actually a *conservative* of an extremist type, although definitions can vary, and there's a subjective element to that.

But there's a degree to which people have to understand that the values of elitism and inequality are morally wrong. The reason we have redirection points for meetings like this is because in the past significant numbers of people wanted to really attack you, because the post-sixties generation that went through the radical Marxist groups really believe that they were attacking evil. That's why they could get so worked up.

Because people in a strange way, when they think they are defending the truth and the light, can do almost anything. And this is the irony about these people who preach humanism and preach universalism and preach the universality of love. Pol Pot, Stalin, Choibalsan, Lenin, Trotsky: all these people preached this sort of thing.

Trotsky said, 'We will have after the people's revolution a Kant on every corner; we will have a Goethe on every corner; we will have a Tolstoy on every corner; we'll have a Shakespeare on every corner; we'll have a Milton on every corner!' Garbage! You won't have any of that! Because if you melt down to nothing you will create a civilization of ants, and you won't create anything of glory at all!

But I mustn't get carried away, because somebody called

---

[12] Maurice Cowling, *The Impact of Hitler: British Politics & British Policy, 1933–1940* (Cambridge: Cambridge University Press, 1975).

[13] Francis George Steiner (1929–2020), Franco-American Jewish literary and cultural critic. See chapter 11 below.

Lee Barnes said on Stormfront that I was a 'rabid fascist.' Rabid! A rabid fascist who shouldn't be listened to, shouldn't be listened to. But you're listening to me, so we'll continue.

Jeffers was a sort of oracular poet, and Colin Falck has chosen two lines of D. H. Lawrence: 'It was a world before and after the god of love.' In other words, Jeffers represents a sensibility—because this is Falck choosing this from Lawrence to talk about Jeffers—it's a sensibility before Christ and before the Christian revelation and after.

Because one of the interesting things about Jeffers is that he predicts Christianity's collapse. Now, you can say that's unoriginal because Nietzsche predicts this collapse amongst others at the end of the nineteenth century. But Jeffers is going even deeper than that because he's predicting its *moral* collapse. The importance of Christianity is its ethical system. The cathedrals are glorious. Much of the art is glorious. It's the ethical system that's *wrong* with this faith, because it's a faith that says ultimately, 'You push me, and I'll feel sorry for you.' When of course you push them *back*, because that's a law of life! And those who don't push back will be eaten: by fate, by destiny, and they'll become compost of other groups.

Our species contains many groups that no longer exist, many cultures that no longer exist. You drill down into the earth, and you find all sorts of individual strata of civilizations and cultures that no longer exist.

The Philistines had quite a significant culture, and another group said they didn't, and that's why we in turn we use that word for anyone who is uncivilized today. So, don't always believe what's on channel five or channel four or one or two or three.

What we have to cleave to in our society are those people about whom our children are never taught. You have to understand that literature today is constructed in a way that will prevent "racism."

There was a debate recently at Oxford University about two or three years ago on the chair of poetry. "Chair"? Not even a chairman, you see? "Chair of poetry." And a third of the dons wanted to give it to Benjamin Zephaniah.[14] They wanted to give it to Benjamin Zephaniah! He was offered an O.B.E. in the same year. He said, 'White man, I spit on your O.B.E.!' The Order of the British Empire? He said, 'We want nothing to do with that empire!'

Now, he lost that Oxford vote, and you bet your bottom dollar that many of the Oxford dons who voted for him had never read a *word* of his dub and ragger and deep bass poetry. They'd never read a single word of it! They were voting ideologically, and they were also voting so that no one in the common room could say, 'He didn't vote for Zephaniah!' 'No, no! I did! Don't hold it against me!' That sort of thing.

In the end, C. H. Sisson[15] won, and C. H. Sisson is actually interesting because in some ways he's a naturalist, a normative conservative, had connections with Wyndham Lewis towards the end of his life. And so in a strange way you actually have a moderate Right-wing poet elected on the flipside of everyone cheering and waving to Zephaniah when they'd never read a word of him.

But it's interesting that many of our people know a lot about black history, which is a pretty short subject, and they know very little about our *own* history and our *own* identity because we, with the odd exception, have created through our cultural elites the greatest literature on Earth, the greatest art on Earth. As Camille Paglia says, ninety percent of that which is of cultural value from the past in present modernity is a creation of dead white European males. Dead white European males. DWEMs they're called in politically correct ideology. And they're people like Jeffers.

Jeffers wrote many poems. Many of them are about nature, which he saw in a manner similar to Ted Hughes.[16] But Ted Hughes, a sort of aboriginal Yorkshireman in a way, had no

---

[14] Benjamin Obadiah Iqbal Zephaniah (born 1958), black British dub poet.

[15] Charles Hubert Sisson (1914–2003), British poet and translator.

[16] Edward James Hughes (1930–1998), English poet, translator, and Poet Laureate 1984–1998.

metaphysical basis. Hughes saw nature *raw*. I remember when I did O Level a long time ago. It's not called O Level anymore. We did a poem called "Pike," which is an amazing poem in a way.[17] It's a sort of primordial and cannibalistic hymn, a paean to the pike. But you always think with Hughes that there isn't a larger or a greater spiritual basis to the nature of the diction, whereas in many ways there is with Jeffers.

Now, Jeffers was lionized in the early 1930s. His first book was privately published and didn't make much of an impact.[18] But this book *Roan Stallion, Tamar, & Other Poems* was taken up. This was published by the Modern Library of New York.[19] This was Penguin Modern Classics. It was hardback then, of course, because they didn't have cheap paperback books so much then. But this was as high as you could get. This was Penguin in every shop in contemporary American terms. New American Library, say, would be the contemporary American equivalent.

The irony is that these sorts of poems were lauded. Some people liked them because they were conservative and non-modernistic, but most people rather liked them because they were *daring*, because they were *transgressive*. There was a moment in the culture of the twentieth century where pagans, particularly before the Second World War, were regarded as a bit shocking, a bit thrilling, a bit erotic, pulling the Victorian underclothes, sort of the way Lawrence was received.

If Lawrence had lived longer there is the possibility that what happened to Jeffers would have happened to him. Because he was known to be slightly partial to certain governments in southern Europe that increasingly became frowned on, and what his attitudes towards things later on would have been one really doesn't know. But one sort of suspects that although he wouldn't have gone quite down the memory hole in the way that Jeffers has in American literature, the same sort of thing could occur.

---

[17] In Ted Hughes, *Lupercal* (London: Faber & Faber, 1960).

[18] Robinson Jeffers, *Flagons & Apples* (Los Angeles: Grafton, 1912).

[19] Robinson Jeffers, *Roan Stallion, Tamar, & Other Poems* (New York: Modern Library, 1953), originally New York: Boni & Liveright, 1925.

Most people actually find his views too much, even the people who explicate them. Let's have a dip in.

> . . . no thought nor emotion
> that all his ancestors since the ice-age
> Could not have comprehended. I call that a good life;
> narrow,
> but vastly better than most
> Men's lives, and beyond comparison more beautiful . . .[20]

Jeffers believes that pain and suffering are morally good. He believed it's ordained by nature. He believes that illness and death are divine, because they're principles of decay. When people say, 'I'm sorry' because you're suffering, his sensibility would say 'That is part of the generality of glory.' We're all going to die. We're all going to suffer. Nietzsche once said that sympathy multiplies misery. These are the reversal of Christian ideas. They believe in *strength* as morality. The liberal view is 'This is harsh; it's inhuman; you're punishing people who are weak, people who are defenseless.' The flipside of this view morally is that those who are weak can be built up towards strength, and that is morality. Rather than sympathize you assist, and if they push the hand away, and they don't want it, well, they don't get it. But if they want to be brought up to strength, that is what morality is.

Right-wing views are more than just opposing the European Union and being against the fact that England's fourteen percent non-white. Right-wing views are spiritual views about nature and man and identity. All groups have a Right wing. And eventually in a couple of decades it won't even be called Right-wing, because these are terms from the French Revolution about who sat to the right and the left of the speaker. The only difference between Left and Right is really moral and spiritual. But they believe equality is a moral good! A *moral good*. And it should be imposed!

The irony is that the contemporary Left is more extreme

---

[20] From Robinson Jeffers, "The Wind-Struck Music."

than the revolutionaries of the nineteenth century. More extreme even than Lenin and Marx. They never denied biological inequality. They believed it should be completely socially re-engineered so as to minimize the cruelty and naturalness of its effects. The contemporary New Left *denies* that there's any biological inequality at all, which is a nonsense! An absolute nonsense! They talk of fairness; they talk of justice.

Jeffers' response is to go around a nursery, to go around the cots of newborn infants. Some are born hale and hearty. Some are going to be spiritually strong, smoke three packs of Capstan Full Strength a day, and die in their bed at ninety. Others don't have eyes and don't have legs and are born misshapen and diseased and malformed. And yes, it's a tragedy. But nature spews out life, all the time, and some are destroyed, and others move towards the sun. This is really what our people believe, or at least feel instinctively. Everyone feels, or most people feel.

Because, let's face it, everyone in this society has accommodated with liberalism in some way. Everybody has, because we have to live in the society as it now is. I'm forty-five this year. 1962 is the year I was born. The year Jeffers died. I've known nothing but liberalism. Nothing my entire life. People who are older have known a sort of slightly more traditionalist Britain that was different. We've never known it, but there are people, of course, who in a sense have reacted against indoctrination. But just to react is not enough. What you have to do in my opinion is to reconnect with that which is primal and that which is glorious. Everyone has it. People basically manifest it at different levels of intellectual complexity, but everyone has primordial emotions.

When I was young, I liked "God Save the Queen" and all the rest of it. But to me it's not *fierce enough*! It's not *powerful enough*! Unfortunately, most English people like it a bit softer, actually. It makes them feel more comfortable. You have to find in some ways a method that makes them feel comfortable about being primal again. That's what the sort of politics that we're involved in is about, really. It's making our people feel comfortable with being militantly themselves to the degree that

if somebody stands on your foot you don't say, 'Oh, sorry.'
You say, *'Get off my foot!'* And that's how we have to be in the
future, because, in actual fact, a terrible sort of divorce of sensibility has occurred in our civilization.

I once had a conversation about this with a printer called
Tony Hancock,[21] and I said to him, "One of the great dilemmas
that we have is the total split between the mind and the body
that exists in people in our group." There you have intellectuals
of extraordinary abstraction and capacity for intellectuality —
someone like Samuel Beckett[22] would be an example — who
create culture totally for other intellectuals, totally introverted
and turned on itself. Very gifted, but completely desiccated and
contrary to the instincts of life.

And you have a mass of people for whom comprehensive
education is to be a great glory, but forty percent of them can't
read, can't write, can't add up! This was brought in by Labour
politicians who prated for decades that they were doing it for
working-class people. They weren't doing any such thing!
They have adopted methodologies whereby people can hardly
have any knowledge of who they are by virtue of the education
they've received. That's a far greater "betrayal" than any snob-
bish Tory ever did to them! That's what they've done to our
people!

What we have to do, particularly what intellectuals have to
do, is recompose the mind and the body together, the fist and
the brain together. As I once said to Hancock in a private conversation, "Too many of those who have courage have no intellect, and too many people with intellect have no courage at
all." *No courage at all!* About anything!

Which is why we're totally leaderless in this society, in the
church, in the government, in the Commons, in the Lords, in
the courts, in the universities, in the media, even in the armed
forces! Look all over the society and there is no leadership at
all! Nobody who says 'I'm bringing the mind and the body together'. Nobody who says 'We're British and European by cul-

---

[21] Anthony Sandford Hancock (1947–2012), printer and publisher.
[22] Samuel Barclay Beckett (1906–1989), Irish playwright.

ture and Caucasian by race. And this is *our* culture and *our* society!'

Our ancestors have created extraordinary things, and our culture is dying around us. When I attend salons and posh parties, people who know who I am cross the room and say, 'We can't associate with this terrible man and his terrible views.' My war against them, just to personalize it through me, is that these are the people in their softness and luxuriance who have an effete view of the values of their own civilization. They'll go and see Aeschylus; they'll go and see Sophocles; they'll go and see Euripides—and Jeffers did a version of one of Euripides' plays—they'll go and see these things, but it's a circus. It's not even a circus, it's a museum. It's a memorialism. You can have that as long as you don't insult anyone else. No, don't insult anyone. But you can have that. You can have Radio 3.

Radio 3 is very interesting actually, because you'll have Wagner, you'll have Bruckner, and then you'll have an Auschwitz hour! And then you'll have Shostakovich, and then you'll end with a bit about Stalin added on for reasons of balance. You know, balance. Then you'll have some Mozart and that sort of thing. You can have the one, but you've got to have the other. What they're doing with that is they say you can *have* a memorial and soft and desiccated version of it.

Matt Tait went to see a Shakespeare play in Stratford-upon-Avon recently. I think it was *Julius Caesar*. Forty percent of the cast was black. Forty percent. I don't remember a black character in *Julius Caesar* actually! I know Orson Welles did a black version of it in Harlem in the 1930s and had to be guarded to the theatre by heavies, because that was the nature of Harlem even then for a man who wasn't black.

But there is a degree to which the fear of self-identification of our own culture, the fear of our own music, the fear of the power of our own art is extraordinary in people. The whole point of multiculturalism is that the thing is mixed together so that no group feels slightly alienated. On the other hand, all groups are simultaneously alienated from their own culture, and us as the indigenous more than anyone, because we are the ones who can't be contributive to it.

I've got a friend in the party that I am in called Eddy Butler.[23] And sometimes Eddy's very practical, very electoral, very focused on 'the meat that's on the street' and this sort of thing. He says the trouble with that is it's all airy-fairy stuff. It's all up in the air. But my view, of course, is what is really wrong with our people? What's really wrong with them? Is it physical? No, it's not. We're essentially much the same as we've always been, really. It's what's up here[24] that's wrong. It's the spiritual mentality of our people that's wrong, that's cowardly, that's weak, that's afraid, that's afraid of life, afraid of people's opinions. *Who gives a damn for other people's opinions?* English and British people have conquered large stretches of the world because we didn't give a damn about other people's opinions.

This is an era when, in a sense, we're living in a very, very chaotic and dangerous time. To just for a moment reintroduce some of the topics that were discussed earlier, there are considerable noises off in foreign and diplomatic circles that Israel has decided on a bombing of Iran later this year or early next. They've got to do it in the next two years because Bush will provide an umbrella for them. But even the Americans won't do it for them. They've got to go alone, and America will support. America will refuel their jets in mid-air. Now, whether it happens or not, one doesn't know. But it may well, and indeed the inclusion of a "far Right" leader in the Israeli government is probably part of a precursor to a consensus within that society for that strike. So, we're living in very, very radical and very, very dangerous times.

The isolationists like Jeffers who opposed American involvement in the Second World War, who opposed American involvement in Vietnam, which was a demonized and yet then came to be an acceptable even progressive opinion, particularly because Democrats supported that war because they had to *prove* that they were anti-communist in relation to conservative critics inside America. Hence Kennedy and Johnson radicalized that war. Jeffers lost. The spirit of this poet, and the spirit of

---

23 Edward Mark Butler (b. 1962).
24 In the head.

people like him lost.

The America that Stoddard and Oliver and Yockey and Lovecraft and Jeffers and Mencken and London and all these other people wanted: that doesn't exist. But I've always had a great sympathy for these deeply white, deeply European, dignified, and highly cultured Americans who, if you like, are un-American now in relation to what's happened in their own society.

This man is a poet of extremity, of sacrifice, of violence, and of joy. He's a man who believes in strength through joy, essentially. Let's just read one poem that I've just chosen in a sort of automatic writing way, page 51:

"Return"

A little too abstract, a little too wise,
It is time for us to kiss the earth again,
It is time to let the leaves rain from the skies,
Let the rich life run to the roots again.
I will go to the lovely Sur Rivers
And dip my arms in them up to the shoulders.
I will find my accounting where the alder leaf quivers
In the ocean wind over the river boulders.
I will touch things and things and no more thoughts,
That breed like mouthless may-flies darkening the sky,
The insect clouds that blind our passionate hawks
So that they cannot strike, hardly can fly.
Things are the hawk's food and noble is the mountain, Oh Noble
Pico Blanco, steep sea-wave of marble.

Let it be! I give you the life of Robinson Jeffers: American misanthrope.

Thank you very much!

Counter-Currents, July 29, 2011

NINETEEN EIGHTY-FOUR & TOTALITARIAN LEFTISM*

I'd like to talk about George Orwell who was one of the major writers of the twentieth century. Many people believe that the political novel *Nineteen Eighty-Four* is in many respects *the* novel of the twentieth century. It is probable that by the middle of this century, at the beginning of the new millennium, this novel will be seen as axiomatic of much of what went on in the era just before.

Orwell was dying when he wrote this work, and he wrote in on the island of Jura; he wrote it in a tent; he wrote it on the island that had been rented to him by the proprietor of a magazine called *The Adelphi*.[1] He was dying when it was written, but it doesn't really bear upon it the impress of a dying man.

Nineteen Eighty-Four has entered into the language of contemporary modernity. Even the word "totalitarianism" was made fashionable by it. The term "Big Brother." The belief in an all-powerful and all-seeing yet strangely unknown party. The invention of Newspeak. The notion of Ingsoc or English socialism.

The extraordinarily famous broadcast in the middle of the 1950s which caused a scandal at the time when the BBC broadcast it with the late Peter Cushing playing Winston Smith in the title role. It is said that one Tory MP got up in the House of Commons and condemned the BBC for having this broadcast because one of his constituents had dropped dead during the middle of

---

* Transcript of Jonathan Bowden's lecture, "*Nineteen Eighty-Four* and Totalitarian Leftism," which was delivered to the twenty-third New Right meeting in London on September 26, 2009, online at the Jonathan Bowden Archive (jonathanbowden.org).

[1] Orwell lived on Jura, in the Inner Hebrides of Scotland intermittently from 1946 to 1949. Orwell lived in the Barnhill farmhouse, not a tent. The house was owned by the Fletcher family. *The Adelphi* or *New Adelphi* was an English literary journal founded by John Middleton Murry (1889–1957) and published between 1923 and 1955.

it. The ultimate critical accolade: dropping dead in the middle of a TV performance. It is quite possible that she dropped dead at the moment when the rats were introduced into the mask to torture Winston at the end, by the party.

If you remember, O'Brien, who is the sort of sadistic Party priest and has an Irish Catholic name of course because there is an anti-Catholic element to the novel, and Blair, or Orwell, was a Scottish Protestant in many respects: that strand is there.

And she dropped dead at the moment when the rats were introduced. Do you remember the moment in the cellars of the Ministry of Love? When O'Brien says to Winston about the thing, the one thing that every individual fears above all, and he knows that in Winston's case it's rats, and rats are introduced into this mask. Richard Burton, of course, played O'Brien in the famous Virgin film, actually, done by Branson's organization, of *Nineteen Eighty-Four* in 1984. Burton was dying of cancer at the time, and it was not just his last great performance but his last performance.

This novel begins with a very famous phrase. I don't usually actually quote in my talks, but I think this is the one occasion when I'll differ from that. This is a triadic novel in accordance with the Dante-esque schema which prevails in a lot of Western literature. You have a tripartite division: the affair between him and Julia, the Party dissident, is in some ways a slightly squalid version of heaven; the purgatorial existence under the rule of the all-seeing Party in the first part of the volume is purgatory; and the last sequence in the always lit, electronically lit cellars of the Ministry of Love, is hell, under the dispensation of O'Brien and the totalitarian Party that he serves.

The novel begins in this way. *Nineteen Eighty-Four* part 1:

It was a bright cold day in April, and the clocks were striking thirteen. Winston Smith, his chin nuzzled into his breast in an effort to escape the vile wind, slipped quickly through the glass doors of Victory Mansions, though not quickly enough to prevent a swirl of gritty dust from entering along with him. The hallway smelt of boiled cabbage and old rag mats. At one end of it a colored poster, too large for indoor display, had been tacked to the wall. It depicted simply an enormous face, more than a meter wide: the face of a man of about forty-five, with a heavy black moustache and ruggedly handsome features. Winston made for the stairs. It was no use trying the lift. Even at the best of times it was seldom working, and at present the electric current was cut off during daylight hours. It was part of the economy drive in preparation for Hate Week. The flat was seven flights up, and Winston, who was thirty-nine and had a varicose ulcer above his right ankle, went slowly, resting several times on the way. On each landing, opposite the lift-shaft, the poster with the enormous face gazed down from the wall. It was one of those pictures which are so contrived that the eyes follow you about when you move. BIG BROTHER IS WATCH-ING YOU, the caption beneath it ran.[2]

Now, of course, that's a portrait, in a cartoon-like way, of Joseph Stalin. Who, if you remember, had the handlebar moustache and the eyes that seemed to follow you around the room in a sort of quasi-Elizabethan painting where the eyes are hollowed out and a spy watches you in between one room and another, and so on. On a personal touch, my mother's stepfather had a portrait of Joseph Stalin on his wall, in the pantry, because he was Communist shop steward in the Avro's works that built the Lancaster bomber in Manchester. And so Stalin gazed down upon the Butties and upon the Eccles cake, and upon the things in that Manchester pantry. Stalin: his hero.

Although he once said if it wasn't Stalin it would be Hitler, because he was one of these individuals who would never be in the middle, you see, and because he was naturally of an illiberal mind. But there we are. Don't forget these individual leaders had enormous cults earlier in the twentieth century. The postmodern people wandering around with their shopping bags this afternoon in central London are living in a totally different time

---

[2] George Orwell, *Nineteen Eighty-Four* (London: Secker *&* Warburg, 1949).

and in a totally different temperature and moral climate.

Now, the novel begins with a lot of sense data which shows that Orwell was a novelist and not a political ideologue. One of the reasons that this novel has lasted is because it is *not* political philosophy translated into novelistic effect. It's a novel infused with political ideas. What most apolitical people remember is the cabbage smell that's everywhere, the dirty mats that are everywhere, whenever you put your hand on something there's dust, and there's dirt. Everything's decrepit and broken down, and yet the Tannoy in the background's pumping out ideology about the glory of socialism and the coming struggle of the masses.

The one thing that's forgotten about this novel is that this novel's a comedy. It's actually an extraordinarily funny book, and Orwell views it in deeply dark satirical terms. The fact that the world has not read it as a comedy, but has actually read it literally as a fact, is a testament partly to the *extraordinary* cynical and dark and treacly nature of Orwells' outlook. Maybe it was also affected by the fact that he was dying at the time that he wrote it.

This novel is a satire on many of the Leftist Hampstead intellectuals that Orwell knew in the thirties and the forties. Robert Conquest, who wrote *The Harvest of Sorrow* and *The Great Terror* about Stalinist atrocities in the Soviet Union,[3] was angered to do so by the mealy-mouthed and appeasing apologetics which he came across in the salons of Hampstead and elsewhere, and Orwell was very similar.

Orwell was a paradoxical man: a socialist of upper-middle-class origins, he was in revolt against the Empire of his day, and he wrote a book called *Burmese Days* which was a testament to that revolt.[4] Yet also, a man who, in some respects, was a "Tory," in inverted commas, was archaic in Leftist terms, was a bit of a

---

[3] George Robert Acworth Conquest (1917–2015), British historian and poet was the author of *The Great Terror: A Reassessment* (Oxford: Oxford University Press, 1968) and *The Harvest of Sorrow: Soviet Collectivization & the Terror-Famine* (Oxford: Oxford University Press, 1986).

[4] George Orwell, *Burmese Days* (London: Victor Gollancz, 1934).

nationalist, and a man who always adored rubbing the fur of his own side backwards. Orwell was one of these people who is an extraordinarily difficult bedfellow, as his fellow Leftists were to discover.

He made his name, amongst other things, for editing Aneurin Bevan's review *Tribune*,[5] on the left of the Labour Party, in the 1930s. But his hostility to Stalinism and to Left totalitarianism, his hostility to the British Communist Party, and his hostility to the tactics Communists used to impose their discipline on others became apparent throughout the 1930s and forties.

They were basically crystallized by his experience in the Spanish Civil War, where — typical of Orwell — he didn't go for any of the Left militias that were most favored and ended up with the POUM[6] which was in the command of somebody called Andreu Nin,[7] who was a minor demi-Trotskyist figure, despised by the anarchists, and by the official Left, and yet to one side of the main socialist bloc fighting in the Republican cause. This is rather typical of Orwell because you know full well that he's aligned himself with the faction that, if crushed in internal Left disputes, would mean that he's actually persecuted by his own side, and this is, of course, what happened.

So, in the July days in Madrid, when the anarchists and the Communists fought with each other inside the Republican zone, when there needed to be a scapegoat for that fighting, they turned on this tiny little party that everyone hated called the POUM, and they became 'fascist apologists,' 'clerical dog-collarists,' 'running dogs of the international bourgeois conspiracy,' and so on. And these individuals were hunted down with extreme ruthlessness, and all those that were found were shot and killed without any sort of a tribunal or trial at all. The leader of

---

[5] Aneurin Bevan (1897–1960), Welsh Labour Party politician, was a board member of *Tribune*, a democratic socialist newspaper published in London founded in 1937.

[6] The Workers' Party of Marxist Unification (Spanish: Partido Obrero de Unificación Marxista)

[7] Andreu Nin Pérez (1892–1937).

this particular sect was tortured to death by the Communist secret police inside the Republican zone.

These incidents traumatized Orwell and made him a sort of critical figure of parts of the Left on the Left. We look back today through rose-tinted spectacles to a degree. When he wrote this sort of material the world was still very much in the balance, and the forces against which he was inveighing in art, novelistically, could well have come to power.

It's also interesting to note that most of Orwell's books are not forgotten today but would have been partly forgotten had he not written the fable *Animal Farm*[8] about the Bolshevik *coup*, and had he not written *Nineteen Eighty-Four* about the texture, and nature, and, what novelists call sense data, of living under a totalitarian Left dictatorship.

One of the interesting things to note is that Eastern European intellectuals, particularly in societies like Hungary and Poland and Czechoslovakia and elsewhere all regarded this book as essentially a factual commentary on their lives, so close was it an imaginary, and yet projected, identification with what it was like to live under Ceausescu's Romania, for example. There are also extraordinary parallels between reality and this novel which, don't forget, was written in 1948 which is why when he needed a title he inverted it and it became *Nineteen Eighty-Four*.

In Ceausescu's Romania almost every telephone conversation was listened to, and if you rang into the country from the outside, the Securitate, the all-pervasive secret police, would break a line—very crude, pre-digital connections—and they would put in a new block of tape to listen to the message again. And you'd have to ring again, and then you would have to ring again, and then they would block the line, and you'd have to ring again, and so on. Because everything was being listened to even when it wasn't. Every café table had a microphone underneath it; but eighty percent of them didn't work; but people couldn't take the chance that it wasn't one of the twenty percent that happened to be working.

---

[8] George Orwell, *Animal Farm: A Fairy Story* (London: Secker & Warburg, 1945).

There are two extraordinary parallelisms between the Ceausescu regime and this novel. One is the endless production of works by the great leader. Ceausescu's collected volumes ran to fifteen to twenty to thirty volumes. Of course, he never wrote a word of it. They were all written for him by communist scribes and apparatchiks. Hoxha in Albania had a similarly unread, cavernous library that was produced, to a boy, by tame scholars who would have been shot, or tortured to death, or their families killed, and their family homes bulldozed so that they'd never existed, hadn't they actually produced this sort of material.

The other parallelism is the pyramids. In this novel, the Party builds four enormous ministries: Ministry of Peace, which is for war; Ministry of Love, which is for torture and oppression of the citizen into the purity of Ingsoc, the ideology of the dictatorship, which is called Ministry of Love because it's the inversion of that. Then there's other ministries: Ministry of Plenty, which deals with economic affairs, usually involving endless braying statistical announcements of pig-iron production which Orwell thought was a hilarious joke from Eastern bloc dictatorships, but actually came quite close to the truth.

Now, in Romania Ceausescu ordered large pyramids to be built in the capital, and these were built and were observable when the regime fell in a *coup* organized by ex-communists and other factors to form what was called the National Salvation Front at that time. Do you remember the scenes on television? When Ceausescu's on the podium surrounded by the Securitate? Many of whom were orphans, many of whom were taken from orphanages directly by the Ceausescu family and impregnated with the idea that they were related to him; that Ceausescu and his ubiquitous wife, who was always with him on all occasions, were their mother and father. That's one of the reasons, psychologically, why the Securitate gunmen fought to the end, unlike many of the other Eastern bloc dictatorship servants who gave up when the going got rather rough.

There's that incredible moment, which is history as it's observed, when Ceausescu was orating about the dangers of fascism, the dangers of revanchism, the dangers of counter-terrorism, the dangers of a new bourgeois elite arriving in Romania, and he suddenly stops. And the Securitate around him start to get worried because the crowd is getting restive. And the crowd is working out that if just a few of them move, nothing will happen, but if they all move together, the security police don't know what to do.

And there's a moment when Ceausescu is looking: 'Do I step back from the microphone? Do I continue my anti-Western rant? Do I go into the helicopter with the Securitate?' And he suddenly decides to go with the Securitate, and they disappear.

And usually, if ever a regime like that's in trouble, there's an immediate cut in the television and a ballet starts. Or something like that. That always used to happen in the Soviet Union: whenever someone was being purged or there was something of moment was going on, a famous feature film would appear, you know, just to fill the gap, just like trooping the color but in Soviet terms. It would just be put up.

But the Romanian television just allowed it to run, and you can see the Ceausescus running across the top of the roof, surrounded by Securitate who had their weapons out by then, and then got into the helicopter and went off, by which time the crowd, or mob if you like, had broken in to the bottom of the building, and was coming up the building, and by then the whole structure was swaying. Later that day, of course, the Securitate got on top of many of the buildings and started firing down on the people, and many of them were determined to bring back the regime.

Now, this novel is interesting because it radicalizes certain elements of Communist rule. One of the ideas that's almost got forgotten about in many treatments of the novel; and filming, and theatrical treatments like the Peter Cushing one and like the John Hurt one, and that sort of thing, can't really deal with this: and this is the language the Party creates called Newspeak. This is this all-purpose, jabbering, ideological, Marxist-Leninist language, sometimes referred to as "duckspeak." Duckspeak is the idea that you quack away, quack away, and your conscious brain is not really involved because your response to everything is a preformatted form of ideology.

If you remember, one of the dictionary makers who befriends

him, he's called Syme, in the grubby canteen where they all have their dinners, in the Ministry of Truth, which of course is to propagate lies on behalf of the regime, and to rewrite the *Times* so that everybody's been purged, at the right place, and if somebody is purged they are now an un-person, a un-person in Ingsoc Newspeak. And you have to go through the records and make sure that it's all filed, so there's no relationship with them, so you can never be accused of thought criminality by virtue of the fact they exist. Every bit of spare paper that relates to an unperson, somebody done away with, you put in the memory hole, which goes down into the furnace, which is everywhere, ubiquitous, behind these pipes, this little grill; it's just like a sort of waste disposal really, but the idea is it's waste disposal of all the lives who are being rewritten continuously, so that the current reality fits in with the Party view at any particular time.

The Party has two sections: the inner Party, which wears black and has special privileges; the inner Party can turn the telescreen off. Like that screen back there, every apartment, every room has a screen, but you can't turn it off, and it watches you as you watch it, so it's two-way. And O'Brien of course in a famous scene in the second section of the book, can turn it off because he's in the inner Party.

For most people, the TV rather than at the end of the room, is in the center of the room on a wall, so it can look down on them, and so it can instruct you — "Citizen!" — in appropriate behavior. Everyone, like in Maoist China, at the beginning of the day in *Nineteen Eighty-Four* by Orwell has to do physical jerks. You have to do physical exercises at the beginning of the day to coordinate yourself for the coming struggle and for the commitment to socialism which will occur throughout all of the hours before you go back to bed again.

Another interesting insight is the relationship that people have with their children. Orwell prefigures the world of bourgeois chaos where parents are frightened to discipline their own children, and which we increasingly see in liberal humanist societies. The parents are preyed upon by the young. One of the first, and great, scenes is with the Parsons family who live just up the corridor in the block, 'cause the Parsons boy is a terror.

He accuses everyone of being . . . 'You're a thought criminal!' he says. 'You're a nasty little vanguard against the Proletariat elite!' He screams that at everyone he meets. And he's got a pop-gun, he says 'You're gonna burn, you're gonna burn, you're going to the camps! You're going down the salt mines now!'

And his mother's terrified of him because to discipline him is to engage in the possibility of a counter-revolutionary act. So he knows that he's got his parents where he wants them by this endless sort of Young Pioneers brigading sort of behavior. And it's a way of corralling the older generation into conformity. Orwell's instinct for particularly Left totalitarian forms of power is very acute here, considering that, except for a small period in Spain, he'd never really been subjected to them.

The other thing which is very interesting, and which Orwell knew extraordinarily well, partly because of his time at the BBC, was the penchant intellectuals have for propaganda. Intellectuals adore the idea that they are independent spirits who are highly individualistic and always *love* gainsaying what anyone else has said to them. In actual fact, Orwell believed that most intellectuals are craven, and deeply conformist, and extraordinarily group oriented.

Orwell wrote BBC propaganda for India during the Second World War. He wrote it in Senate House, which is in Malet Street, which is where the Central London university buildings are, the sort of whitewashed, slightly authoritarian sort of twenties, thirties type of heavy modern building. And there's a Room 101 in that, because all of the BBC offices had numbers, and the torture scene with O'Brien was the same room from which he broadcast anti-Axis propaganda to India, where, of course, Gandhian pacifism, and the Indian National Army that supported the Axis, and so on, were active, and the BBC needed people to bring propaganda over to that part of the world during the Second World War.

Now, there's an individual in this book called Syme who's an etymologist. He's writing the eleventh *Dictionary of Newspeak*, and Syme meets Winston Smith in the grubby canteen. You remember the food they have? Your lunch would be a Brillo Pad, which is sort of pork or something, surrounded by bloody stew, surrounded by bits of decaying vegetable, all in a broth, and you sort of eat it down with Victory Tea in a chipped mug, and it's really hot because there's no milk in it, and it's just sort of filth really. But you've just got to sling it down because it keeps you going. And all the time Syme is talking about the eleventh *Dictionary of Newspeak*.

He says, 'We're going to totally eradicate intellectual freedom of thought.' This is an intellectual. He says, 'We're going to so restrict, methodologically, the linguistic compass of the human, so that people won't even be able to think independently of Party rule.' Because to be able to think, you have to have not just a concept but the language to express it. 'We will so restrict language to the possibility that the signifier can never go beyond that which is signified. There can only be concrete concepts even for ideology. So that the mind works in a totally binary way, and you've filtered out the prospect of chaos and thought criminality before you've even uttered a word.' And, of course, this is an intellectual who's devoted to the mind but finds in his own imprisonment and self-torture a strange pleasure.

Orwell has realized that there's a penchant in many intellectuals to weave the bamboo of their own cage in ever more fascinating shapes. And it's this extraordinary percipience in the way in which his own group behaves that gives the novel a particular power. Whether Syme is based on an academic called Ronald Syme who wrote a famous book about Roman history in the 1930s, which was about the concept of Caesarism,[9] I don't know, or whether it's accidental. There are others, like Tillotson and various other Party weavers, and so on.

There's a great moment of illumination as they're biting into one of these meat sort of burgers, you know, and yet look around you. Just over there, the masses in a society like this will be eating meat that isn't meat. Don't you know that when you go to Kentucky Fried Chicken that many of the trays contain food that isn't food? A lot of junk food is gas. It's chemicals, has no food

---

[9] Sir Ronald Syme (1903–1989), New Zealand-born classicist and historian of Ancient Rome, published *The Roman Revolution* (Oxford: Oxford University Press, 1939).

at all. There was an American television program a couple of years ago . . . well, you know what Americans are like. A fifth of them are so obese they could hardly fit through that door. I saw a man in America who was so fat that I thought to myself, if you fired a bullet through his body—I have these thoughts—you wouldn't hit a bone because he was so fat. And that's because he's spent his entire life eating that sort of muck.

But it's the same muck that the Party apparatchiks eat, and say that they like it, in the canteen in the Ministry of Truth. And Syme, he's sort of spitting out this gristly non-meat as he's talking, you know; these are probably imagined dinners in the BBC sort of re-filtered through a novelist's imagination. And he's going, 'This is marvelous, Winston,' he says, 'marvelous. In Ingsoc, no freedom at all, the individual will be completely restructured and inert. Imagine a baby with its limbs cut off just quacking away ideologically, it's marvelous! Have another bit of chicken,' you know? Because Syme is sold totally on the idea that his liberation is more and more enslavement, sort of anti-hermeneutically, to the minutiae of the Party's lexicographical control of man.

Now, to the non-intellectuals, to the mass of the population who are known as the proles—for whom the socialist revolution was created of course—none of this matters at all, and Orwell's extraordinarily aware of the ultimate class split, which isn't really about poverty but is about the mind. This split between people who live for and use the mind, and those who are purely physical.

One of the slogans of people who want change in *Nineteen Eighty-Four* is 'The future is the proles.' They look at the proles, and all of them are looked at in a degraded way. One of the things that socialist and Left critics, such as Professor Raymond Williams,[10] have always said about *Nineteen Eighty-Four* and related books is that they are degrading to working-class people, that they are an attitude of bourgeois snobs in their ivory towers, liberals really, cracking on about theory, condemning those who

---

[10] Raymond Henry Williams (1921–1988) was a Welsh socialist academic and novelist.

are struggling for a better world. Williams, who was a sort of communist fellow traveler or crypto-communist, from his berth at Oxford, of course, for many years deep down had this view of Orwell and expresses it in the Fontana Modern Masters about Orwell.[11] Interestingly, Fontana gave the Lenin volume to Robert Conquest,[12] which is an absolute hatchet job, and they gave the Orwell volume to Williams, which is a mild hatchet job because Orwell couldn't be criticized too much.

Now, this desire for intellectuals to torment themselves and the division between them and those who are purely physical in this life is one of the cardinal themes in *Nineteen Eighty-Four*. There's a moment when Winston — and Orwell partly identifies with Winston, although it's not an absolute fit, obviously; but he invests a certain emotional power that clearly comes from himself within the narrative into the Winston figure — there's a moment when he looks out — I think it's during a scene when he's about to have sex, you can't really say "love," with Julia, his lover in the novel — and he looks out and sees a proletarian washer-woman with some pegs putting some laundry on a line. And she sings a love song, 'It was only an 'opeless fancy,' and all this, you know. It's a musical, it's a vaudeville turn. And Winston looks out at her and says, 'If there's any hope, it lies with the proles.'

Now, one of the most interesting features ideologically in *Nineteen Eighty-Four* is that the Party creates its own dissent; the Party creates its own past; it creates its own present; it creates its own future. Because it controls the mind, the mental regime that people use to think about the past, the present, and the future. And it also creates its own dissent. All the dissenters use a book called *The Theory and Practice of Oligarchical Collectivism* by Emmanuel Goldstein, who of course is Trotsky. And the Two Minutes Hate is oriented towards Trotsky.

The Two Minutes Hate is very funny. In the Ministry, all the chairs are lined up for the Hate, and you get like a sort of performance, or giving a speech in the company office, you know?

---

[11] Raymond Williams, *Orwell* (London: Fontana, 1971).

[12] Robert Conquest, *Lenin* (London: Fontana, 1972).

There's a certain buildup of tension in the bureaucracy prior to the Hate, and they all sit in these rows.

And all of the blocs are at war with each other. Because there's Oceania; there's Eurasia; there's East Asia. Three great totalitarian socialist regimes dominate the world. Sort of North America/Latino bloc, European bloc, Asiatic bloc, and they just divide it, Africa and the rest of it. They're not even mentioned. Poor old Africans don't even get a mention.

And initially the Hate begins with millions of Eurasian troops, you know, sort of the depiction of North Koreans or the Vietcong during those particular wars of American power, you know, faceless, merciless Asiatic masses marching towards you tommy gun out, all depersonalised and impersonal. And then, Trotsky's features will appear on the screen, and they all start hissing immediately; women, uncontrollable, have sort of negative orgasms, and roam about throwing things at the screen, 'Beast! Beast!' they scream. And the Hate's beginning you see, and the Party officials are pointing out the Goldstein figure, because Goldstein wrote the book that defines the Party's negation.

But the inner truth is the Party wrote that book, because they control the mind even of their enemies. And there's an amazing scene with O'Brien in his Ministry, where he's turned the screen off so they can't be listened to, and he's dressed in black. And Julia and Winston, who he knows are lovers, dressed in denim, dressed in blue serge, are with him in the office. And they talk about Goldstein's book, and O'Brien says later on, "I partly wrote that book of course."

But no book's written by an individual. Books are written by committees, because the individual mind can never be trusted, so everything's done by committee. So his outlook is true: the Party degrades itself, denigrates itself, tells you pretty explicitly what's going on and why, but never why they're doing it. So if you provide your opposition with the mental feed that they need in order to oppose you, you partly control them. This is a very old idea, but in the twentieth century, when mass propaganda became available for the manipulation of the masses, this was an extraordinary way of behaving. You actually create your own inversions so you can control them.

Now, Trotsky/Goldstein is a figure of the early Party who provides the figure of the renegade, the running dog, the one who turns against the purity of the Party position, and also the scapegoat, the goat that's actually tied with the rope to the tree. All the hatred, all the failures, all the espionage that goes wrong, every battle that's lost: it's the fault of Goldstein and the deviationists. They are the ones; they are the traitors. In every word, behind every lie, behind every false sausage, behind every false statistic, the traitors lurk. Sin, secularized sin really, lurks everywhere, always to be purged, purged in the Hate, purged through self-criticism.

Under communist regimes, individual Party members had to undergo self-criticism on a regular basis. You'd be forced. 'Self-criticism is expected comrade.' You'd be forced to stand up in front of the others and to engage in dialectical critique: 'I had moments of class evasiveness. I suffered from moments of false consciousness. I had certain religious moments where I denied the material nature of reality and the glory of the Party's ascendency.' And everyone would be going, 'Mmm, yes.' It's all very serious, you know. And under certain regimes this could be life or death.

Like many Polish people, post-Gomułka and after 1948 . . . I went to a Catholic school. You did religion four periods a week. But in those ex-Catholic schools in Poland you did Marxist-Leninism four periods a week. And you had to get those lessons right. It was very important. If you made a mistake about the 1844 Paris manuscripts in relation to *Grundrisse*, you were *in error*, and that was a serious matter.

Most of the liberals smile cynically about all this because they've never really had to live under the pressure of those sorts of institutions and don't understand what it's like to have to play all those dialectical games and engulf yourself in all those sorts of lies.

The irony is that, broadly speaking, working class children weren't exempt, but as long as they just prated a few simplistic slogans it was alright, because they weren't the ones for whom it was done. The Party wanted to control the minds of people who could think, not those who, in a sense, follow, and who are physical and who need an architecture within which to be. So the very modern totalitarianism understands that you have to control the mind first. Control the mind, you control the body; control the present, you control the past, you dictate the future. The future is the Party.

The Party has three slogans: War is Peace; Ignorance is Strength; Freedom is Slavery. And those are on everything. They're on every beermat. They're on every watch. They're on every tablecloth. They're on every flag. War is Peace; Ignorance is Strength; Freedom is Slavery. And then there's the ubiquitous "Big Brother is watching you." And Stalin's heavy Georgian features—although some people say he's an Ossetian—his heavy features looking down on you. That sort of power, that sort of insistence, that sort of mask, because he was wearing a mask.

There is an extraordinary picture of Stalin after Sergei Kirov's death.[13] Kirov was the Leningrad Party leader, who was assassinated in mysterious circumstances, and it's probable there were lots of Western Marxists and liberals who couldn't, who didn't understand what was going on. And, of course, Kirov was killed on Stalin's orders to set off the purge which sort of begins, if you exempt the Ukrainian famine, from the panoply of a politically-oriented purge.

Kirov was killed to provide an excuse for mass terror, less in the society than over the elite: terror over the bureaucracy, terror over the army, terror over the KGB, or one of its incarnations itself. Because Kirov was so high up in the regime that if he had been got to, it must be because of conspiratorial forces of an anti-revolutionary tendency at the heart of the republic. This means that no one was safe, and that you look for the treason and the traitors right at the top, not at the bottom or in the middle.

The mass shootings and killings and tortures beforehand that got rid of between a third of a million and a million Party members, higher to middling apparatchiks, and members of the armed forces, and that decimated the Soviet higher command before Barbarossa, and were one of the many reasons—partly

---

[13] Sergei Mironovich Kirov (1886–1934), Russian revolutionary and Soviet politician.

because the army was in the wrong position in relation to the invasion because they were planning to attack Germany themselves and were caught unawares, and so on—but one of the many reasons for their collapse in the early days was because vast numbers of their officers had been purged, undergone self-criticism, failed self-criticism, down the plug.

But, of course, executioners and torturers and invigilators and those who interviewed those who were going to the camps or going to be shot, they themselves could be found guilty of deviation, because if they made a mistake, or if they had an elision of consciousness, or if they showed too much zeal in certain circumstances, if Party ideology shifted slightly in a subsequent moment, they themselves could be before the committees. It's just like the French Revolution but using sort of mass death technology in a way, and it's all quite deliberate.

And there is this amazing moment when Stalin looks down on Kirov, in this orthodox way when the body is laid out in the casket, and he looks down on Kirov, and it's a Mafia boss looking at a subaltern that he's had killed in order to start a war between clans, and you can see it. I mean it's just a subjective way of looking at reality, but you can see that Stalin knows in his face what he has done.

And Stalin is this odd character. Western propaganda about Stalin has been based on Trotskyism for most of the twentieth century. Stalin was actually an interesting and slightly creative man who was also a brigand and an *extreme* criminal, addicted psychopathologically, very like Mao, to extremes of sadism and slaughter which he positively enjoyed, positively enjoyed, and gained pleasure from.

Mao certainly had pronounced sadistic features and used to enjoy the physical torment of former Party members who had fallen out with him. Their bodies, mutilated, would often be exhibited in the streets in order to terrorize the masses into obedience with socialist logic. It's probable that psychologically many Chinese have not recovered from this. The full extent of the terror that was represented in Asia by the Cultural Revolution is still not really explored, even by quite radical and mainstream Western historiography.

Certainly, many people in Hong Kong saw enormous numbers of bodies floating out to them, when Hong Kong was under British rule, of course. Many of these bodies were partly eaten as well, and many of them were Red Guards who started fighting with each other about moments of dialectical purity, because these bureaucracies have a tendency to start sort of ravening like dogs. They get so wild they start attacking themselves if there's no object to attack at a particular time.

This phenomenon also fed through into many other things, the collapse of discipline that was also ordered, a sort of planned chaos, particularly in relation to the mass rape of German women at the end of the Second World War by Soviet troops, which even today Premier Putin says never occurred: 'Never occurred, Western lies fed by the enemies of Russia.' Russia is a nationalist country now, and Putin in many ways is a man to be admired in certain respects, but their old ways die hard in many ways.

The interesting thing about those mass rapes, which certainly occurred — to the degree that the German communists pleaded with the Soviets to stop them because they were preventing the creation of Ulbricht's state in occupied East Germany — the reason they occurred was because commissars ordered them, and at the same time there was such a breakdown in order that that order was itself part of the chaos with which it ramified.

All of Stalin's atrocities are ordered and are written down. The Katyn forest massacre of the Polish officer corps. There's an interesting quasi-revisionist Polish national film called *Katyn* which is available now in certain art cinemas, not getting general release. But who in the multiplexes would see it, let's face it? But it is available through art cinemas. It's very gruesome at the end, very truthful at the end. Now, the whole Politburo ordered that. All of their signatures are on the death order, including Krushchev's, and the later thawists and reformists. Stalin's name — bigger than all the others, graphologically — is at the bottom: Stalin.

Because they thought they were going to win and that history was on their side, and that all the records of the elite of the masses should be there for people to see, for history to judge: 'We have to wade through feces and blood and filth to create socialism and glory. Because heaven can come down onto the Earth. But you've got to wade through the blood to get it. Heaven is coming down but first: the abattoir. Onwards!'

Orwell in a sense understood the logic of many of these processes of purges and trials within regimes. Within months the men like Vyshinsky in the thirties at the show trials, screaming at the victims, certain of their subordinates could be on the other side being screamed at and could be executed very quickly.

The interesting thing about this novel is that actually, Orwell, apart from in Spain for a few brief months before he got out, never really experienced the rigors of communism. There will be many Leftists who say it's a fantasy. It's an artist's metaphorization of what occurred in certain Eastern European societies, particularly certain societies that were less controlled by Soviet power: Hoxha's Albania, parts of Yugoslavia, and Ceausescu's Romania, where there were indigenous communist, terrorist, army-based, and paramilitary movements who came to power without necessarily the intervention of the Red Army. Sometimes you see purer forms of communism built to excess of a sort that occupied Eastern Europe didn't always equate to, because there were certain balancing elements in occupied Eastern Europe. In the Soviet Union of course, Soviet power and pure communism had been completely uncontrolled from the very beginning.

The term "Bolshevik revolution" is itself a misnomer. There was no revolution. It was a *coup* by the armed wing of the Bolshevik Party, and was thought of at the time by the people who did it. There was a moment when Trotsky, Lenin, and Stalin slept together in a room about as big as this after they had seized Kerensky's palace, and with newspaper on the ground. It was the first day, after being up for over twenty hours, and after they had had a couple of hours sleep, Lenin got up and said, 'Comrades, we have achieved a great thing. We have been in power for one day.' Because power is what it's all about in relation to this ideology, which ramifies with what O'Brien says to Winston at the end.

The point is that Winston has intellectually denied the sovereignty of the Party's rule over the mind. Therefore he's far more important than some prole who just rebels physically against the Party. With them you break their arms or their legs or send them to a camp; that's of no importance. What matters is the mind that controls the body. So before they kill Winston they will torture him into submission: he must love Big Brother before they execute him; he must be reworked.

There's a famous moment, isn't there, when all his teeth are rotten, and O'Brien pulls all the teeth out—snap!—in one go, and pulls them out of the mouth, and he says, 'Look what you've done to yourself; look how you've destroyed yourself.' And Winston (John Hurt's always playing the victim, isn't he?) says, 'You've done it to me, you've done it to me,' and O'Brien says, 'No! No, no, no, no, no, you've done it to yourself by denying *the love of the Party*!' Do you remember that line, 'You're just a cell, Winston'? He says, 'You're a cell. The individual has long ceased to exist in history as we define it. You're just an individual cell within the body of the Party. Your death, your life is of no significance; you're just a cell. Do you die when you cut your fingernails?'

I say this in this theatrical manner because I've played O'Brien. When I was eighteen we had a school play, and it was quite interesting. There was a very bad actor called—someone I won't name—whose surname was Smith, who played Winston Smith. And I played O'Brien dressed all in black. And we didn't have any girls in the school so we had one homosexual in the sixth form dressed up as a girl who played Julia. And there's this strange moment, because this is an all-boys school, and all the Catholic brothers are down there, and it's all very odd. I'm one of the few Protestants there, there's a transvestite on the stage, and a bloke who can't act, and we're playing *Nineteen Eighty-Four*; it's typical. And when Julia comes on there's this great wolf-whistle that then dies in its own throes, do you know what I mean, when they all realize, 'Good Lord, it's so-and-so dressed up!' And there's a moment of horror and terror, in which you see all these grammar school boys, about seventeen, you know, quite funny actually.

O'Brien is one hell of a part. I mean he really is, let's face it. Because he's attracted to O'Brien from the earliest stages because

O'Brien is a priest who believes in nothing but the ideology of the Party, and who is genuine. He's not a fraud. He wrote *The Theory and Practice of Oligarchical Collectivism*. He believes in torturing Winston as a cog in the machine because it doesn't matter. You see, it's the futility of the absence of negation. They could just shoot Winston and have done with it. Why go through all these games?

But the games are important because they prove the meaning of meaninglessness, if you like. That's the point, because all of these ideologies are totally atheistic, totally anti-transcendental, totally mechanistic, and totally material. It's a sort of revenge of matter upon itself, if you like. It's the churning of matter, and he's the scientific non-priest of the churning of matter, human matter.

There is a slogan of the Czechoslovak secret police where they used to say, 'We are the engineers of human souls.' And there's a famous Czech dissident novel called that, or uses it in the title.[14] And that's how they really saw themselves. They saw themselves as a vanguard in history. The working class had been oppressed. They'd been degraded. They're being decanted from the agricultural state—this is in classical Marxist theory—into the industrial one. The industrial civilization creates its negation through social renewal and the creation of a vanguard which is drawn from all classes, particularly from bohemian, outsider intellectuals. Half of them are Jews, although they don't say that in the ideology. Half of them are Gentiles who want to destroy their own society because they hate it for various reasons, and want to tear it down, and want to see themselves—largely marginal figures hitherto—promoted to serious posts.

This is why ideology is so important for these sorts of regimes, because it's committees and groups of quasi-intellectuals fighting with each other about meaning and purpose, and plotting against each other, and doing each other down, and releasing statements to the secret police so they can all be purged, so I can get his job, so I can edit this magazine, so I can overstep him,

---

[14] Josef Škvorecký, *The Engineer of Human Souls*, trans. Paul Wilson (Funks Grove, Illinois: Dalkey Archive Press, 1999).

and so on. It's the universalization — with a ruthless and very violent terrorism added on — of the struggles that go on in your average university department today. But that sort of engine of destruction isn't added on. Orwell's extraordinary insight is his ability to see these processes at work.

Don't forget communism is one of the most extraordinary stories of modern man. Here is a movement that emerges with almost no social support at all, and a few fringe ideologues around it, in the middle of the nineteenth century. By the first third of the following century, just passed, it controls vast stretches of the world; it kills tens of millions of human beings; it launches enormous wars; it creates enormous social structures; and then it fails, virtually, and deconstructs, morally and structurally of itself, almost as if no longer believes in its own lies any more.

It's quite clear that Gorbachev was in many ways a liberal, or a Social Democrat in an old/new way, who allowed it to go. Because no reform of that system is possible unless you want to use violence and ferocious force, which Honecker wanted to do when the crowds began to come out in Germany prior to the deconstruction of the wall. Honecker's first instinct is the Stasi on the streets, fire, fire again, fire again, step on the bodies of those that are covered in blood and fire on them and step on their bodies: Socialism! Imposed on the masses! Because we are the masters of fate and history.

And it's only because Gorbachev said the Red Army will not back the Stasi up in the streets that Honecker remembered he was feeling a bit ill and had a bit of cancer on the way, and so they allowed him to clear off to Chile. And slightly more reformist, Euro-Communist types took over. And eventually sections of the wall were opened. Remember those incredibly dramatic moments when the bulldozers and so on brought down sections of the wall and the Stasis and the [unintelligible] came out and stood with their Kalashnikovs, and the Germans came through the gaps that had been created? And the Westerners were on the other side cheering and this sort of thing.

When the Soviet Union collapsed there was a British trade unionist leader called Ken Gill who was the leader of TASS, a certain section of the electrical engineering union.[15] And he said that when the Soviet Union collapsed — a bloke with a broad Wiltshire accent, a genuinely working-class communist — Gill said, 'A light went out for humanity when the Soviet Union went down.' A light went out, and he died soon after. Because, you see, for people like him it was a pseudo-religion, and it was a belief in a radiant future as they used to call it in the ideology: *a radiant future for the masses*! And there was a belief in it.

It's why all of these people spied and so on. Of course many of them did it because they owed money; they were perverts; they were rebels against their own system. But never forget that many of them converted to it like a quasi-religious conversion. Donald Maclean,[16] who was part of the Kim Philby[17] ring at Cambridge, read an incredibly boring book called *Materialism and Empirio-Criticism* by Lenin which is based upon the materialism of a scientist at the beginning of the twentieth century called Ernst Mach, and the light came into his eyes:

> 'Now, history is clear to me. There is a plan! There is progress from the agricultural to the industrial state, through the dialectical reversal via the vanguard that creates socialism that is above the masses. And eventually all the apparatus that is needed to install this — the terror, the lies, the propaganda, the secret police, the endless purging, the mass graves — will all fade away, all fade away, and be replaced by love. And by the encomium of forgiveness, as all members in all classes embraced each other, and there's no division. There's no division of race, of kind, of class, of gender, of ideology; all are one. All are one in the radiant future.'

---

[15] Ken Gill (1927–2009), British trade unionist, was General Secretary of the Technical, Administrative and Supervisory Section (TASS).

[16] Donald Maclean (1913–1983), British diplomat and Soviet spy, was a member of the Cambridge Five spy ring.

[17] Harold Adrian Russell "Kim" Philby (1912–1988), British intelligence officer, Soviet spy, and member of the Cambridge Five spy ring.

And that's socialism, you see.

And there's a stage even beyond socialism: communism. Because if you listen to communist parties when they're in power, they will say that socialism is just an approximation of that which exists beyond them. Another quasi-religious idea, really a quasi-idealistic conception, whereby the perfection of the future is still to be announced, and in that moment the state itself will wither away. There'll be no secret policemen. They'll start kissing their rubber truncheons, and this sort of thing, and throwing them away. It's all going to die before the dispensation of love, and that sort of thing. But down in the abattoir, you know, comrades have got some dirty work to do in the name of progress.

It is, if you look at it, an enormous sort of materialist Greek tragedy acted out over about a century and a half, because it affected and changed the whole nature of the world, this ideology. China, of course, has done a reverse trick. They've kept an authoritarian, technocratic regime that's frozen the ideology like a theology it no longer even listens to, and it's introduced the most aggressive form of capitalism on Earth, using the very structures of authoritarian rule that were supposed to bring in its opposite. So there's a strange hybrid.

Then you have these sort of dinosaur states like North Korea which strongly resembles in the cult of the Emperor/the Kim Il Sung figure who's worshipped like a god. Didn't you know he discovered the light bulb? Didn't you know he wrote all the books in the British Library? Didn't you know that he painted, personally, the roof of the Sistine Chapel? Didn't you know that virtually every scientific development has been done by Kim Il Sung and his semi-dead son? Because most North Koreans are taught this all the time.

There are also very interesting elements in the fugitiveness of communist ideology where you do wonder whether it's a materialist belief system at all. In camps in North Korea, if a dissident has a child, a woman, often the child will be killed by a commissar. The child will be born. The child will be presented as the child of a deviant and of a thought criminal. This is the doctrine of hereditarianism isn't it? This is the doctrine that the child inherits the social and secular sins of the parent. This isn't a Left-wing idea at all, essentially, so it's very odd, mentally. And the child, the commissar will step on its neck and crack it, break it in front of the camp. 'Death of a deviant! Aliens of socialism and the praxis of the masses! I do not this as a crime. I kill not a human. I kill an enemy of the human.'

When Yugoslav trials killed a large number of people in 1945/46 – "trials" – they were described not as trials of people, but as enemies of the people. The communist jurists would get up in the dock and say, 'You are an enemy of the people,' you know what that meant: not long to go; let's hope it's over quick. That's what people really thought when they were subjected to this.

What this novel does is it draws out the psychological, linguistic, and mental processes of what's going on in those quicker, enemy-of-the-people type trials which, of course, Ceausescu and his type got at the end. There is an occult principle isn't there, "What goes around comes around," as the hippies in the sixties used to say. And I remember when Ceausescu and his wife were tried the trial lasted for three hours. There wasn't much of a defense, just a bloke jabbering a bit, pushed to the side by the military policeman. They were dragged out of the court and shot. And shot as terrorists by the National Salvation Front, two thirds of whom were ex-communists.

And remember there was that moment when the camera goes towards them as they're lying on the ground and the camera flicks onto the faces? The BBC, ITV, and CNN (if CNN existed then) cut that, because it was too distressing for Western audiences. Too distressing for Western audiences. But you could see the blood on the ground, and they were dead. So they got the trial that they gave many others. And the Securitate, their bastard children, ideologically as well as structurally, fought to the end and died in burning buildings to keep it going.

Hoxha's Albania was an even more extreme example of that. You could be arrested in Hoxha's Albania for owning an orange. Because it obviously hadn't been grown there, and you'd imported something from the regime's of the class enemy. So you were even a criminal for owning a bit of fruit. And that's why, if you view it in a cross-conscious European way, a very scandalous way, many European politicians from the comfortable West, like Kohl and so on—do you remember he went to East Berlin waving bananas? Waving great bunches of fruit saying, "You haven't seen this have you, you poor little people? You haven't seen this stuff for fifty years." Extraordinarily condescending, but the liberal materialism was at a much higher level. That's one of the reasons why they collapsed further east.

But the interesting thing is that communism is really the product of intellectuals. It's almost a sort of revenge of the intellectuals as a class upon life. The interesting thing is that some of the softest elements of Western societies, some of the most long-in-the-tooth elements, also some of the most economically comfortable elements are the people who pushed the Western/Eastern version of these ideas when they came to power.

There's a famous story of Jean Cocteau which may well be apocryphal, the French artist and poet and writer and film director, and all the rest of it. It's about 1910, and Lenin was certainly around then in Parisian salons as were many other people. Don't forget Stalin was in Vienna. There are rumors that Hitler, Stalin, and Lenin once sat in a street in Vienna in different cafés, and they didn't know the other from the other, all developing their thinking. And you never know, because many of these bohemian undercurrents mix with each other in that decade of proto-revolution between 1900 and 1910, revolving around the Soviet proto-revolution of 1906, the early Soviet attempt at revolutionism.

I personally think, in a totally differentiated way, we're in a similar era now. We're on the threshold of enormous changes, of Herculean changes, the nature of which we don't really understand yet. And I think, very like the first decade of the last century, we're looking out on what's coming. Because quite clearly an attack upon Iran is prefigured by much of the rhetoric that's going on now, and much of which is being prepared now. They say they can't weaponize it by 2014 but who knows?

So, the interesting thing is the support of the wealthy and intellectual outsider for a belief system that materially offered them very little, but intellectually offered them power. Power! Winston says at the end, 'What's it all about?' to O'Brien. 'What's all the hunger and the torture and the endless war and the propaganda and torturing me to death for a cause I don't really believe in to say "I love Big Brother," and then I do, and then you shoot me. What's it all for?' And O'Brien says, 'It's for power. Power,' he says. 'Power and more power. Power as a dialectical principle.' You remember that great line? 'If you want the future of the human race, Winston, imagine a boot, a boot, stamping on a human face forever!' And it's a sort of satire of a sort egomaniacal intellectual power using ideology purely as a vehicle.

And there's a very interesting insight into communism there. At the end Mao lived like a potentate. He lived like an ancient Persian or Egyptian Emperor. He was surrounded by women. He was surrounded by bastard children that he created. The Politburo used to meet him around his bed. Mao was quite a beast towards the end, and he used to say to Western correspondents he cleaned himself in his women. This is the great champion of humanity, the great anti-sexist, you see. This is what they're like when they're in power. Surrounded by Marxist books.

Have you ever seen pictures of his bedroom? There'd be this enormous bed, like that of an emperor, with all these women and children around, and the secret police in their caps with the red star further back? And then these volumes of Marxist prose behind the Red Books, his own work allegedly, to the front. And then he'd be lying on this bed dictating to the others like a sort of overgrown child, like an ideological version of a mad Roman Emperor, essentially, because that's how it ended up. And probably the ideology had ceased to matter by then hadn't it? It had become a sort of mental chess that you played with yourself and with others for reasons of pure power.

Because these economies weren't making anything except more weapons, and the idea of Marxist critique of capitalism, that the proletariat is degraded because of the distinction between price and value, and that the surplus product is ripped out of the proletariat and invested by capitalists abroad in empire. When Lenin wrote *Imperialism* in 1916 this is why he explained that revolution hasn't happened yet. It hasn't happened yet because they displaced the capital they have stolen from the people, stolen from the proletariat. And the irony was that extreme communism was an extreme version of what Marxism had criticized Western societies for: total degradation of the peasantry and proletariat, total ripping out of surplus value. Used to create more and more weapons in order to build more and more forms of power: pure power as an end in itself, but always at a material level because the ideology could only justify itself in material terms.

I think, to close, the interesting thing about *Nineteen Eighty-Four* is that what lingers in my mind is the sense data. When Winston's in the Ministry of Truth and he needs to use the intercom he has to clean the holes in the device because they're full of dirt. It's that grubby dirt-under-the-fingernails element that you get in state socialism, even in Western societies.

Anyone who's ever queued in a DHSS[18] queue—the glass in the office is cracked, there are no plants, there's no carpet. Everything's unnaturally cold and grubby. You know, your substandard, sub-standard NHS[19] ward, you know what I mean? Everything's slightly out of focus. No one listens to you. Half of them are foreign anyway. No one really listens to you when you say something to them. They exist for you, don't they, not the other way 'round?

There's this logic, the state socialist logic, the logic of the producer writ large. You couldn't buy anything in shops in the Soviet Union at the end, but the Party could. You had a card, and you went to a special shop where you could get razor blades; you could get boots; you could get the niceties, soap, things you need to live, basically, in any sort of industrial society. And the masses would queue.

Anthony Burgess who wrote *A Clockwork Orange* once went to a restaurant in Moscow, and you sat there for five hours! 'Can I get some service now?' 'Screw you, we're the staff! You'll *wait* there for five hours.' And then, after five-and-a-quarter hours, you get this sort of cabbage soup, which is just a bit of cabbage

---

[18] Department of Health and Social Services.
[19] National Health Service.

in a bit of hot water with a sprig of parsley in it, sort of chucked at you, you know. It's like in Western restaurants now isn't it?

But it's that sort of idea of the grubbiness of its texture, when you've got this ideology of idealism and universal brotherhood, and yet you return to the cabbage soup and the smell in the dysfunctional lift and the hair floating in your soup, and you know that state socialism of that sort, imposed by a party, a bureaucracy, an army has gone, and in all probability won't come back.

And yet the real point of *Nineteen Eighty-Four* and the reason why this novel lives, and still probably frightens people in a way, is the ubiquity of its concern with mental processes, and the belief that when humans, in many ways, reject the philosophies of the past they will try to subordinate the present to them. Communism has died.

It maybe killed a hundred million in the twentieth century, or more. It had to be fought. The tendency of which we are in some ways a part is accused by many out there of beastliness, of nonhumanism, and all the rest of it. But I would say that there was a time when the forces of the Right had to be as ferocious, had to be almost as nasty as what they were attacking, and was attacking them, otherwise they would have been completely destroyed by it. This was an ideology that preached utopia but believed that the ends justified the means in a manner that's beyond that of a mafia don.

Do you remember the scene in Mario Puzo's *The Godfather* with the Jewish Hollywood producer, who's a pedophile, and the Irish-German *consigliere* of the mafia clan? And they talk about him, and he's racially abusive to people of Italian and Germanic and Irish ancestry and all the rest of it. And the don waves that away. He's not bothered with all that. And Brando, big figure then, bit of a better actor then, said, 'What does this man love?' And he loves a horse. So the mob cuts off the head of the horse and puts it in his bed. Why? Because the don is saying, 'I am a man beyond all law, beyond all morality, beyond anything you could even think of. I can strike at you in a way you don't even understand. Because I have no limits. No limits.'

And there was a time when communism, before it froze into a bureaucracy, had no limits at all. I'll close with Lenin's remark.

Don't forget the Cheka, the secret police was created momentarily. It was said it would be dissolved in a few years like the Terror under Robespierre. 'It's just to impose discipline upon the class enemies so that paradise can begin.' Towards his death in 1924 Lenin's brain was liquified. Many medical historians believe that at least half of it was liquid. And at the height of the terror and the war between the Red and the White, which of course the Whites lost, Lenin said to one of his aides, 'Now is the time. There's maximum chaos, total starvation, the complete collapse of the Russian economy and civil war. Now is the time.'

And the aide said, 'Time for what?' And he said, 'Time to seize all the assets of the Orthodox Church. Time to seize all their churches. Time to turn them into granaries and barns and shops, and places where we put tap paths and tractors.' And the aide said, 'Why?' And Lenin said, 'Why not? *Why not?* We are history, we do what we wish.' Lenin believed that in a moment of chaos you extirpate the *meaning* of the prior order that the chaos was destroying, because they always worked on the mind before they worked on the body.

Thank you very much!

Counter-Currents, August 11, 2014

THE SOVIET GULAG*

I have spoken with you before about elements of the Soviet Union, a regime which has now passed into the dust, but this time I am going to concentrate on the Soviet gulag.

No one knows the number of victims of the Soviet gulag. It's still indeterminate really. No one can lose their academic career, however, by projecting for a sort of minimum total or a maximum total.

I think the thing to look about the Soviet Union and Stalinist oppression in particular is the fact that it dates from the very beginning of the regime, the first day that the Bolsheviks came in. And the Bolshevik Revolution was never a social revolution. It was a *coup*. It was a *coup d'état* by the armed wing of the Bolshevik Party that had nine, ten, eleven, twelve percent of the vote, but no more at that time after the first Duma elections, which had put in a socialist revolutionary, a social democrat in Western terms, called Kerensky.

Now, when the Bolsheviks came in they immediately instituted a revolutionary committee for the protection of the state and revolution, which is known as the Cheka. The Cheka began the instrumentality of terror that certainly pre-dates Stalin. There is a Left-wing myth that essentially Stalin is the cause of all the problems, and that, in a sense, Lenin can be regarded as a semi-sacred, secular figure prior to Stalin's overall rule.

Stalin took a long time to consolidate his power within the bureaucracy and gradually chipped away at the Trotskyist bureaucracy and didn't really obtain complete power inside the Soviet Union until 1928, after which the Left opposition, the Trotskyite faction, was dispensed with, and Trotsky became a Goldstein-type figure rather like the figure in George Orwell's famous novel and confabulation *Nineteen Eighty-Four*.

---

* Transcript by V.S. of Jonathan Bowden's New Right lecture of February 4, 2012, online at the Jonathan Bowden Archive (jonathanbowden.org). I want to thank Michèle Renouf for making the recording available.

The camp system was set up initially for the nearest Left opposition to the Bolsheviks. That means Social Democrats, Social Revolutionaries, Kerenskyites, and various Mensheviks were amongst the first individuals to be put in the camps. But gradually the camps extended out their remit to include all elements of Soviet life.

One of the most extraordinary things about the camp infrastructure was that it paralleled the existence of mainstream Soviet society. Nobody knows how many people passed through the camps. The revisionist or lower estimate is about sixteen to seventeen million. The higher estimate is about twenty-eight million. You're dealing with a society the best part of two-hundred million, so you see that the "gulag archipelago," as Solzhenitsyn called it, serves as an enormous island of reserve population inside the Soviet Union.

It's estimated that perhaps a quarter to a fifth of all male Russian lives were affected by the gulags in one form or another. At the height of the Terror in the 1930s, a man who was late three times for work could be sent to a correctional institution, and a man who was related to somebody who had been sent to a correctional institution could also be put in a camp himself.

Many of the designations for how you got to end up in a camp were actually quite irrational, such as being related to a thought criminal or related to an oppositionalist or related to somebody in another national group that needed to be purged as part of the rolling series of purges — national, ethnic, sociological, class-based, peasant-oriented — that occurred throughout the 1930s.

The terror, of course, also extended into the party itself, into the inner bureaucracy itself, into the military, into the infrastructure of the state, into the army most especially, and even amongst the executioners. Nobody could be invulnerable in Stalin's Russia. Only one man, the Iron Man, as he was regarded, the Iron Man of Socialism, was invulnerable from the attacks of the multiple purges that he instituted.

Why go down that particular road? The Leninist pattern of atrocity had some logic to it. The basic atrocity was the killing of political opponents and killing of Whites, that's Russians on the opposition or counter-revolutionary side during the Russian Civil

War between about 1917 and 1921. It's estimated that the Bolsheviks killed maybe one-and-a-half million prisoners of war and the Whites killed one-and-a-quarter million prisoners of war, because both sides massacred each other's prisoners. Indeed, that's what a lot of the military fighting in the Russian Civil War consisted of.

Circumadjacent to the Russian Civil War and its atrocities in relation to troops on troops and troops on civilians was famine and the partial collectivization that Lenin instituted prior to his reversal of this with the famous party congress in 1921, the revolutionary third party congress, part of whose deliberations were concealed and secret and were not revealed until years later when the Soviet Union collapsed.

One of the interesting byproducts of the 1921 party congress was the fact that Lenin advocated a tacit alliance with nationalists in Germany in order to bring down the then-nascent Weimar Republic so that they could fight over the spoils later. That's a deeply non-Leninist and politically incorrect and Machiavellian decision that causes quite a few Leninists considerable problems retrospectively. It also foreshadows, of course, the Nazi-Soviet Pact, which was entered into by both sides to dismember Poland, but also as an alliance of convenience prior to the fact that they knew they were going to fall upon each other at a later date.

The deaths from the "war communist famine," as it was called in the early 1920s and late teens, is difficult to determine. The BBC puts the figure at one-and-a-half million, but other figures go up to about seven million. The total death total for the regime as a whole from 1917 until its virtual collapse in 1990 was twenty million according to *The Black Book of Communism*[1] and possibly more. But Robert Conquest in his book, *The Great Terror*,[2] adduces the idea that twenty million persons died from the Stalinist period alone. The mainstream Western equivalent is now disputed, and

---

[1] Stéphane Courtois, ed., *The Black Book of Communism* (1997), trans. Jonathan Murphy and Mark Kramer (Cambridge: Harvard University Press, 1999).

[2] Robert Conquest, *The Great Terror: A Reassessment* (Oxford: Oxford University Press, 1968).

people think the figure of twenty million is too high and was influenced by Cold War propaganda.

Alec Nove,[3] who was a professor of Soviet studies at the University of Glasgow for many years, led a rather fellow traveling and Sovietphilic group of historians, but they estimated the death total for the Stalinist regime at ten to twelve million, which is hardly too revisionist but was widely regarded as such at the time. Many mainstream Western historians now believe that this figure is actually closer to the truth.

What I tend to do in relation to all these figures is to give a range of figures. The truth is that no one will entirely know. When the KGB archives were opened up at the Lubyanka in the 1990s, during a very confused period under Yeltsin, the figures that the NKVD, a forerunner of the bureaucracy known as the KGB later on, preserved tend to be in the middle range of historical variables. In other words, KGB and security organ figures for those who perished in the camps were largely halfway between the minimal, or revisionist figures, that were spread on the whole by more Sovietphilic elements in the West, and the exterminationist figures, if we may call them that, which were largely pushed by ultra-conservatives and Right-wing anti-communists and those who would be regarded as Cold War warriors.

So, in a strange way, the truth seemed to be somewhere in the middle. But there are many mainstream historians who do not accept the KGB's figures for those who suffered and died.

The Stalinist Terror after 1928–29 when Stalin gained an iron grip upon the whole of the Soviet bureaucracy, basically falls into various waves. All the time throughout this period, certain people who were regarded as refractory or socially dissentient were sent to camps, but there were periods of acceleration, and there were periods of deceleration throughout this entire period.

The problem that Communism had was that it was a total answer to the human possibility, but what do you do with all of

---

[3] Alexander Nove (1915–1994), Russian-born Professor of Economics at the University of Glasgow, specialized in Russian and Soviet history.

those people who don't fit into the total answer to the human possibility? An enormous swathe of traditional and religious believers of one sort or another did not find their way into the then-current Soviet utopia. You had large criminal underclasses in all of the major cities and, to a lesser extent, in the rural areas.

You had refractory levels of peasants collectively known by the system as *kulaks* who were very, very resistant to the idea that their status—namely that their tiny little individual holding, allotment, quasi-farm, and actual farm—might well be taken from them. This class would be highly resistant to the doctrine of collectivization of agriculture that was spread in the Soviet Union in the late 1920s and early to mid-1930s.

The prospect of de-kulakization, as it was called in the ideology, terrified much of the upper strata of the peasantry, and it is no exaggeration to say that Stalin's bureaucracy declared war upon the upper tier of the peasantry and regarded it as such in its own propaganda. The number of *kulaks* who suffered is anywhere between three to five to eight million. Large numbers were sent to camps all over Eurasia and all over the deepest Soviet Union.

Many of these camps, despite fifty years of Cold War propaganda, are still not known in the West. The most notorious camp is probably Kolyma, which in *zek* (prisoner) history was regarded as the most extreme of all of the isolation camps. In these camps, people were basically given a ration of a quarter of a cabbage and some gruel or porridge every day and would have to work a sixteen-hour shift in biting conditions of extreme Arctic temperature guarded by NKVD officers with light machine guns and dogs.

There were escapes, and there were rebellions in certain camps. Certain camps were closed down, and certain individuals—upwards of three million of them—were inducted into the Red Army from the camp system when Nazi Germany invaded the Soviet Union in the early 1940s. So, there was lots of displacement, and there was lots of movement. The camps were essentially dynamic rather than static. Prisons tend to be very static in most societies, whereas the camps were highly fluid in terms of their in-take and out-take. A large number of people served short sentences in the camps and were then released. It was as if they came to be associated with a revolutionary dynamic which was existing in the society as a whole.

There is no doubt that Stalin's psychopathological personality had an enormous degree to do with the extension and remit of the camp system. Before he took over and clamped down over all aspects of Soviet life, the camps were much more rudimentary, much smaller, much more finite, and seemed keyed into certain economic prospects that relate to normal imprisonment. After the Stalinist experience of the early thirties, the number of people flushed down the sewage system of the camp structure — as Solzhenitsyn refers to it in the beginning of the first volume of *The Gulag Archipelago* — increased exponentially.

The purpose of the camps was to inculcate the values of socialist man, and these were being inculcated through extreme hard labor of a sort that was basically . . . For a man who wasn't in the peak of physical fitness when he was admitted to the camps and wasn't suffering from a prior disease, survival was just about possible. But for anyone who tipped under that particular score or threshold — who was suffering from a particular illness, had a generic complaint, was slightly too elderly, was relatively infirm or unfit — the camps in many ways encoded a death sentence. The number of people who died in the camps is still indeterminate. During the course of this discussion, I will look at the range of figures which are available.

Why did the Communist system under Stalin do this when it is not entirely necessary? Why did the Maoist system under Mao Zedong in Communist China ape the Stalinist system to a considerable degree? Even in today's China there are large labor camps and prison camps which are screened from the rest of the world, despite the open access to many cities as China invests in a high-tech capitalism in order to power its new twenty-first century super-power status. Western thermal imaging from satellites above the heavens shows quite clearly the existence of large-scale mass camps in China, and to this day it is not entirely clear how many Chinese are incarcerated in these camps. The more realistic figure is six-hundred thousand. The less realistic, more fanciful figure is six million.

But the range of figures that are adduced in this respect are always slightly unbelievable. This is why when very Christian, conservative, and anti-Bolshevik sources of opinion in the Western world began trumpeting the scale of Soviet atrocity from the early 1920s onwards they were widely disbelieved outside their own circles. Partly because the numbers involved appeared to be unbelievable.

But when you bear in mind there was no prior codification of human or civil rights, there was no right of *habeas corpus* in law, and there was also a complete control by the state of almost every aspect of an individual's life from cradle to grave, the prospect of being incarcerated in the gulag, in the operating camp system was an ever-present reality to anyone who lived in the Soviet Union in the 1920s, 1930s, and 1940s.

It is also interesting to point out that the thaw begins immediately after Stalin dies. It is as if, in a system as beholden to sort of Byzantine power intrigues as that, the top man is crucial. When he goes, the entire timber and caliber of the system didn't collapse but altered radically.

Khrushchev was once asked, 'Why did you remain silent in the Politburo? Why did you do nothing while all of these events were occurring?' And he just responded that everyone was terrified. Everyone was terrified and was looking over his own shoulder, because every remark could be used against you in the manner that everybody was an auxiliary NKVD or OGPU spy, and you never could trust anyone including people in your own families. This is widely believed to be the system that exists in North Korea, where if somebody sins against the regime, the family as a whole is collectively punished.

There was this concept in the 1930s in the Soviet Union of the "unperson" and the "ex-people." People were described as ex-people and were decanted into the camp system. There are many famous photographs of high schools and Bolshevik dignitary parties and even just social events where the shoulders and heads of various people are cut out of all sorts of obligatory photographs. These photos would then be put on display. There wasn't a system in which it was denied that these people had given up civic dignity or been otherwise disposed of. It was admitted that they had once existed, but they had ceased to exist within the socialist project.

There's also a degree to which the Terror could devour its own children. Nobody in the party was safe. No one in the inner party was safe, certainly during the events of 1936–1937–1938. No one in the party *cum* army was safe. And nobody amongst the executioners or even the torturers were safe.

This was also proved by the ethnic games that Stalin used to play in relation to different parts of the Soviet Union where he would play off one group against another. One classic example is he used Ashkenazi Jews for some of the dirtiest work in the camps as commanders and then to turn around and say that they'd had an excess of revolutionary zeal for which they should be punished, and the system would tack in a more chauvinistic and Russian direction, and such individuals would be purged and replaced by others who only got those posts because they'd been involved in a prior purge of those who were themselves purgers. And so it went on and on and on.

In some ways, what is happening is a psychological disturbance of almost everybody. There's nobody in the society that can rest easy. There's nobody in the society that can rest on their laurels. Even to hide amongst the executioners and the torturers is no guarantee that one won't be purged at a later date.

In the Red Army, of course, traditionally, in the Russian Civil War and in the wars after it, commissars would stand eight paces or its equivalent behind the front line. Anyone who retreated on your own side would be killed. Tens of thousands of Soviet troops were killed at Stalingrad for retreating, and they would be killed by their own commissariat and the NKVD troops and elite forces that would exist behind them. So, the Soviet Union often went to war against its own army in order to prop it up in terms of total victory. If they fled from the Germans they would be killed by their own side.

This is why Stalin got an enormous number of Russians who fought on the German side as a paradox. Of course, if they were ever captured they'd either immediately be put back in punishment battalions right at the front of the line or they themselves would be exterminated. The extraordinary high death total in nearly all Soviet wars, particularly in the Great Patriotic War as the Second World War was called in the Soviet Union, is partly because of the infliction of mass torment on one's own side.

In a talk at the last meeting that I attended, we had the idea that Soviet pilots bombed Red Army prison camps behind German lines during the early months of the German invasion of the greater Soviet Union. These events certainly happened, because the first ideology of Stalinist-Communism was to protect your own base. Therefore, men who surrendered needed to be punished in accordance with certain primal Soviet attitudes, so that others would not take from their example, and they would fight to the last man way into greater Russian and Soviet territory.

This idea that you purge your own core first, so that your vanguard is pure, before you go out and then attack the enemy was a key part of Stalinist ideology.

This also made slight sense when one interprets the fact that people could be held collectively responsible for anti-socialist agitation and propaganda. So, if you were found guilty, everyone in this room would be guilty through you. Everyone you knew socially would share in that guilt, and all family members and extended family members could often be purged subsequently with you could share that guilt as well. So, you have this strange ramifying and interconnected concept of collective guilt often for transgressions and crimes which were themselves imaginary.

The bulk of the people who were interned in the camps were in no ways enemies of the regime. There was a quota of dissidents; there was a quota of old tsarists; there was a quota of all sorts of low-level officials and so on who had different views. But the bulk of people were ordinary Soviet citizens who were just taken up by the meat grinder — as ordinary Russians called this system — and were laid waste within it, prior to their decanting back into the society as aged husks and wrecks *or* their death in captivity in the Siberian outer wastes.

The system also seemed quite irrational. Many enormous projects of public improvement, such as dams and dikes and great civic adornments, were built by slave labor from the concentration camps, from the gulag proper. And yet, many of these were white elephants that have later been discarded in accordance with Russian process. It was almost as if you have great big motorway half-sections built into the distance which are never completed and then, just like in some sort of J. G. Ballard novel, just exist as structures of their own, which never progress and are left as strange mausoleums to a previous and slightly delinquent form of planning which they are the arbitrary representative of. And a lot of these gulag projects never went anywhere and served no ultimate purpose but the methodology of the gulag itself, which was to use up more and more prisoners and was to take more and more individuals from out of socialist life.

Why was it done? I think it's partly the methodology of Communism itself. The imperfectability of man is so blatant that an attempt to create an allegedly perfect society will come a cropper very early on. What the Soviet Union did, instead of giving up on its project and just installing a regime in perpetuity, it tried to change the nature of man by introducing pressure onto the citizenry. You often have in science-fiction films the mythology whereby the walls creep in on somebody, and the floor and the ceiling creep down on somebody, and that was what the Soviet Union was doing to the private citizen, particularly between about 1931–32 and 1953–54. Pressure was being applied to the psychology of ordinary Soviet citizens to get them to behave in different ways.

It was also a form of *action*. The regime preached action at all possible opportunities, as if inaction was itself a sort of reactionary and almost religious and counter-system complaint. And action meant acting on the human scale, acting to the degree to which the individual must serve the interests of the state.

Stalin had no concept of individual life at all. He believed that all individuals essentially were there to serve the state, and the state was there to serve the socialist ideal. The image that we have of Stalin has changed to a large degree in the last twenty years. Most Western propaganda accepted the Trotskyist evaluation of Stalin as a teenage boy in boots with a mustache, an overgrown sadistic psychopath who launched the Soviet Union into a disastrous course. This has only been re-evaluated in the last twenty years with major books written by Simon Sebag Montefiore and others about the young Stalin[4] and his early caucus and his later

---

[4] Simon Sebag Montefiore, *Young Stalin* (New York: Random House, 2007).

court, "the court of the red tsar,"[5] as it was widely termed at the time, something Stalin never entirely repudiated.

In Eisenstein's film, *Ivan the Terrible*, which of course is metaphorically a comment on the Stalinist era, Ivan is depicted as a great spider at the heart of Russia, particularly in *Ivan the Terrible*, Part II that was later banned in the Soviet Union. Although tsar Stalin had a private viewing because he rather liked the image of Ivan upon whom he identified himself. Ivan, of course, terrorized and decimated the boyars, the nobles of old Russia, and began the centralization of the Russian state and also made Russia feared and powerful: all the things with which Stalin implicitly identified.

There's a great moment in the film where Ivan, bearded, dances that sort of Russian dance where you go down on your haunches and you kick your heels. He's all dressed in black, and he dances before the boyars in a great, powerful, triumphant vein, almost like a big, dark spider — "*pauk*" [spider] I think it's called in Russian — whereby you leap and dance about.[6]

Pauk was the name the KGB gave to Solzhenitsyn later on for revealing the true extent of the camp system. It's important to realize that in an era where all media was closed, and there was no internet, way into the 1960s people only had their personal memories of the gulag. Almost everyone knew it existed, because it had touched almost every family in Russia, Greater Russia, and the Soviet Union. However, most people were undecided about what they could talk about, didn't wish to talk about it to outsiders, and would rarely talk about it even when people who were members of their own family returned from the camps. So, Solzhenitsyn's books came as a revelation and were deeply damaging to the regime.

When the Nobel laureate for literature Doris Lessing[7] said that

---

[5] Simon Sebag Montefiore, *Stalin: The Court of the Red Tsar* (New York: Alfred A. Knopf, 2003).

[6] The dance is called "*gopak*."

[7] Doris Lessing (1919–2013), British novelist and winner of the 2007 Nobel Prize in Literature.

Aleksandr Solzhenitsyn caused the death of an empire, she is exaggerating and engaging in literary hyperbole. But there is a degree to which she has also grasped a salient truth. In Russia, where politicians are accorded scant respect unless they're feared, writers are seen as beacons of truthfulness and repositories of popular wisdom.

Solzhenitsyn's book, *One Day in the Life of Ivan Denisovich*,[8] which follows an average camp day from beginning to end with all its sordidness and boredom and cruelty and coldness and just the dogged human desire to survive this pretty perishing and terrible experience, was allowed by a journal called *New World* (*Novy Mir*), which was a reformist and "liberal" journal within the Communist matrix. The decision to publish went to Khrushchev himself, who allowed it so long as there were a few lines introduced in the story condemning Ukrainian nationalism. A point which we'll come onto in a little while.

The Gulag Archipelago by Solzhenitsyn,[9] which was the main statement of alternative opposition to the camps that came out of them, appeared in three volumes, later condensed into two, and later in the West condensed into one. It's interesting to note that Solzhenitsyn was highly persecuted by the KGB after he left Russia. Something which is not widely known in the West and indeed is slightly, exasperatingly misinterpreted. He initially lived in Switzerland but fled from Switzerland due to KGB harassment, particularly ordered by Andropov. He later settled in Vermont in the United States in a private villa with fencing and barbed wire all around. Every day the KGB used to send him and his agent in Switzerland pictures of mutilations and dead bodies and cancer cells in the human body.

Don't forget that Solzhenitsyn had survived cancer and turned

---

[8] Alexander Solzhenitsyn (1918–2008), *One Day in the Life of Ivan Denisovich* (1962), trans. Ralph Parker (New York: Dutton, 1963). Solzhentisyn won the 1970 Nobel Prize in Literature primarily for this work.

[9] Solzhenitsyn, *The Gulag Archipelago: An Experiment in Literary Investigation* (1973), 3 vols., trans. Thomas P. Whitney (New York: Harper & Row, 1974).

it back as his novel, partly autobiographical, *Cancer Ward*, attests.[10] These were moments of psychological warfare which the KGB used against Solzhenitsyn, whom they regarded as a very dangerous man because writers in the Russian tradition are accorded a heroic and transvaluating status that Western writers do not have. This is why Solzhenitsyn became, after a period, the most dangerous man. They never assassinated him because they knew they would be blamed for it, and in the end the texts were written, and they were out there.

The irony is that under Putin, Solzhenitsyn's key texts are integrated into the Russian school syllabus and are now taught to people. Maybe that will deaden their impact over time as often happens when people are put on the school syllabus. But it's an interesting transformation.

Solzhenitsyn, of course, went from the most dissident of dissidents to being a mild supporter of the Putin government. Something that shocked other dissidents and liberals in the ex-Soviet Union. Solzhenitsyn, of course, was never a liberal but was a conservative nationalist in Russian terms, a Christian Orthodox conservative nationalist, essentially.

He wasn't liked when he came to the West either, because his diatribes against what he termed the decadence and materialism of Western life. After a while, the KGB ceased to persecute Solzhenitsyn, because they believed he had become so unpopular in the United States because of his denunciation of what passed for American popular culture. They interpreted his isolation in modern America as partly a repudiation of him and his views by modern America, and they were not entirely incorrect.

Solzhenitsyn resembled a biblical Old Testament prophet in many ways. Bearded, lashing his audience with invective and splenetic rage. Solzhenitsyn, in some ways, was part of a great Orthodox tradition of outsiders and religious teachers who would march into the innermost enclave and lay down the law as to what should occur. He was also quite unpopular when he returned to Russia, although he was given a television program of his own for

---

[10] Solzhenitsyn *Cancer Ward* (1966), trans. Nicholas Bethell and David Burg (London: The Bodley Head, 1968).

a while that was repeatedly unwatched.

A large number of the generations that suffered during the massive terrors that convulsed the society from the early twenties until the mid-fifties don't want to talk about it, and even to this day there have been no reparations paid. There have been no festivals of remembrance, except for a few, mostly as a result of private money and donations and extracurricular activities undertaken on by human rights groups and university departments. There is no national day for the victims of any Soviet-communist atrocity, no matter how many one wishes to look at.

You look at the de-kulakization, you look at the Ukrainian Famine or Holodomor, you look at the famine that occurred in Kazakhstan and Greater Russia circumadjacent to the Ukrainian terror famine, you look at the mass shootings and the killing of upwards of a million alleged political dissidents in 1937–38 at the high point of the Terror, what Robert Conquest in his book called "the Great Terror," you look at the enormous waves of prisoners and others who were inducted into the camp system during the war, and in 1948 when the Cold War began and there was an immediate closing of the door inside the Soviet Union in relation to the relative thaw that had occurred a couple of years previously after the victory over the Axis powers when Stalin felt more certain of his ground and Europe was half under the control of the Red Army.

Now, there's also a degree to which the Terror was extended into Soviet satellite states, such as Mongolia, and also took up a disconnected sampling in Eastern and Greater Europe. None of the systems in Eastern Europe, even Ceauşescu's or Tito's which were slightly outside the Soviet bloc, registered on the Richter scale of Stalinist atrocity. And yet there is a degree to which all of the Communist regimes, in Poland under Gomułka from 1948 and elsewhere mirrored what was going on in the Soviet Union. All of them had their camps, all of them had their dissidents, all of them used psychiatry as a political weapon, although that largely occurred after Stalin. Although the Doctor's Plot at the end of Stalin's life was beginning to presage that.

The waves of individuals incarcerated in the camp system didn't let up really until the dictator's death. After that there's a stasis in the system, and the system begins to grind down, although it is not until the 1990s that major political reparations are accorded. The Communist Party, of course, was banned for a period under Yeltsin and was tried largely by the Russian media in absentia for many crimes, which were then subsequently forgotten about.

During the chaotic Yeltsin period, the most liberal parts of the Russian polity, the bloc known as Yabloko, wished to make sure that the restitution of the past and the victims wasn't forgotten. But because of the economic chaos and extreme hardship during the 1990s and because of the failure of the big bang capitalism that the Yeltsin clique tried to impose, those ideas became discredited with the Yeltsin circus, and Putin's more authoritarian, Kremlin-oriented type of politics that replaced the Yeltsin years has largely put a halter on the culture of fear, trembling, and remembrance which has convulsed post-war Germany, for example. There is no comparison whatsoever.

Stalin is still slightly praised in the contemporary Russian context as a great Russian war leader, and the Russian leadership is determined not to engage in what you might call the rhetoric of self-hatred. Because the irony is that nearly all of these atrocities, even when they were inflicted upon the Ukrainian peasants, were internal. After all, they were all citizens of the Soviet Union, and the bulk of the victims ultimately were Russian, particularly in the greater gulag system, both of special and of general camps. So, this was a war that was inflicted by the Soviet elite and their attendant military and security bureaucracies on the Russian and Greater Russian and Soviet populations as well as certain more militant ethnic minorities.

It's not widely known that all the Tatars, for example, were all depopulated and shoved into Siberia in one go in cattle trucks. As were all the Chechens, who were transplanted in one go from Chechnya to Siberia. They made their way back almost without state edict after Stalin died. Indeed, there's a day of remembrance in Chechnya where everyone wears a black armband and black flags fly from buildings to attest to the depopulation of Chechnya. No one knows how many Chechens died. The figure of 350,000 is adduced in Chechen nationalist circles.

The population of Greater Russia found itself totally beholden to state power in a manner which is difficult for people who live in Western democracies to understand. The individual had no rights and no recourse to any state institution. There was no court of appeal, and there was no legal process, although a sort of trial would be gone through. In the sixteen to seventeen million that passed through, on the lower estimates, the Soviet camp system under Stalin, from about 1929 until 1953, only about three to four million actually had a conviction. But these would be convictions for an enemy conversation, conversation with a class enemy, conversation pursuant to an absence of dignity of the socialist republic.

Solzhenitsyn was given eight years in a prison labor camp, despite having an exemplary war record in the artillery and despite at that time being a relatively firm Marxist-Leninist in terms of personal belief, having lost the Christianity of his early phase. It's very important to realize that Solzhenitsyn was a believer who turned on the system in relation to the way in which he had been treated, as is quite understandable. He wrote several letters to a colleague behind the front describing Stalin as the chief bandit, which was a term of relatively mild scorn and abuse that was used and that also conflated with his Georgian and possibly Ossetian origins.

There's a dispute about this. Sometimes Stalin described himself as an Ossetian and sometimes he described himself as a Georgian. But, of course, Ossetia is part of Georgia as Georgians claim. Many Ossetians don't want to be a part of Georgia, of course, and this is an on-running dispute with Russia that's flared up recently, but it's always part of these disputes that exist when peoples live amongst each other and claim loyalty to a much larger country that lies on that country's borders.

Stalin had a madcap attitude towards the exercision of political power. That much is certain. At times, Stalin could be warm and bucolic, at times coldly murderous. It's well known that in the trials of the Old Bolsheviks, for example, during the Great Terror in 1937 to 1938, Stalin had a booth constructed for himself at the top of the court with a glass screen that was frosted that he could shove either way and look down into the body of the court to see the Old Bolsheviks, his old colleagues from the revolutionary Leninist years, being punished and done to death.

It was widely regarded that a light would go on in this little booth at the top of the court when a judgment from the people's court with Vyshinsky, the Soviet state prosecutor, screaming for the death penalty or for execution or for torture before execution or for gulag followed by torture followed by execution. These were the options that would be given to various unfortunates who were in the dock. It was always said that Stalin looked down upon this with the cold, egregious look of an ultimate avenger.

Stalin never forgot a slight and never forgot a word out of place. And in politics there are lots of slights and lots of words out of place. Anyone who had ever, on his way up to the top of the greasy pole, slighted Stalin in any way, shape, or form would be remembered and would be dealt a crippling blow at a later date.

This is why he even came to purge his own purgers during the logic of this sort of socialist pyrotechnicon whereby people would be ostracized, integrated again, shot, then their families would be put in the gulag, then they would be released. All as part of an endless cycle of unsettling and desensitizing people in relation to the organs of state power.

When Orwell wrote *Nineteen Eighty-Four* and samizdat versions of it flourished in Eastern Europe and further afield in the Soviet Union from the 1950s, it was regarded as extraordinary that a Western writer should be so prescient about what the psychologically oppressive lifestyle was like in the Soviet Union, particularly under harsh Stalinist terror. Later, it became a softer, more Brezhnevite, conformist Soviet Union whereby infractions were not punished to the same degree, and the gulag system was allowed to fall, partly through a natural wastage, in its own terms.

Stalin was quite capable of embracing a man, with the Russian kisses and all this, and then say, "Have him killed." Just like that to some KGB or NKVD flunky that was nearby. The fact that everybody was on edge in relation to what he would do and what he would not do is part and parcel of the metaphysic of terror, the almost piratical way in which he ran the Soviet state.

He would occasionally ring up artists and get them to come, and he would play the piano to them. And lo and behold if anyone said to him that he couldn't play the piano particularly well. The people in the audience would be Shostakovich, would be Khachaturian, the Armenian composer, and he would play the piano—*clunk, clunk, clunk, clunk*—and they would have to say, "What a marvelous rendition!" of some Russian folk song he'd given.

Talking of folk music, there was a moment where he had almost all of the folk musicians outside of Russia in the Soviet Union shot. Or that was the plan. Folk music was at one madcap moment, in the days of cultural struggle in the early 1930s, described as mad, reactionary music that needs to be purged from the hinterland of the Soviet masses. So, large numbers of folk musicians were gathered, particularly from the Eurasiatic republics, and they were then all shot. Shostakovich burst into tears when he heard this, although many folk artists survived because they realized the untenderhearted underpinnings to this mobilization of their talents.

Stalin regarded the Ukrainian famine as a direct attempt to break the back of the Ukrainian peasantry. The Ukrainian famine is the only event in the Soviet Union which is described by some of the United Nations—particularly the Western powers on the Security Council—as a genocide.

If you remember, the Genocide Convention which came in 1949 refers exclusively to crimes which are ethnic, which are racial, which are religious, which are folk-oriented, and which are an attempt to exterminate a people. Class-based crimes or sociological crimes whereby entire groups may be done to death or exterminated were deliberately excluded—partly because of the presence of the Soviet Union on the Security Council at the time—from the remit of genocide. But the Ukrainian crimes are crimes against a nationality, and this is widely perceived as such in the contemporary Ukraine.

In the Ukraine, you see a sort of thought criminality in reverse subsequent to the Orange Revolution whereby the entire Soviet metaphysic has been thrown over, and a subculture has emerged of the Holodomor, for example, which is now accepted as a genocide by twenty-seven countries, nearly all of them Western, including the Vatican. This causes a headache for Russia, because until 1990 the Russian organs of what was then the Soviet Union denied the existence of the Ukrainian famine. The Ukrainian famine was a lie spread by fascist perverts and their Western ideological champions.

The Ukrainian Communist Party's central committee admitted to the Ukrainian famine in 1990–1991, but even then they said it wasn't directed against Ukrainians. It was actually a part of a general series of massacres which affected Kazakhstan and Russia as well. That is true. The Western totals for deaths in the famines of the 1930s is eight million. That is the un-revisionist and un-exterminationist middle-ground position. Russia tentatively accepts that this may well be true.

President Medvedev caused quite a stir when he stood before the Holodomor victims memorial in Kiev in the Ukraine with a whole Russian delegation during a previous period of his presidency, the first major Russian leader ever to do so or ever to accede to the Ukraine that a quasi-genocide or an actual genocide had been committed on their territory.

The Russian view is that the victims were the victims of inhuman state totalitarianism that was the formation of the Communist Party of the Soviet Union at that time and were not Russian crimes and cannot be blamed upon Russia, and Russia refuses to pay any reparation in relation to these crimes.

However, there is a lot more counter-cultural material circulating in Greater Russia now, and there is a much greater awareness of the Holodomor than there has ever been in the past. Although many Russians are defensive about these crimes, because one of the areas of complicity between victim and violator in relation to Soviet atrocity is that so many people passed through the camps, so many people were involved in the repression, so many people were related to people that were involved in the repression, so many people were related to people who were repressed, that it's an enormous stain in the society. Many people would rather not know about it.

The Russian attitude is largely a shrugging of the shoulders They're fifty or sixty years on now or more. What can they do about it? And there's a sort of slight patriotic refusal to engage in an enormous game of blame and recrimination when for many people the collapse of the Soviet Union, the actual implosion and downfall of what appeared to be a totalitarian state at the time, is the punishment for all of the crimes that it inflicted. Twenty years on, it's as if it's gone down like a slow-motion shot of a building being demolished as it comes down in stages, when the engineers occasion an explosion for it to collapse. Most people consider that the Soviet Union has fallen in that way and that draws a red line, if you like, under the past.

The Putin administration is Janus-faced. On the one hand, Stalin is praised as a great war leader and super-Russian patriot who saw off the fascists in the Great Patriotic War and laid the foundations for Russia, as the Soviet Union, to put men into space and so on. But on the other hand, Solzhenitsyn's texts are allowed on the school syllabus as a reminder to those who suffered under pitiless totalitarianism. So, Russia in its present incarnation is in many ways playing a double game.

What they don't want to do is humiliate themselves before the bar of world history and drag themselves along the ground as if they feel worthless and put upon and pejorated. In some ways it's quite a clever and slightly patriotic course to blame it all on Soviet Communism, to blame it all on the Iron Man Stalin, and to, if you like, withdraw Russian responsibility for what went on.

Certainly the tsarist camps that did exist and were run by the Okhrana, the forerunner of its much more ferocious and generalized Soviet examples of state terror, were infinitesimal in comparison to their Soviet counterparts.

When Dostoyevsky was sent to Siberia for being involved in a very minor Decembrist flirtation with opposition and he was mock executed — he was stood against a wall and they fired over his head — and he then had to serve a period of imprisonment in what was then essentially a tsarist labor camp in Greater Siberia, out of which he wrote a book called *The House of the Dead*,[11] which was his first great publication.

Again, an example of the literary writer who stands at the bar of history and accords truth and solemnity that it ought to witness. Dostoyevsky is part of that grand tradition of great Russian

---

[11] Fyodor Dostoevsky (1821–1881), *The House of the Dead: or, Prison Life in Siberia; A Novel in Two Parts* (1860–1862), trans. Constance Garnett (New York: Macmillan, 1915).

voices and writers that it seems can't be stilled and almost have a religious passion accorded to them in Russia, the Soviet Union, and now the Russian Federation coming after the Soviet Union.

In relation to the Ukrainian famine or Holodomor, which means "terror famine" or "death by famine" or "genocidal famine." It's a kind of compound Ukrainian word which is designed to indicate that it was volitional. The Ukrainian sensibility of the present hour—with the possible exception of those Russians who live in the Ukraine and take a slightly more revisionist and differentiated view of these events not to deny them but to excuse themselves and their presence as Russians inside Ukraine—is that seven to ten million perished in this famine. The Western estimates are different. The West states between three-and-a-half million and five-and-a-half million perished in this famine, with three million dying elsewhere in the Soviet Union of similar famine-related causes.

The famine was created by the state. There were geographical and climatic reasons for a famine in Ukraine and elsewhere in the early 1930s. But one has to understand that all of agriculture was collectivized in one fell swoop. All farms were seized. All peasants were forced by the NKVD and Ministry of the Interior troops into state collectivized farms. People who didn't go along with this were immediately dispatched to the gulag or shot. There was also a degree to which the state insisted on taking from farms which had been collectivized the bulk of the grain, some of which was exported.

Rations were set in the Ukraine artificially low. Certainly they were not enough for people who were infirm or in any way ill to survive upon. There's a degree also to which peasants could be sent to the gulag for the crime of "stealing socialist grain." This was stealing a particular husk of grain from a silo or from a bin or from a village which had been collectivized, and millions were sent to the gulag for these imagined crimes against Soviet produce whilst the regime, of course, lived in the relative lap of luxury, although no one lived in luxurious circumstances even in Stalin's circle because the hand of fear could always come in at any time and pluck somebody from the golden circle and plunge them into the outer darkness of the gulag or beyond.

The KGB as it then was, the NKVD, was organized into various directorates, the internal directorate of which was responsible for the absence of sabotage and the absence of spying and the absence of counter-revolution inside the state socialist republics. It took on an enormous and bloated and bureaucratic form during the years of the Terror to such a degree that most of the statistics which were recorded by the NKVD probably have a degree of truth to them, because the Soviets always wrote everything down.

Just as the Katyn forest massacre of the Polish officer corps was ordered by Stalin. Everything was written down. Each member of the Politburo signed the death order, including Khrushchev, because the Soviets had the view that their system would last forever, and what they were doing was of unique human importance, and therefore everything that they did needed to be preserved. Rather than hide things away, things were definitely not hidden away in terms of Soviet bureaucracy. That's why when the archives were opened in the 1990s for a brief period under Yeltsin—Putin has largely closed those archives now—much of what occurred was revealed.

It appears that in 1937–38 about 1.1 million were shot by the NKVD pursuant of political crimes. These were the mass trials that began with the Old Bolsheviks, who were despised as class traitors, early nationalists, renegade fascistic traitors, anti-Soviet lowlifes, and various forms of un-socialist reprobates. Their shooting paved the way for an enormous clearing out of the Soviet bureaucracy and the army.

There are some dissident historians who maintain that the purges stiffened and emboldened the Red Army and enabled them to fight more effectively, but this is an extraordinarily minor view. The basic Western historiographical perspective is that the Red Army was virtually ruined for several years by these purges, had been decapitated at source, and was no match for the invading Germans. It's widely believed, of course, that one of the reasons that the Soviet formations at the time of Barbarossa were in the format that they were was they were preparing themselves for an attack upon Nazi Germany and were caught unawares by the speed of the German attack, which possibly came six to eight months ahead of what they expected.

The rough Soviet tactic, which was to throw as many men into the breach as possible, to retreat, to pull heavy industry back into Eurasiatic Russia to bring the Germans in, to rely on winter and partisanship behind the lines to whittle away at the German spearheads and to ultimately reinforce the cities so that they could serve as bridgeheads and blockades that the German Panzer spearheads would break on largely proved to be the winning recipe in relation to the Eastern Front of the Second World War.

Now, how far Stalin is personally responsible for directing the war is difficult to imagine, but certainly the development of elite Soviet tanks by the end of the war had a lot to do with the relocation of massive industrial projects in Greater European Russia.

Russia is a society that's gone through immense torment and pain, unlike most Western societies to whom its immediate history cannot really be compared. The Russian sensibility is very, very different from that which prevails in the Western side of the continent, and part of the unrecognized sensibility of the modern Russian identity has to do with the gulag and has to do with the gulag archipelago, which remains a sort of albatross around the Greater Russian neck. Many believe that it will take a long time for Russia to come to terms with what happened during the course of these mass killings and mass expulsions.

Don't forget that when all of these was being done Western Communists and liberals believed that this was a doctrine of love, believed that it was a doctrine of human brotherhood, believed the Soviet Union was a beacon to humanity and a beacon to the world, that it was peace-loving country among the peace-loving peoples of modernity, that it didn't threaten any of its neighbors, that it was internally at peace with itself.

All sorts of Western idiots, as they now appear even in contemporary liberal jargon of our own era, like the Webbs[12] and so on, crowded into the Soviet Union looking at the factories, looking at the plants, even approximating to look at the softest end of the gu-

---

[12] Sidney Webb (1859–1947) and his wife Beatrice Webb (1858–1943) were English socialists who helped found the London School of Economics and the Fabian Society.

lag, which was prepared for foreign visits, and were totally unaware, or seemed to be totally unaware, of this enormous archipelago of internal camps in the frozen tundra and wastes of the inner
Soviet Union whereby an enormous amount of sort of mole-like
economic activity — much of it with no economic desiderata — was
occurring. These people were totally taken in by Soviet propaganda.

Although many Western journalists who said, "There is no
famine in the Ukraine, nothing is happening, the Old Bolsheviks
were guilty" were actually, like Walter Duranty,[13] paid by the
KGB in order to spread this disinformation in Western societies.

One of the things that perplexed people for a long time, as a
Western social democrat like George Orwell pointed out, was
why people confessed to all sorts of crimes at their trials, or mock
trials, that were obviously fake. This is partly the refusal of the
liberal mindset to understand the psychopathological reality of
such a totalitarian regime.

The Old Bolsheviks were told that all of their families would
be killed or family members would be tortured before they were
killed, the houses that they'd lived in would be blown up, there
would be no records of the fact that they'd ever lived, and in comparison to what was then offered, that if you sign these docu-
ments which say that you've contributed to anti-socialist sabotage
and to say that you've allowed these dissident pamphlets to be
published and so on, you yourself may get ten years in a gulag,
but your family will be let off.

That is the reason that many people signed these affidavits
claiming that they'd committed all sorts of anti-socialist abuse. It's
because people couldn't put themselves in the position of people
who had no cards with which to play, had no defense lawyers in
the Western or general meaning of the term. It's only when you
realize that, that much of what occurred becomes explicable.

Amongst the special camps — six million or so in prison there
on top of the sixteen to seventeen million in the general camps

---

[13] Walter Duranty (1884–1957), an Anglo-American journalist,
served as Moscow bureau chief of the *New York Times* (1922–1936) and
won a Pulitzer Prize for passing off Communist propaganda as news.

during the Stalinist period—it's estimated that another one million to one-and-a-quarter million may have perished, and in the sixteen to seventeen million in the general camp system it is estimated that ten percent died in the camps, so that's about 1.6 million. The figure which is adduced now for mass shootings and camp deaths is 4.25 million perished under the raw Stalinist period, 1929 to his death in the early 1950s.

However, to that you have to add the famine deaths from the state inculcated famine, which will probably be declared a genocide by the United Nations at some time in the near future. The future of Russia, of course, will determine whether that happens or not. Russia does not regard it as a genocide, but as a human atrocity, because of course on these terms and their definitions and the splits that occur between and around their definitions, states rely for their moral purpose in this world.

The Turks regard the genocide of the Armenians, as many Westerners call it, at the end of the Great War, as to be part of the ongoing struggle, part of the greater violence of the Great War, whereas most Western nations now sign up to a discourse embraced by the Californian legislature, the American congress, and the French parliament that this is a genocide. A genocide involves the doctrine of intentionality, that there is prior intent to exterminate, and it is widely believed that it can be proved to be prior determination to exterminate in relation to the Ukrainian famine because of the collecting of Ukrainian grain. Grain was actually stolen from the Ukraine and taken into the greater Soviet Union at a time when there was known to be mass starvation. This proves in an *a priori* way that there was a plan to decimate the Ukrainian peasantry as the basis of Ukrainian nationalism.

The irony is that the Soviet Union throughout much of its history always regarded itself as endangered and enfeebled and surrounded by enemies, external and internal, when the system itself to the Western gaze looked impenetrable, permafrost, and totalitarian in its tidiness and ferocity and rigor. Stalin always thought they could lose the Ukraine, which given the circumstances of Soviet politics in the 1930s was quite extraordinary.

The Stalinist Terror of 1937 to 1938 involved mass killing in relation to a death of the Soviet party boss. This was Sergei Kirov, who died in Leningrad. No one knows whether Kirov was killed on Stalin's orders as a pretext to the great repression. A lot of Western historiography believe that this was indeed the case. There's an extraordinarily revealing photo of Stalin stood next to Kirov's bier, and Kirov's [arms are] folded over, looking very Russian Orthodox in actual fact, despite this being a secular event, and Stalin is stood next to him

And Stalin, for all the world, in this photo looks like a figure from *The Godfather*. He looks like a mafioso who's had a fellow mafioso done in for internal family reasons, and he's stood there brooding and looking down on the body in the coffin, because whether he was responsible for it or not, the death of Kirov seemed to "shock" the internal Soviet bureaucracy and terror mechanisms which had not been released to the same degree since the Russian Civil War. The right of the Cheka to basically root around in Soviet society unchecked by any humanist standards whatsoever then became the order of the day.

What do we have in the Western world as a record of the Soviet gulag? There are the three volumes of Solzhenitsyn's *The Gulag Archipelago*. There's a book by Norman Naimark called *Stalin's Genocides*.[14] There's the work *Gulag* by Anne Applebaum.[15] There's Robert Conquest's *The Great Terror* and *The Harvest of Sorrow*,[16] which concentrates primarily but not exclusively on the Ukrainian famine. There irony is that these are, on the whole, great works. There's no need for a plethora of other works, although such works now do exist in many Slavic languages including Russian.

The lesson I would draw from this is that Left-wing utopianism based on materialism is bound to fail, because the ideals for human conduct which it set were so high that they are insupportable by the biological evidence of human life.

Counter-Currents, October 13, 2015

---

[14] Norman Naimark, *Stalin's Genocides* (Princeton: Princeton University Press, 2010).

[15] Anne Applebaum, *Gulag: A History* (New York: Doubleday, 2003).

[16] Robert Conquest, *The Harvest of Sorrow: Soviet Collectivization & the Terror-Famine* (Oxford: Oxford University Press, 1986).

LILITH BEFORE EVE[*]

This talk is called "Lilith before Eve," which is a bit of a joke title in a way, because in the Old Testament Apocrypha Lilith is the mother of all evil and the mother of all demons and the mother of all vampires and mythologically is Adam's first wife, and she's created from mud, unlike Eve who's taken from the rib in mythology. So, it's a joke title in a way, because I'm going to talk about feminism and about the feminist movement.

I'll dispense with the Shirley Williams[1] idea about feminism that it's just equal pay for equal measures and equal work done, that it's just a sort of form of generalized, pre-packaged egalitarianism between the genders, because that's not very interesting. What I'm going to do in this talk is look at the most extreme and marginal elements in feminism which you can't entirely categorize as Left or Right because it's a movement off to one side by itself to a degree. And I'm going to look through them, probably going from the most extreme to more moderate examples of same.

What is the most extreme piece of new wave feminism from the 1960s and 1970s? Probably it's the *S.C.U.M. Manifesto.*[2] The *SCUM Manifesto*, that's what it's called. Yes, the Society for Cutting Up Men, which was published by Verso which was New Left Books and was produced by Valerie Solanas, who was a sort of artistic lesbian in Andy Warhol's circle in relation to The Factory movement.

She shot Warhol actually, so she put theory into practice, because he wouldn't publish a play by her. In actual fact, it was quite a serious incident, because Warhol almost died and was never the same again afterwards, according to people who were associated

[*] Transcript by V.S. of Bowden lecturing at the London Forum in London on September 24, 2011, online at the Jonathan Bowden Archive (jonathanbowden.org).

[1] Shirley Williams (1930–2021), British politician and academic.

[2] Valerie Jean Solanas (1936–1988), American feminist and artist, author of the *S.C.U.M. Manifesto: Society for Cutting up Men* (New York: Olympia Press, 1968).

with him during that period. She also wounded two other people, but because she was a paranoid schizophrenic she got three years in prison. She later surrendered to a policeman that very same day.

The Society for Cutting Up Men, which was her own abstraction, was a piece of extreme misandry, which is not really heard of very much but which is the opposite of misogyny, and it's extreme hatred of men. In this text, Solanas advocated the eradication of men as a gender, who she described as having a perverse chromosome which makes us unfeminine and therefore differentiated.

This text—which is still available in very alternative, Left-wing bookshops, those that are left—is probably the most extreme and sort of delusional, counter-factual, and virtual-reality piece of feminism that was ever created. It's a quite literate text. It's not just sort of belly-aching ranting. It also talks about the entire re-structuring of society and deals with essentially lesbian separatism or female-female bonding away from heterosexual norms or family-based societies as traditionally supposed.

Separatism is actually a key part of the more biological elements in the feminist movement. Feminism has achieved most of its mainstream goals, which is why the WLM, the Women's Liberation Movement, has largely been curtailed. Or so the sixties generation of radicalized students that provided most of the camp followers have themselves grown old and long in the tooth.

Some people may know that there's a separatist feminist book shop on the Charing Cross Road called Silver Moon which traditionally doesn't like men to go in it, and so when the odd male student on a dare and that sort of thing goes into Silver Moon there is a prescribed policy to be as frigid, to be as hostile, and to be as nasty as possible until the man leaves, because they can't deny male entry into the shop under equality law, which of course technically feminism is actually in favor of. So, you have this reverse principle going on there.

Separatism of the Solanas type is very extreme and very radical and was disputed by other feminists, of course, such as social-ist feminists and certain Marxist feminists who don't necessarily believe that men are the enemy. So-called "rooted," or biological, feminism, which actually is not a biological discourse, it's a discourse about biology, perceives an endless gender war and a conflict between men and women in all social areas. "Radical feminism" is the term that's usually given to this tendency.

The issue of lesbianism, in a sense, has to be dealt with because there are two types of lesbianism in relation to this type of politics. The first is so-called political lesbianism where a woman doesn't have those desires herself, but because of a rejection of patriarchy, refuses congress with men and therefore has two options: either inversion (lesbianism) or celibacy. So, the idea of political lesbianism grew up in the 1960s and seventies in the women's liberation movement, although later was questioned by the majority of democratic and socialist feminists who believed that women have a majority instinct to be heterosexual. That was alright as long as they entered into non-patriarchal relations with men. That was ultimately, democratically, the majority tendency that the women's liberation movement adopted.

But separatist currents have always existed, and there's the concept of a lesbian nation as it's called. *Lesbian Nation*,[3] which was quite a well-known feminist book in the 1970s, posits the twin-track strategy for lesbianism in a political context.

The other, of course, is women who are born inverted and who were born that way and who adopt lesbianism as a norm, but they would be a minority of the activists who advocated complete surrender to the world of matriarchy and so complete avoidance of congress and intimacy with men on all fronts.

Radical feminism also was very keen on the abortion of males, particularly after abortion was achieved, largely due to social democratic and liberal pressures in the 1960s and thereafter. Abortion was, of course, achieved in law. It's always existed in the back streets but had never become an ordered part of the health services of Western Europe and North America until the social and cultural revolutions of the 1960s. And it was militantly supported by all feminist movements. Indeed, abortion is a key

---

[3] Jill Johnston (1929–2010), British-born American feminist author of *Lesbian Nation: The Feminist Solution* (New York: Simon & Schuster, 1973).

issue for mainstream, second-wave feminism because it deals with autonomy, the autonomy of the female without male coercion or control and the extreme individualism, but without femininity, is at the core of many of these movements and is actually probably the tendency that draws together anarchists, feminists, radical feminists of a semi-biological type of the sort that I've enunciated, socialists, Marxian and communistic feminists, and their more mainstream liberal equivalents.

There are people who basically say that even the Margaret Thatchers of this world have a feminist element to them because, after all, women have to have the vote and have to be able to engage in political activity for somebody to rise to be the leader of a center-Right political party such as she did in the mid-1970s becoming the first female premier in Britain's history a couple of years thereafter.

But for the purposes of this analysis, I'll exclude that normative talk whereby very, very mainstream liberal humanist demands are conflated in with the feminist movement, which regarded them as just the softest edge of their more radical currents.

One of the most famous feminists in the 1970s and eighties, who received acreage of print on her death a few years ago, was Andrea Dworkin.[4] Andrea Dworkin, who was an obese individual, wrote a series of quite famous books, *Pornography: Men Possessing Women*,[5] a book on Right-wing conservative female activists in the Republican Party in the United States called *Right-Wing Women*,[6] and certain quite scatological novels, actually, such as *Ice & Fire*,[7] and various other works of what she called "explicit anti-pornography."

One of the great failures of the feminist movement that has succeeded in many other areas is their campaigns against pornog-

---

[4] Andrea Dworkin (1946–2005), American Jewish radical feminist.

[5] Andrea Dworkin, *Pornography: Men Possessing Women* (New York: Putnam, 1981).

[6] Andrea Dworkin, *Right-Wing Women: The Politics of Domesticated Females* (London: The Women's Press, 1983).

[7] Andrea Dworkin, *Ice & Fire: A Novel* (London: Secker & Warburg, 1986).

raphy and the sex industry. Socialist feminists, fearful of the accusation of Puritanism, have tended to shy away from some of those discourses. But feminism as a whole is deeply opposed to the commercialization of sexuality and to the commercialization of the female image as a result of that. In the 1960s, a whole potpourri of different Left-libertarian and Trotskyite notions came up, and some of them were in conflict with each other. Sexual libertarianism and extreme freedom and extreme hedonism clash violently with the neo-Puritanism of quite a lot of the feminist movement.

In their campaigns and strictures against pornography — from page three in the *Sun*[8] through to so-called and alleged snuff movies and everything in between — feminism has distinctively failed. It's failed to make any inroads on the commercial activities of pornographers. It's failed to decrease the profitability of these areas. People will be aware that large parts of the British print media are now owned by pornographers or ex-pornographers as the fortunes of these people have been mainstreamed since Paul Raymond and David Sullivan[9] and others started these businesses over forty years ago. Again, allowed to do this by the social reforms of the 1960s.

Many feminists used to have "Reclaim the Night" marches, as they used to call them. Reclaim the Night, where they used to go around with candles and various torches late at night. Particularly in the sort of pornographic or sin bin areas, the red zones that exist in all cities. There's one in London, of course, sort of equidistant with the streets around a particular district of Soho. It's probably about a quarter of a mile square. Traditionally, feminist marches used to go around these areas. Sometimes "actions" would be engaged in, which are socially and civically illegal such as the supergluing of the locks of various pornographic book shops and film distributing agencies and that sort of thing.

---

[8] Page three is the "boobs page" of the *Sun* tabloid.

[9] Paul Raymond (born Geoffrey Anthony Quinn, 1925–2008), was an English strip-club owner, pornographer, and property developer known as the "King of Soho." David Sullivan (born 1949) is a Welsh pornographer and sports team owner.

One of the more interesting corollaries is that the feminist movement took a very radical turn in Northern Europe or Scandinavia simultaneously with commercialization of the hardest type of pornography in those same countries. So, you see a culturally schizoid phenomenon going on there where the sixties led amongst the people who came out of them in quite contrary and diverse directions. You see one tendency of opinion, militant feminism, that wants to close the sex industry down and does not regard it as a legitimate form of capitalist enterprise (this is irrespective of criticisms they have of capitalism that they have more generally), and you also have an enormous range of Left-libertarian and more liberal spokesmen and women who regard pornography as essentially legitimate.

But it is interesting that feminism has had such an utter defeat there. Although most far-Left movements retain a certain Puritanism in relation to sex industry issues. The Trotskyist Left on the whole regarded the emotional pornography that women read, romance fiction and that sort of thing, as on a par with male pornography and hates to make moral judgments of a bourgeois character. But most traditional Communist movements, if they can be described as traditional — most authoritarian and Stalinoid type movements — banned pornography, as indeed the Soviet Union did basically from the Stalinist period after Trotsky was defeated internally in the internal battles with Stalin after 1928.

The Soviet Union is an interesting example of the sexual politics of the extreme Left. Between 1918 and 1928, almost all inhibitions were flouted, at least in law, although the effect of that on Soviet life was more marginal. And almost every sexual tendency was permitted between about 1918 and 1928. You moved from a tsarist, conservative, and highly socially authoritarian, conventionalist, and conservative apparatus to almost complete libertarianism in these years.

One feminist that was very important for the Bolshevik movement was Alexandra Kollontai, who was an ex-aristocrat who later became ambassador to Mexico, partly to get her out of the Stalinist purges, and was regarded as a Bolshevik heroine not least for her taste in young Soviet sailors of a *Battleship Potemkin* type. Now, she wrote a quite well-known novelized state socialist fiction called *Love of Worker Bees*[10] in which men and women live in Spartiate-type communes and don't intermarry with each other and engage in what is called free love, the doctrine of free love between men and women. In other words, no traditional family structure, no monogamy, no heterosexual bonding, and a looser sort of infinite rather than finite relations. It goes back to most forms of utopian Leftism in the nineteenth century and underground and bohemian movements and resurfaces in the 1920s, resurfaces again in the 1960s.

Wyndham Lewis, who's a modernist, Right-wing intellectual who has influenced me quite a lot in my life,[11] had the theory that radical counter-culturalism from the Left has three phases in Western society in the last two-hundred years, although he never lived to see the third one. The first one is in the 1890s in which you have an elitist zone of decadence, if you like, a bohemian radicalism. The next one is in the 1920s, the so-called Jazz Age, where there's a blowout culturally from the devastation of the Great War. You have a sort of endless party on easy credit that the Great Depression brings to an end in 1929–30. That could be considered to be a bourgeois or a middle-class version of the more upper-class decadence of the 1890s.

The next great splurge is the baby boomer generation in the 1960s, who, in a sense, have a lower middle-class, bourgeois, and proletarian Bohemia, a mass Bohemia based upon student activity and based upon all of the economic privileges which in a sense accrued in the post-war era and which are now being taken away, because of course you could do degrees virtually for free then. You had several years to engage in radical critique of bourgeois society without really doing any meaningful work.

Now students are £30,000 down just for a very moderate degree from an ex-polytechnic, as all degrees are commercialized along the American lines, and that's one of the reasons for the

---

[10] Alexandra Kollontai (1872–1952), Russian revolutionary, diplomat, and novelist, authored *Love of Worker Bees*, trans. Cathy Porter (London: Virago, 1977).

[11] See Bowden's writings on Wyndham Lewis in *Reactionary Modernism*.

complete deradicalization of contemporary students, which is very noticeable. Apart from animal rights, some residual feminism, and ecological activity, there's almost very little radicalism going on in the universities outside of what certain radical Muslims get up to, watched by the security services.

The feminist movement influenced all forms of Leftism with the possible exception of the old Stalinist model with the Communist Party of Great Britain. But even then the influence of anti-sexism, as it would be called, was palpable. Almost no institutional, ideological tendency on the Left was immune from feminist critique, and this changed attitudes on a whole range of issues from property rights to divorce, from abortion to so-called child's rights, to the rearing of children, to attitudes towards pornography, to attitudes towards heterosexuality and attitudes toward men.

The broad socialist/humanist Left never went along with the idea that men are the enemy. There used to be, of course, in traditional feminist congresses and so on chanting that men were the enemy, and if ever a boyfriend or a husband or whatever turned up at the end of a meeting to take somebody home in a car there would be quite a scene. So, separatism was sort of enforced but was also a dividing line between the very radical feminists and those of, if you like, a more assimilationist and more gradualist character.

Like all movements, it was plagued with an enormous number of personality clashes and splits, and it had its star turns and star theorists who remained media characters and representatives of feminist opinion long after the movement had begun to dip down. The media had a schizophrenic attitude towards feminism. On the one hand, they were good copy, and feminist intellectuals and ideologues were given a lot of space.

Probably the most famous ideologue in Britain of this type was Germaine Greer whose book *The Female Eunuch*[12] caused outrage and sensation in various ways. She was an Australian don, who

---

[12] Germaine Greer (born 1939), Australian feminist, most famous for *The Female Eunuch* (London: MacGibbon & Kee, 1970).

now teaches, I think, at Oxford and has been through several permutations. Indeed, her theory is dialectical. The first book was a very radical piece of feminism, almost on the cusp of "all men are rapists" ideology that Marilyn French disseminated through her novel *The Women's Room*.[13]

A lot of this material was very mainstream. In the 1960s, seventies, and eighties, you could get it from Smith's.[14] This is the one thing that's interesting about the feminist movement: the belief that women wanted this material and that certain dissentient Leftwing men wanted this material if only to peruse it, was very much of the moment. This material was available in the women's section in most, not newsagents, but most mainstream bookshops. You didn't have to go to obscure sources to obtain this material, and, although the number of people who ever read this material was very small, its influence in the general culture has been very pervasive. Probably no movement has influenced society more in a soft power way than feminism since the Second World War.

Unlike almost any other tendency of opinion, its erosion of traditional and patriarchal structures, to use its own terminology, has been very extensive and very deconstructive, and it has almost, to use a seventeenth-century phrase, turned the world upside down in fifty to sixty years. If you consider that all laws in relation to divorce, in relation to abortion, in relation to pornography, in relation to most mainstream male-female relations, and most of those relations *per se* were the opposite or, slightly less tendentiously, the semi-opposite of what they are now before I was born.

I was born in 1962. In 1962, abortion was illegal, divorce was very difficult to come by, contraception was difficult and highly medicalized and somewhat obscure, relations between men and women were quite traditional, mass mainstream pornography and the growth of the so-called sex industry and its invasion of all other medias — because one of the tricks is the contemporary media now resembles the pornography of the 1960s and seventies,

---

[13] Marilyn French (1929–2009), American feminist, authored *The Women's Room* (New York: Simon & Schuster, 1977).

[14] WHSmith, mainstream UK high street bookseller.

because the pornographificization of mass media is, again, one of the most salient factors which has occurred in the last forty to fifty to sixty years. It's almost a shock to point it out now, because the process has become so all-encompassing and so gradually obtainable that the fact that *Cosmopolitan* is as extreme as most forms of male soft pornography now, which it certainly wasn't when it started. Whereas the sort of pornography that *Playboy* once represented, in other words, very soft, is now so mainstream that it's almost on television nightly.

One can argue that forces of the counter-factual sexual revolution of the 1960s have not been in women's interests at all, and there are certain dissident feminists who turned back to slightly more conservative social positions, later in life usually, who sometimes ruefully admit that this is the case.

Probably the destructivity of the feminist movement, particularly the second wave from the sixties and seventies, is seen in the enormous divorce rate and the enormous non-marriage rate which now exists. The deconstruction and whittling down and whittling out of the society like a piece of wooden sculpture is well under way.

No politician now can criticize the single-parent family, because so many people are involved in them, and they are so much part of the constituent electorate to which one has to appeal. Marriage itself has been relativized almost to a point of semi-invisibility within the culture, although there are still quite strong ideological pressures to keep it as a gold standard or as an ideal. But the very difficulty that a policy as tame as giving tax breaks or exemptions to married families that the Cameron government has tried to instigate around the margins shows you the difficulty in a lone area of plowing back on what has occurred in all other areas.

The radical social, sexual, and libertarian agendas of the 1960s ramified with feminism in various ways and yet never lived up to the utopianism of the feminist movement. Feminism remains in some respects, particularly in its second generational aspect, a utopian movement, a belief in total transformation of woman, of man, and of social and civic and lived circumstances.

One of feminism's radicalisms is the idea that the personal is the political. When people leave a room like this, or whatever tendency of opinion they support, they drop their politics away from them in their private life or the way in which they actually live their own lives. That would be true of many people who have even quite pronounced political views.

Feminism is based on the idea that everything that one does, from the smallest interfamily relationship and so on, is actually deeply political, and the belief that the personal is political, and the personal is even more important in its politicization than what is customarily regarded as politics.

Certainly electoral politics has had enormous soft power gains. By soft power, I mean cultural power. The ability that feminism has had retrospectively to engender terror in normal relations where quite ordinary and normal people without any ideology at all weigh sexism and weigh whether one remark was more sexist than another as a criterion of social acceptability. Few people would have heard of this terminology before the 1960s or the 1970s. Today, in certain areas of employment, it's quite a serious matter to be accused of institutional sexism or to be accused of sexism *per se*, and as with the corollary, racism, an enormous bureaucracy has grown up to police particularly academic discourse.

There is a certain *Nineteen Eighty-Four* or Orwellian element to this where in the academic life, where people are mentally trained for the attitudes that they will carry through as educators in the future, people are taught the correct responses in a post-religious, secular, and multicultural age. An enormous number of university lecturers have gotten into trouble over a sort of feminist and PC agenda to such a degree now that many will only interview female students with the door open or with a woman colleague present in case they are accused of making a remark of detrimental, objectifying, patriarchal, or sexually genocidal character. This can be quite an innocent and freeborn remark in relation to what would be regarded as old-fashioned masculinity. But old-fashioned masculinity is something that's probably not too much to be found in many institutions of higher learning.

Traditional colleges were segregated along gender lines. Traditional Oxford and Cambridge colleges were segregated along gender lines, certainly. There were single-sex female colleges well into the 1980s. Again, a strange byproduct of feminist success is the deconstruction of the old-fashioned, all-female institutions, many of which were actually in female interests.

So, feminism's successes have been multiple, but the detriment to society as a whole has been massive. Happiness can never really be measured, but from a personal, subjective way of looking at things, I would not characterize this as a particularly happy or successful era or a particularly happy or successful culture. I think the fact that almost one out of two marriages are now ending in divorce, and there's an enormous amount of dissatisfaction which, in some respects, the two genders may have with each other. Many of these issues are not discussed.

Feminism and male reactions to feminism, some of which have not been too brilliant, are actually part and parcel of many of the ongoing problems in this age. I think childlessness, radical single living, the decline in the family as a model, intergenerational decline, whereby the idea was your grandparents looked after the children and that sort of thing rather than hired help, that you didn't necessarily need two incomes in order to survive in an average mortgage property, which is now no longer the case, have all contrived to bring about feminist victories in ways that undercut the utopianism that that movement once espoused.

Is feminism a Left-wing movement? Only in part. Although it's very difficult for the Right to agglomerate its ideas in with certainly second-wave or second-generation feminism. Yet, traditionally, gender and the politics of the personal, being all-pervasive, is something for which Marxism has little time. Only postdated non-Stalinist and Trotskyist types of Marxism were able to meld sexual-political, anthropological, and environmental concerns in with themselves. Traditional Marxism has had no time for these bourgeois deviations. Green politics is no account; industrialization is a moral good in accordance with mainstream Marxism. Similarly, semi-biological ideas about women have no place in an order which is totally socially ameliorated and understood as such. So, traditionally, Marxism had little time for feminist politics, although acceding to radical female wishes in relation to the restructuring of society such as occurred in the Soviet

Union after 1917.

The interesting thing which occurred is that despite the lifting of almost all psychological, social, and familial restrictions between 1918 and 1928, Soviet life did not change particularly dramatically, partly because most people were struggling to survive, and these legal changes only had marginal impact.

After 1928, everything was reversed, and Stalin introduced a form of neo-conservatism in the personal and political area. Family life was re-encouraged. After the Second World War, the enormous devastation inside the Soviet Union meant that motherhood was prized. Women who had over ten children and contributed to feelings of Soviet warriorship by providing men to work in factories and so on were given medals by the state.

Everyone knows the extreme prudery of the Communist bureaucracies in post-war Eastern Europe, far more extreme than their Western equivalents. Indeed, the media in traditional Communist societies after the first revolutionary phase is over often resembles the Western media in the early part of the twentieth century, when you largely had a conservative bias, and you had a conservative society with a very small "c" rather than a liberal one tending to the Left. In my opinion, up until the 1950s in most Western societies, if you analyze the mass media, you have mainstream conservative (small "c") attitudes. Whereas after that you have mainstream Left-liberal and mildly libertarian social attitudes.

This is why these radical movements cut very deep. But they never achieve entirely everything that they want. What they do is that they are the radical vanguards, they are the diamond drills, they are the teeth in the flesh that pushed the thing, pushed the unwieldy social contract in a particular direction. Without all of these radical movements, the enormous social, cultural, and exhibitionistic changes which we've seen would not have occurred. Therefore, these radicals are themselves the splinters that give off the energy that corrals other tendencies of opinion and pushes them into the mainstream. These are the ideas that are then taken up by people in a very jaundiced and hazy way. But the very fact that a television executive could be sacked today for making a program that evinced the traditional values of the 1950s is emblematic of the fact that enormous societal and structural and psychological set of changes has occurred.

The breakdown of the Women's Liberation Movement is partly due to the success of that tendency of opinion despite many of the contradictions which were involved. The most famous British feminist publishing house is Virago, which was set up by a committee of women about thirty-odd years ago now, quite late in the day, but most of the books that Virago produced were quite conservative literary works written by upper-class women between about 1890 and 1940. So, you had this strange lag, basically, where the culture of the suffragettes was brought back by second-wave feminist publishing, because that's what they had to publish.

The key feminist text from the past is Mary Wollstonecraft's *Rights of Woman*,[15] which is a feminist version of Tom Paine's.[16] She, of course, was founder of a famous, in that era, Left-wing family which consisted of Shelley, Mary Shelley (the second wife who wrote *Frankenstein*), and of William Godwin, the mild but evident political anarchist who wrote *Political Justice*.[17]

The key texts in feminism move from a belief in equal rights to the exchangeability of men and women. One of the more radical (small "r") feminist demands is that men are feminized to the degree that women are masculinized. This is an ultimate end in sort of egalitarian social pressures. Hence all sort of outrider movements have been supported that disprivilege traditional forms of masculinity.

The deconstruction of the traditional heroic male images that accounted for most of Western media up until the 1950s and early 1960s is all part of that project. If you analyzed Hollywood films even today in comparison to what they were before 1960 you see a reversal which is almost an inversion, although strands of what

---

[15] Mary Wollstonecraft (1759–1797), *A Vindication of the Rights of Woman: with Strictures on Political and Moral Subjects* (1792).

[16] Thomas Paine (1737–1809), *Rights of Man* (1791).

[17] William Godwin (1756–1836), *An Enquiry Concerning Political Justice and its Influence on Morals and Happiness* (1793).

was to occur later on were widely discernible even going back to the thirties. But again, up until about 1960, the norms of a socially conservative culture survived.

Britain in the 1950s is a world away from the society that we have now. Indeed, the libertarian-Left pressures are such that we've received a total inversion, or sort of psychological auto-mutilation, which has occurred between then and now. The interesting thing is that most people regard what exists now . . . they regard the content of *The Daily Mirror* on a daily basis, as semi-normal, whereas *The Daily Mirror* in 1960 was almost a completely different type of newspaper, a slightly socially conservative, center-Left newspaper, that supported anti-Communist trade union leaders and the Right wing of the Labour Party. Now, you can argue that that Hugh Cudlipp model,[18] a sort of MI5-prescribed Labour model, which it was, was an establishmentarian ploy of that era. But the content of mass media now is so unsubtle and so pervasive in its change as to exemplify all of the tendencies of opinion which won through in the 1960s and thereafter.

The irony is that many of these vanguard movements would regard the popular media of today as a sink of iniquity. This is one of the paradoxes. Adorno and the Frankfurt School are totally critical of modern mass media, are totally critical of what they consider to be the cultural industry by which the masses are enslaved, and yet at the same time the tendencies that they represented in a purified and vanguard form have broken through, albeit moderated and assimilated, to such a degree that they partly got what they wanted, but in a way in which they can never appreciate. It's almost as if everyone gets partly what they want and don't want combined in equal measures.

The only tendencies in the West that haven't gotten what they want at all are the radical Right and various forms of religious fundamentalism which remain outside the circle and are conceptually demonized, because they cannot be assimilated.

One of the radical ideas in the sixties and seventies, a post-Marxist idea, was the cultural notion of Situationism. This is the

---

[18] Hubert Cudlipp (1913–1998), Welsh journalist and newspaper editor noted for his work on the *Daily Mirror* in the 1950s and 1960s.

idea that everything is mixed together and one has a society of the spectacle and of mass media and of postmodern interchange of image upon image and thought upon thought almost with the instantaneity with which someone can control their mobile phone or some application on it.

This type of tendentious and voyeuristic media feeds on images and ideas that were released by the vanguard movements of the sixties and seventies, but they've been commercialized. This is the interesting thing which the feminist movement never realized. Indeed, sexual liberation movements in the 1960s never realized that the commercialization and the commercial exploitation of the body and all of its resources in mass advertising and elsewhere would be what would occur. There was hence an innocent-mindedness in a strange prurient way to these people and their ideas.

They never thought that the beneficiaries of many of their notions would be pornographers like Raymond and Sullivan who are traditionally villains or semi-criminal figures in a far-Left lexicon. Indeed, the criminal, drug-dealing, prostitutory fringes of capitalism shading into criminality are traditionally stereotypical images of capitalist and center-Right evil in far-Left terms.

But the sixties introduced so many social waves and so many subcultural changes that when *Oz* magazine and various other things broke taboos, and were pleased to do so from a Hippie or Yippie sort of Left student perspective, they never realized that the beneficiaries of these changes would be the man who presently owns *The Daily Express* and *The Sunday Express* and related media. The Richard Desmonds[19] of this world are the monsters that have been created by the free-for-all in image and fact and the change in the reference points of sexual politics which the sixties introduced.

I once visited, for my sins, the National Union of Students building in Manchester on the Oxford Road, and they had a newsagent's there, and it was the most Puritanical newsagent's I've ever been in. Usually when you go into a newsagent's, even if you

---

[19] Richard Desmond (born 1951), British pornographer and media magnate.

just want stamps or something, you know, there's an enormous wall of flesh essentially, even in the more moderate titles, which superficially have little to do with sexuality, because that's how things are marketed today. Before 1960, they certainly wouldn't have been marketed quite in that way, and yet there was none of this at all in this NUS prescribed building because they had been through every tendency of opinion from innocent listings magazines in Manchester right the way out to the fringes, and everything had been judged in accordance with how objectifying, how masculinist, how stereotypical, how Patriarchal (with a large "P") all of this media had been. That which fell on one side of this particular sort of red line went into the dustbin or was returned, and that which was regarded as acceptable . . . and there was hardly anything that was regarded as acceptable, actually, so there was almost a complete absence of media in this media shop. This is one of the great ironies of the entire development of what's gone on.

There was an attempt about twenty years ago now to found a Left-wing paper on Sunday called *News on Sunday* which only lasted a couple of issues, and one of the problems they had was capitalization and distribution and all the normal, rather boring things. But one of the internal reasons that it failed is because nearly all of the comment by quite traditional Left-wing writers and famous Left-wing cartoonists like Ralph Steadman[20] was regarded as politically incorrect. Indeed, Steadman's sort of quite German expressionist cartoons about Margaret Thatcher and so on—they sort of looked like George Grosz[21] and people in the twenties and thirties in Weimar Germany who pioneered that type of very aggressive, graphic sort of illustration—was regarded as so sexist and anti-humanist and patriarchal that it couldn't be permitted.

---

[20] Ralph Steadman (born 1936) is a British cartoonist and illustrator best known for his collaboration with American writer Hunter S. Thompson (1937–2005).

[21] George Grosz (1893–1959) was a German artist and caricaturist affiliated with the Dada and New Objectivity (Neue Sachlichkeit) movements.

So, what tends to happen is the Left devours itself when it really gets going. Between the tendencies of new-formed and new-fangled censorship, which are very extreme, and tendencies of total anarchy, nihilism, and near depravity that wants to let everything rip and basically believes there are almost no standards and no limits at all nor should there ever be.

This tension that does exist and is still there in nearly all forms of feminist critique of media plagues the Left to this day. But what they are doing is they are arguing from a position of semi-victory whereby each new film and each new magazine is considered in accordance with how correct and/or incorrect it actually is.

The criteria for correctness and incorrectness have also changed. The so-called "girl power" culture of the 1990s, where teenage and sort of ladette women insisted that they wanted to be female in their own way has also played havoc with some of these post-sixties norms. In the realm of mass culture, wave follows wave, and the standardized ethos from one era can be overthrown by new concepts and precepts that come up.

There's been no attempt to roll the clock back to before the psychological and cultural changes of the 1960s. In this sense, feminism has achieved a partial victory. The interesting thing is how male structures of traditional ways of looking at things acceded to these wishes. Many men are deeply confused at the present time and have been for several generations, and yet, because gender is biological, the recrudescence of core male and female attributes survives, free-floating and irrespective of all theory.

However, most men have acceded to feminist demands because they feel there's no alternative to them. To stand out against the culture of egalitarianism is to render yourself demonic, and this is particularly so in private relations. You'll often find that people are far more nervous of intruding their values into private relations where you can pay a considerable price if things go wrong. This is where the idea that the personal is political is so extraordinarily powerful.

It was said earlier on that one of the subtexts for this particular meeting is why are women not extraordinarily involved in Right-wing politics? That's complicated. When Right-wing political movements break through, a large number of women become involved. Success, power, the trappings of getting somewhere all interest a significant part of the population and interest everybody. Everyone begins to agree with you when you start to be successful.

I remember when I attended the Red, White, and Blue once in Paris. The mainstreaming of that movement after some of its major electoral successes was quite evident. All politics is vanguard led. You begin with small little groups that implant their ideas within the general culture. They have to engage in some intellectual prior positioning, otherwise it's just an empty populism which becomes the jester politics of the fringe and ends up largely with an empty protest and people who are elected in the end, end up in the mainstream parties whether they like it or not, whether they even choose to join them or not. But if you do the intellectual prior positioning and you then break through on the crest of a wave — that will always moderate the utopian demands that exist in any absolutist and radical tendency of opinion — you do begin to get somewhere.

Feminism has now triumphed in the West in particular to such a degree that it's causing new convulsions with the mass of the immigrants who have come in, most of whom come in from socially conservative and/or religiously defined cultures elsewhere in the world. One of the things that was most shocking to unassimilated to assimilated, Westernized immigrants is the social and cultural revolutions of the 1960s, which most of them, traditionally the older generations, just ignored and lived in their own mental space as if they weren't actually cohabitating the society in which these things had gone on. This is less so now.

And what you see among younger immigrants is a dialecticism whereby amongst the young they either become very Western and reject their own parents and reject the assumptions of their own communities, or they engage in a militancy grounded in their own communities or grounded in their own faith systems. So, people are either going back to the traditional structures in a more radical way without the social conservatism of their elders, or they assimilate completely into post-sixties Western norms, which are now so pervasive that most people don't bother to reject them, even in their own mind.

Because to actually reject many of them you would have to turn off mass media. You would have to engage in processes of alienation in a way from what now exists. And that's very difficult for many people, and nor do they want to be regarded as odd or socially reclusive or corralled into a space or ghettoized in their own life. The bulk of people conform to the energies and pressures that they now feel themselves living under.

Wyndham Lewis wrote a text in 1926 called *The Art of Being Ruled*,[22] and he said that the idea that women will go out to work and completely compete in a male way and on a male basis would be the most easy and requisite way to undermine the family that had ever been created, far more radical in its excesses than all of the feminist and Left-wing marches put together, and this is indeed what has occurred.

We live, as I've often said in these talks, in a strange, hybridized society where the economics of the center-Right and the social, cultural, and soft power prerequisites of the center-Left have fused and merged into a Left-wing capitalism, which would have been regarded as absurd in the early part of the last century.

When Right-wing and Left-wing intellectuals actually used to meet with each other . . . This hardly occurs today except in media set piece battles, which are largely orchestrated from beforehand, the results of which are unsatisfactory. When Chesterton and Belloc and Shaw and Wells used to actually have debates with each other in the early part of the twentieth century, the idea that you would end up with a Left-wing capitalism would have been regarded as utterly absurd. Utterly absurd.

And yet this is what we have, because the market has realized that you can clear at the lowest common denominator level and you can clear to a market expectancy of maximum profit by often pitching things at a low to middle common denominator and that you never go bankrupt by underestimating the taste of the generality. Therefore, you can always push things lower, and you can

---

[22] Wyndham Lewis, *The Art of Being Ruled* (London: Chatto & Windus, 1926).

always achieve a maximum payout by making sure the thing is tilted to the lowest common denominator, up to a point. You have to be careful [not] to go too low, where you become unacceptable and outside the frame of what is commercially convenient, but the tendency and the drift is always downwards.

So, you have egalitarianism, downwards drift, and the desire to make money of a maximum sort combined in a poisonous and rather noxious brew. All over the economy . . . And don't forget we're living in a society where we make very little, and everything is traded on services and secondary and tertiary forms of production and added value, fueled by debt and based upon an interchangeable, moveable capital economy where the movement of labor, namely mass immigration, is just one tool in the general game. So, we have a situation where the deconstruction of traditional ideas of masculinity and femininity and the disavowal of the idea that they are biologically based, even though many of the critics now believe that they may well be, is part and parcel of the atomized and alienated world with which we find ourselves surrounded.

Feminism has thus done much of the groundwork and the spadework for radical forms of libertarian individualism that it doesn't really agree with, because much of the objectification of women that's resulted in mass media is something that feminism's been traditionally opposed to and yet has inexorably led to.

I also think that a lot of men have taken advantage of the choices and expectations that feminism has aroused, and this has led to a general coarsening of relations between men and women which has occurred. People don't like being done down, or perceived that they have been, and they often get back in niggardly and low-grade ways which are not too transparent or necessarily courageous. And I think there's a degree to which that has also occurred. The traditional male role models did involve heroic and self-sacrificial elements, even though, as in all human affairs, hypocrisy and venality doubtless played a part.

But the degree to which many men feel relatively powerless in the present situation and somewhat embittered is again not a tendency that you can base political idealism on. People who are narrow-minded, feel they have a grievance, and are embittered *may* radicalize, but they may not necessarily be in a particular state to adopt a heroic attitude towards their radicalization, which is ultimately what you want.

I remember the late John Tyndall once said that you can never do anything with somebody whose politics just begins and ends with a whining about immigration, if that's all it is, because it's purely negative. When in fact what you have to be is heroic about your own nation, your own culture, its own history, your own ethnicity. These are the things you have to be positive about. Otherwise, there is almost no point in being negative about the other, because you have nothing to replace what exists now.

I think it's also true of relations between men and women. This is a very difficult area, politically, because none of the mainstream parties, apart from acceding to the post-dated egalitarian attitudes of the past, have a policy about these things. There's been a Left-liberal drift in all of them now, bearing in mind the conservatives would have at one time opposed the quickie divorces; they would have opposed mass abortion, at least apart from a small minority of their libertarian MPs. Now the party basically supports all of these things because they're fearful of not getting females votes if they don't.

And yet the irony is that men and women are keenly divided on abortion. Seventy percent of women support abortion according to most deep Gallup polls, but twenty percent of that support is actually very, very thin. Men split fifty-fifty. These debates are very aggressive and very toxic. One of the reasons that mainstream politicians rarely address them, because these are primal issues — or at least they tend to the primal — and if you upset people on primal issues, they will never forgive you if they don't already accede to your notions, and you've lost them in relation to all other areas of the spectrum.

This is why immigration, the politics of the personal, Europe, and a few other issues are the issues about which mainstream politicians wish to speak least, because they are the most difficult, the most problematical, the most toxic issues, the issues that ultimately will galvanize the population to be interested in politics again. And that's why they are not mentioned.

I think the feminist movement's success shows the success of cultural struggle as New Left Marxists would call it. Cultural struggle is what this group and other groups like it are involved in and is in some ways the only show in town for our tendency of opinion at the present time. Feminism has shown if you go with the grain of a culture, as they did after the 1960s, what can be achieved by militant movements. Few women today know the names of the key feminist theoreticians such as Orbach,[23] such as Greer, such as Millett,[24] such as Solanas, and so on. Few people know their names, but the tendencies of opinion that their books influenced have proved highly decisive in the way in which people live their own lives.

The trick is to have one's vanguard notions integrate with the *Zeitgeist*. The problem is that the liberal society has probably not reached its apogee even yet and is churning away and becoming yet even more radical and more deconstructive. However, all one can do at this present time is to put out contrary ideas.

When people say that the traditional Right wishes to subordinate women to men, the Right has always traditionally responded that it is in favor of masculinity and femininity and sees that men and women have fundamentally different roles in society. This is not enough for many contemporary women, who wish to see a less patriarchal bias from what they perceive to be Right-wing opinions.

But deep down these things are more powerful than reason. One of my principal views about politics is that people are attracted to politics only with a small percentage of their reason. The bulk of their attraction is emotional and pre-rational and irrational. The more that you appeal to these notions, the more you will actually appeal to the generality of people.

One of the most powerful political discourses that can ever be enunciated is traditional male and female role models which are positive for both. This goes with the clock of biology and goes

---

[23] Susie Orbach (born 1946), British Jewish psychoanalyst and feminist author.

[24] Kate Millett (1934–2017), American feminist author and academic.

with the instinctualism of biology. Everything that goes with biology may be deeply unacceptable at the present hour, but it's probably the most powerful type of politics that occurs and that can occur.

Lots of people will actually be quite impressed and emotionally entranced by the rejection of contemporary sexual-political norms as currently perceived, but they would also be shocked and be deeply scandalized with the politically correct and rational part of their intelligence. Don't forget, almost everyone who's educated now has been through the politically correct filter and only perceives reality in that way.

Yet everybody has a prior, largely biological identity, and if that particular identity is appeased by image, by word, by association, and by the absence of grievance, then you will see people come to you. My view is that the more one attempts to rescue female and male ideas of a traditional sort from the maw of the New Left and from second-generation feminism, the more you will have the implicit and the intuitive support of generations as yet unborn.

Thank you very much!

Counter-Currents, January 15, 2015

AESCHYLUS' *AGAMEMNON:*
THE MULTIPLE USES OF GREEK TRAGEDY

Greek tragedy is all but forgotten in mainstream culture, but there is a very good reason for looking at it again with fresh eyes. The reasons for this are manifold, but they basically have to do with anti-materialism and the culture of compression. To put it bluntly, reading Greek tragedy can give literally anyone a crash course in Western civilization which is short, pithy, and terribly apt.

Let's take—for purposes of illustration—the first part of the *Oresteia* by Aeschylus, which concentrates on Agamemnon's murder by his wife Clytemnestra. This work would take about two hours to read in a verse translation by Lewis Campbell (say).[1] You will learn more about the civilization in those two hours than many a university foundation course, or hour after hour of public television, are capable of giving you.

The real reason for perusing this material, however, is the sense of excitement which it is capable of generating. Agamemnon and his entourage have returned to Argos after the successful sack of Troy and the destruction of Priam's city.

A series of torches across the Greek peninsula announces the triumph, and the Watchman on the palace roof is the first to bear witness to the signal. The Chorus of Argive Elders soon gathers and is addressed in turn by a herald and then Clytemnestra. She swears undying loyalty to her husband (falsely) and makes way for his triumphant entry, although for those with acute ears there is a sense of foreboding in the imagery and early language of the play.

Agamemnon enters and speaks of his victories, but is ill-disposed to walk on the purple vestments that his wife has had strewn on the ground. He considers them unworthy or liable to damage his standing with the Gods. Clytemnestra seems to

---

[1] *Aeschylus: The Seven Plays in English Verse,* trans. Lewis Campbell (1831–1910), revised ed. (Oxford: Oxford University Press, 1906).

want her husband to behave more like an Eastern potentate than a Greek monarch. After much show of reluctance—he accedes to his wife's wishes, kicks off his sandals, and walks on the Imperial purple . . . in a manner that Clytemnestra knows will antagonize the Gods. She wishes this due to the future assassination which she has in view.

The prophetess Cassandra is then introduced from Agamemnon's car, and she outlines—in ecstatic asides and verbal follies—the likelihood of her paramour's death at the hands of his wife. She also speculates on the origin of the curse deep in the history of the House of Atreus—when Thyestes' own children were baked in a pie for the edification of their father in revenge for adultery. This sets in train the codex of revenge and hatred which inundates the House's walls with blood and gore and sets the ground for new horrors at a later date. Cassandra, surrounded by the near-seeing and purblind chorus, goes into the House where her Fate is sealed.

After a discrete interval, Clytemnestra emerges in one of the most dramatic sequences in all of Western art. She clutches a dagger in one hand and is partly covered in blood; whereas Agamemnon, her previous lord and husband, lies dead inside the folds of a net, with Cassandra raving and raving over him. The prototype for Lady Macbeth and every other three-dimensional female villain, Clytemnestra boasts of her deed and how she executed it—to the shock, horror, and awe of the Argive elders.

The killing is justified—in her eyes at least—by the sacrifice of her daughter, Iphigenia, to make the wind change its direction when the Greek fleet is becalmed at Aulis on the way to Troy. For this wilful act of child-murder, Clytemnestra has lain in wait with her lover, Aegisthus, to slay the King of Argos. (Aegisthus is descended from Thyestes and has his own reasons for wishing doom to the House of Atreus.)

This particular play ends with a confrontation between Aegisthus' soldiers and the elderly members of the Chorus, but Clytemnestra—by now sick of bloodshed and desiring peace—intervenes so as to prevent further conflict. The play concludes with the two tyrants, surrounded by their mercenaries, walking back towards the palace where they will rule over the Argives.

The question is always raised in modernity: Why bother with this material now? The real reason is the abundant ethnic and racial health of ancient Greek culture. Although tragic, blood-thirsty, and mordant in tone, it is abundantly alive at several different levels. It also exists as the prototype for so much Western culture, whether high or low.

As I have already intimated, a two-hour read is broadly equivalent to a short university course in and of itself. Also, the pre-Christian semantics of this material speaks across two-and-a-half thousand years very directly to us today, certainly in the post-Christian context of Western Europe. Another reason for parents reading this material to adolescent children (at the very least) is its pagan immediacy. This is not cultural fare that can be dismissed as lacking pathos, blood and guts, or a sense of reality, if not normalcy.

Another reason for refusing to give this work a wide berth has to be the fact that various forces which were outgunned and defeated in the twentieth century definitely took the *Greek* side in various cultural debates. This can also be seen in Wyndham Lewis' *Childermass* which I reviewed,[2] where the chorus of opposition to the Humanist Bailiff (a sort of democratic Punch) has to be the philosopher Hesperides and his band of Greeks.

The culture of the Greeks still has dangers associated with it, hence the re-routing of Classics to a netherworld in the Western academy. Yet the refutation of Bernal's *Black Athena*[3] is still everywhere around us; as long as people have the wit to pick up the plays of Aeschylus and read.

Counter-Currents, August 3, 2011

---

[2] Jonathan Bowden, "Wyndham Lewis' *Childermass*: Black Metal, without the Music," in *Reactionary Modernism*, ed. Greg Johnson (San Francisco: Counter-Currents, 2022).

[3] Martin Bernal, *Black Athena: The Afroasiatic Roots of Classical Civilization*, 3 vols. (New Brunswick, New Jersey: Rutgers University Press, 1987–2006).

A POLYP DEVOURS ITS FEED, PARACELSUS UNZIPPED:
AN ANALYSIS OF F. W. MURNAU'S FILM NOSFERATU

F. W. Murnau's 1922 movie *Nosferatu*, starring Max Schreck, begins with bourgeois sentimentality or its tableau. Yet this comfortable familiarity can be vitiated by intrusion, even obtrusion. Darkness occurs amid light; there is a hint of delirium, as well as madness and despair. All of this has to be presaged by Knock—a villainous, if expressive, land agent. (Note: he doesn't figure in Bram Stoker's *Dracula*, from which the screenplay comes, and has more to do with Hans Prinzhorn's *The Art of the Insane*.[1])

A sweep of the Carpathian hills follows on—and it indicates simple pleasures, often obscured. A negation (this is) that takes a wolf's form; and possibly it's a lynx, a wolverine, coyote, or mink. Certainly, it happens to be a wildcat who brings cold air; the latter forcing old peasants to cross themselves.

Whilst the young Jonathan Hutter, the land agent's assistant, settles down to some reading. Has it taken root in his hand? One doesn't know; but what becomes clear is its involvement with vampirism, a hidden necropolis, and even Satanism.

Dawn's freshness brings relief, however, and it clusters around light or its foreknowledge. It is more than enough to illuminate one's toilet or wash. He (Hutter or Harker) hastens to a trap or brig, and the camera snatches away so as to glimpse a dark mountain. It—a sinister Carpathian pile—gives purchase to a glinting storm. At last the coach driver refuses to

---

[1] Hans Prinzhorn (1886–1933), *Bildnerei der Geisteskranken. Ein Beitrag zur Psychologie und Psychopatologie der Gestaltung* (1922). Translated as *Artistry of the Mentally Ill: A Contribution to the Psychology and Psychopathology of Configuration*, trans. Eric von Brockdorff (New York: Springer-Verlag, 1995).

go any further, and he cites as his reason that: "The land of Phantoms begins here . . ."

We gain our first glimpse of Castle Dracula or Orloc, and this involves a speeded-up approach by a coach. It was seen—like a racing car—through a reverse periscope. For, as Stoker declares in his horror novel, "the dead travel fast." Now we discern the first vision of Orloc in an abandoned Castle Dracula, and he comes across as a wizened old man. In all honesty, "it" looks like a Giacometti sculpture, a signification of the outsider, or a Kafkaesque bogle. Similarly, a distinct resemblance to the Khazar or Eugène Sue's *The Wandering Jew*[2] is unfurled—especially in relation to the Weimar lore into which this film was dropped.

Orloc, *ceteris paribus*, exists in a grieving age or time. He senses his guest's fear of midnight: the former resounding from a clock with skeletal figures. Needless to say, a cut at the dining-room table, inflicted using a knife, leads to a dénouement or its non-reconciliation. It also unleashes a miasma in a world of lucid dreaming. "Let us stay up till midnight," mimes the feaster, and no one doubts the healing power of the sun. Castle Dracula finds itself relieved, yet none can deny their subdued intimacy over a bite . . . even though a meal awaits. Renfield's agent makes a joyful repast (thereupon).

He later approaches a belltower or keep, so as to examine the Carpathians at his leisure . . . but disconcertingly, the very spot is haunted by flies or mosquitoes. They suck the blood (you see). Nonetheless, a Gypsy who passes by was given a letter to send, and this occurred under a hebetude of storm.

Whilst Orloc (during the next night) is entranced by his guest's beloved. "Your wife possesses a beautiful neck . . . ," are the only words he can utter. In a strange way, Jonathan Hutter finds himself perturbed by this incident involving a miniature portrait. It is now past midnight *tout court* . . . and this draws attention to a book on *Vampires* in a Gothic script. Thereafter, he attempts to bolt a door that's deep within the

---

[2] Marie-Joseph "Eugène" Sue (1804–1857), *Le Juif errant*, 10 vols. (1844–1845).

castle, as the noise of midnight reverberates around.

Then, in an Expressionist masterpiece of mesmerism, Nosferatu emerges from behind an unbolted door. He appears to be silent within an all-encompassing greed. Likewise, and in a shift back home, his wife Ellen (Mina) seems to be sleep-walking over a ledge. Can anyone really come to her rescue? Eventually, two hands cling to the raiment of these claws, and they exhibit sympathetic magic—even amid its expiration.

Back at Castle Dracula, *per se*, Nosferatu waxes triumphant, stoic, bizarrely stayed, expectant, and bat-like. He refuses to give up—even when the door is shaped like a coffin lid. It doubles as a pall and closes on its victim with crisp finality.

A while later Hutter is wide awake—albeit with a residual pain in his neck. He manages to force open the tomb or mausoleum which is outside the Castle's doorway, and he creeps down into a silent crypt. In such a grotto, he prises up a coffin-lid and spies the master of the house. At last our visitant understands *why*, rests for a period, and then sees laborers down below who work at double-time. Could it be a gloomy premonition? Resultantly, then, he scales the tower using some sheets and falls to the ground precipitously . . . whether asleep or torpid!

Various raftsmen carry Orloc (Dracula) downriver towards Hutter's tower [thereafter]. He revives, distraught, in a hospital bed—while bargemen hurry these coffers to their destination. They are beset or imperiled by rats.

Meanwhile, a mysterious Professor Bulwer—a mystic or Paracelsian—sets the scene. He uses a Venus flytrap to metaphoricize Dracula. Whilst Knock, the former land agent, is out of his mind in a padded cell. He catches flies in his hands and crams them into his mouth . . . so as to absorb their "power" inside. The maniac has transformed himself into a cannibal or an autophagous; and he's a man-eater (you see), if only of drosophilae. To wit: a wag in an "O"-level lesson can call him a lord of the bluebottles, albeit using a porcine head on a stick!

Still, Professor Bulwer addresses his students over polyp life and he examines it microscopically . . . as Dracula's boat gets nearer. *Touché!* For the madcap—see the example of Gaius Cibber's *Melancholy* and *Raving Madness* (outside the Imperial War Museum) — writhes in his cell. He exhibits both the agony and the ecstasy, in Irving Stone's words,[3] while a dark lord promises developments from afar. Likewise, a letter was delivered to Ellen (Mina) on the sea's very edge, and it tells of her fiancé's recovery from his malaise. Already now, the land agent's assistant makes ready to leave a Catholic hospice. Won't he make the decision to travel by boat?

Further on, Knock's lunacy grows apace within a sensory deprivation chamber, while newspapers shout and blare. They are heralding "a new plague that baffles science." Our Bedlamite understands this by snatching a tabloid from one of his warders. Resultantly, a vessel on the high seas approaches its port, and already the sailors or crew were dropping like skittles. It's the many coffers or sarcophagi behind a flitting Nosferatu which focuses anxiety, and Orloc flutters around a camera. This is transparently so . . . and, as time goes by, each new Jack Tar was committed to the waves.

Finally, a redeemer seeks out the bacillus' source or "eye" — as with a boil's apex — and he's armed *avec* a halberd. Slowly, oh so slowly — the vampire emerges perpendicularly out of his coffin; and he comes straight up as death's visitation. At one level, it combines the character of Barlow in Stephen King's *Salem's Lot* with Emily Dickinson's morbidity. To be sure: our vessel of a thousand fools (even in plague) has a new captain, Nosferatu. Whereupon this lemur or toy boat docks in a Baltic cove . . . why, it carries Beowulf from the North with its facsimile of a long prow.

Likewise, we find Mina (Ellen) all alone and waiting via some erotic filigree. Such a mysterious clarion must come to her from across the waves. Doesn't the ocean swell within a periscope's compass or crosshairs . . . at least in terms of a magic 'scope? Anyway, she asseverates the following — even oneirically. It's all a dream after Dalí's fancy — don't you see a Ouija board moving so?

---

[3] Irving Stone, *The Agony & the Ecstasy* (New York: Doubleday, 1961), biographical novel of Michaelangelo.

"I must go to him," she remarks sleepily, "the master is approaching us all!" Surely, to paraphrase John Cowper Powys, we sense a medley of *Oxtiern*, or *Isabella of Bavaria*, *A Dialogue between a Priest and a Dying Man*, plus *The One Hundred and Twenty Days of Sodom*.[4] It can only be seen at the depths of Remenham's caves *vis-à-vis* the Hellfire Club. Let it pass, metaphorically so —.

Now then, the trees roundabout are given to swirling (expectantly), and a four-sail rig floats in. It berths in a coastal town. Already a lycanthrope (Knock) twirls, gibbers, or capers with glee. "Our Rex Vivant is coming. He invades this space," chunters our roadster in his cell. A schooner finally docks as a sleek craft, by the by, and Count Orloc emerges silently from its hold. In the meantime, however, a loon escapes his cage and makes off over the roofs.

By a Tarot card's turn, a textbook explains the misadventures of Science, *à la* Paracelsus. Whilst — simultaneously with the previous — Orloc carries coffers into the Berg. He positions them amid the pink raiment of so many rats . . . rather like a nineteenth-century photogravure *avec* Sir Henry Irving.[5] (An image which captures the spice of a wizened Scotch earl; at once resourceful, wry, eldritch, or Mephisto'd.) Yet again, "he" flits through the shadows as a lucid dream or a participant in Artaud's Theatre of Cruelty — perhaps it speaks to Paul Nash[6] or Leonara Carrington.[7]

Pursuant to any twist, Hutter travels home on a salient brig. Will he be in time? For Orloc, a cadaverous imp of envy, reaches a neighboring courtyard in relation to *chez* Hutter. He's arrived in order to reclaim a history — even from itself. Soon the house opposite or its ruined hulk is alive, and strange lights flit aslant its windows. They mismatch the even-tide of these drop-

---

[4] Four works by the Marquis de Sade.

[5] Sir Henry Irving (1838–1905), English stage actor of the Victorian era.

[6] Paul Nash (1889–1946), British Surrealist painter.

[7] Leonora Carrington (1917–2011), British-born Mexican Surrealist painter and novelist.

lets (all black) by crossing ebon glass. Surely now, Dracula approaches it by transmigration—in that he moves hither and thither in a pall of grey.

Back at the docks, the pilot of the ruined vessel is found dead or otherwise lashed to the wheel. Various officials then go below so as to inspect the hold, while the ship's captain was laid out and his logbook confiscated. This will be examined at a later date by urban worthies gathered to do so. Presently, these mugwumps raise the gangplank and go ashore.

Yet what's Professor Bulwer, the metaphysician, been up to during this advent? Why, our worthy boffin examines the log—but not blog. And it reveals that the plague or Black Death stalks abroad. A proclamation is then delivered by town criers who broadcast it across this imaginary Gotham . . .

Speaking of which, the comic strips of Bob Kane illuminate Murnau's mound, in that they feast on a poster-paint medley. These graphic novels indicate a palsy or cinematic bite—after Edward Muybridge's sequential photography. Also, the colors are garish in their brightness—at once a lurid yellow, red, sapphire, orange, tangerine, gorse, or puce. They surge forwards—dealing with a Bat-man rather than a Man-bat—and yet Nosferatu's symmetry with the Joker is complete. For both are living corpses or blanched idols that adopt a violent disregard o'er the future . . . Might the one's green hair, purple suit, and clown's face (frozen) merge into the other's longitudinal shadow? It testifies to a cadaverous slide; plus red eyes, long nails, a nineteenth-century waistcoat, and a glabrous skull whose skin's calcified in milk. Does its X-rated certificate surprise you?

By any account, the windows in all dwellings are to remain shut—irrespective of any mephitic vapors inside. A municipal official goes around and secures each door, as, amid flickering torches or brands, the dead are carried out in their boxes. Meanwhile, Ellen (Mina) looks at a bibliographical rarity—*The Book of Vampires*—which her husband has smuggled back from the Carpathians. Whilst the manse opposite "feeds" on her every night, and it exists like a cannibal, or an Animist freak-show.

Its happenstance delivers a blow at many distinct levels.

Since Hutter moves slowly away from this aperture, or open window, in order to splurge upon a divan. Moreover, an "un-answered" bed cannot save him from a hypnotic pull over the way, and a dark mesmerism emanates from this Marsten House. It catapults Nosferatu's persecution of his victims into stone and mortar, in other words.

Likewise, Ellen contracts a fever which goes abroad — it de-notes a miasma, a tincture of ochre or sand, and even a Giant's exhalation. By day, a procession of coffins marches through the town . . . and they adopt a concert of snakes without the lad-ders. Do you remember a children's game of yore? It was played on a checker board.

Irrespective of this, Ellen (Mina) reads that a woman must sacrifice her blood, willingly, in order to assuage a vampire. She comes across this advice in her Gothic tome — and might it have been a secret script, or lexicon, her husband brought back from Translyvania? For a moment (just) one imagines him carving a message into the clay of his cell — albeit with dirtied nails. On other fronts, the people seek out a scapegoat, and they pursue Knock, the madcap.

They want to lynch him or apply tar-and-feathers, as in a Mark Twain short story. He makes off like a ruined Vaudeville turn; at once hobbled and hawking. While — simultaneously with the above — Ellen (Mina) waxes neurasthenic in a nine-teenth-century way. She suffers from the erotic delirium of Vampiredom, you see . . . even as Knock's pursued avaunt a stump. All of an instant (and peeping out from behind a frond) our jester gibbers unceasingly, as the *canaille* seize a scarecrow . . . They wish to tear "it" to pieces without respite. At this veri-est instant, Mina (Ellen) finds herself "seduced" by Dracula be-yond the glass, and no Plexiglas can prevent her from shedding blood.

As her husband slumbers, she attempts to open sultry veins to a Man-bat over the way. Let it fall sheer — since his intima-tion is to ride out towards an unseen bite. Yet Jonathan Hutter (Harker) wakes so as to foil the schema which would see her descend into those Hellfire caves. These once belonged to an eighteenth-century club[8] that recalled Robert Louis Stevenson's *The Suicide Club*.[9] In any event, a nubile figure lies on a stone crypt deep underground . . . and a hermaphrodite Beast-god gazes down.

Metaphorically speaking, the tapers are out or find themselves gripped by an eldritch glow. All remains still—and Jonathan Hutter's unquestioned answer is to call for Professor Bulwer! We have the power now . . . *quod* a window lies open afore the breeze, and Mina (Ellen) starts her vampiric egress once more. A shadow stands out against a startled emptiness—albeit in the manner of a silent cinema's shimmer. It subsists along the following hurdy-gurdy rides, in terms of the Western symphony's origin. Do you reconnoiter such black-and-white classics as *Rio Grande, He Who Gets Slapped, Faust, Stagecoach, Dick Tracy in Gruesome, The Three Musketeers* (with John Wayne) Parts 1 & 2, *A Woman in Green*, and *The Man Who Knew Too Much*?

Anyway, Count Orloc beckons to her from across the way, involuntarily, and his spindly fingers intimate a presentiment. Could this be a bloodsport, necessarily? Might Max Schreck's Nosferatu throw a penumbra upon the stairwell . . . i.e., one that's elongated, decisive, pinioned, ascending, and yet lice-ridden? It lets out a sarcophagus' expiration—despite its revolutionary selfishness. Does the director (F. W. Murnau) want it to pant at a meaty retrieval?

Over the way, though, Professor Bulwer has been rescued from his study by Jonathan Hutter. They rush back towards his wife as a cock begins to crow. While—within the asylum's walls—a recaptured Knock squeals at the advent of day. "Beware, Master!" he admonishes. The attendants within the madhouse strive to subdue a kook at a signal of time's nemesis. May such a sandstorm (inside an hourglass) have failed to depart?

Already, the Vampire finds himself trapped by the morn,

---

[8] Francis Dashwood, 11th Baron le Despencer (1708–1781), founder of the Order of the Friars of St. Francis of Wycombe, also known as the Hellfire Club.

[9] Robert Louis Stevenson, *The Suicide Club*, first published in *The London Magazine*, 1878.

and it rushes upon him like a vinegary sponge. Almost immediately, he becomes transfixed or glued to the light—this subdues him *à la* a photograph's negative or converse. It distills or decants his essence—possibly its negation.

And finally we recognize that a female sacrifice has worked, the town is saved, or an Undead parasite's been forever stilled. The maniac or Tom o' Bedlam breathes his last, however, and this occurs inside Horst Bienek's[10] cells. Not even its bars may chisel at Knock's Parthian shot, though. "Our Dark Lord has died under the incense of a golden lotus," he lisps prior to collapse. Might this axiom concur with Phil Baker's biography of Dennis Wheatley, *The Devil is a Gentleman*?[11]

Ellen then expires herself—in an orgasmic rapture or *auto-da-fé*—once count Orloc has been sent eastwards. He shrivels after a drying mummy in the wind . . . what with Walter Sickert's[12] morbid entombment of demi-mondes. These were ripped out of place *vis-à-vis* the Ripper murders—but without Stephen Knight's[13] reductions. Nor can a conspiratorial logic quell the pain in one's chest, even though her spouse, Jonathan Hutter, and the benign occultist do their best. The good Professor has at last arrived—isn't he named after Bulwer Lytton, the author of *Zanoni*?[14] In any event, no Bowie knife severs a mummified head, girt in lintel *à la* Boris Karloff, and portending to the azure. It labors the point of Stoker's finale, in terms of the physicality of John Cowper Powys' *Wood & Stone*.[15]

---

[10] Horst Bienek (1930–1990), German novelist and poet. Bowden may be alluding to his death from AIDS.

[11] Dennis Wheatley (1897–1977), British author of thrillers and occult novels. Phil Baker, *The Devil is a Gentleman: The Life & Times of Dennis Wheatley* (Sawtry, UK: Dedalus, 2009).

[12] Walter Sickert (1860–1942), German-born British painter and printmaker.

[13] Stephen Knight (1951–1985), *Jack the Ripper: The Final Solution* (New York: McKay, 1976).

[14] Edward Bulwer-Lytton (1803–1873), *Zanoni: A Rosicrucian Tale* (1842).

[15] John Cowper Powys (1872–1963), *Wood & Stone* (New York: G. A. Shaw, 1915).

Finally, Count Orloc's castle collapses into dust akin to an explosion on one of Gerry Anderson's miniature sets. Doesn't it convince us that the truth proves to be ashen, mimetic, non-providential, and ill-foretold? To re-adapt Dion Fortune,[16] even a psychic vampire requires a host to batten upon *à la* Eugène Sue.

Counter-Currents, September 1, 2010

---

[16] Dion Fortune (1890–1946), British occultist, magician, novelist, and writer.

GEORGE STEINER'S
THE PORTAGE TO SAN CRISTOBAL OF A.H.

George Steiner's novella, *The Portage to San Cristobal of A.H.*,[1] was published about three decades back and encodes a large number of the author's non-fiction books which were released beforehand. This is especially pertinent to the analysis published in *In Bluebeard's Castle*,[2] for instance.

For our purposes in this review, the dramatic or theatrical presentation of Steiner's brief work is almost as important as the text itself. It was dramatized (the only one of the Professor's works to be treated in this way) by the socialist playwright Christopher Hampton, and, on a personal note, I actually saw it in 1981–82.

The drama starred Alec McCowen as Adolf Hitler in a production which lasted around an hour-and-a-half. He was later awarded the *Evening Standard* theatre award for his riveting performance—particularly his oracular testimony or speech at the play's close. The critical record suggests that it was performed at the Mermaid Theatre, but I seem to recall seeing it at the Riverside studios in west London. I went with a girl that I was rather keen on at the time, but she was nauseated by the whole thing and fell asleep.

To cut to the chase: I believe that this is largely a work by and about George Steiner rather than the personalities or historical personages with whom he deals. Steiner is an "ultra-civilized" liberal, a polyglot, and an Encyclopaedist who has made a personal or subjective religion out of Western high culture. His play—and the short novel which gave it birth—are his

---

[1] George Steiner, *The Portage to San Cristobal of A.H.* (New York: Simon and Schuster, 1982).

[2] George Steiner, *In Bluebeard's Castle: Some Notes Towards the Redefinition of Culture* (London: Faber & Faber, 1971).

attempts to deal with the fact that no matter how knowledgeable or assimilated he becomes he always remains an outsider . . . an Ashkenazic amongst Gentiles.

What differentiates Steiner from most of his group is that he has not chosen to identify himself with the major pathways that various vanguards usually choose. Not for him, in other words, the ways of commerce, gross materialist accumulation, or gain; militant Leftism or anti-system revolt; or active and intentional Zionism.

The elements in the play which appear shocking, "transgressive," non-humanitarian, anti-Zionist, and even "self-hating" in Jewish terms, are quite understandable when you reckon on Steiner's own sensibility. A pure intellectual who incarnates the mind-body split, Steiner actively dislikes Israel, Ashkenazic enthusiasm, and the normalcy, almost semi-Gentile qualities, of nationalism and group adherence. Like an ultra-liberal in the West, an active vision of Hell would be national service in the armed forces — that is, having to endure the relative crudity, non-sophistication, and "political incorrectness" of all and sundry. Steiner, in other words, wishes to assimilate on his own terms — most of which are basically specific to himself.

His culture is actually quite a small sliver of land that articulates the integrative energies of mid-European Jews from around 1880 to 1940. For him, authors like Karl Kraus,[3] Franz Kafka, and Paul Celan[4] are European culture *tout court*. Likewise, a special endorsement will always be given to those superior Gentiles and cultural creators (Goethe, Tolstoy, Beethoven, and so forth) who make ready the path of assimilation through humane artistry.

In a manner which is typical of the radical liberals who dominate the cultural space in the West today, Steiner is truly horrified by man's brutality, ferocity, hatred, and capacity for endless sadism. A keen dualist, many of Steiner's books contain long, anguished discourses about the Marquis de Sade, for

---

[3] Karl Kraus (1874–1936), Austrian Jewish writer and journalist.
[4] Paul Celan (1920–1970), Romanian Jewish German-language poet and translator.

example. De Sade, in gigantic works of megalomania like *The 120 Days of Sodom*, is rarely pithy or gnomic. But one of his remarks bears recording: when he declares that civilization is an exercise in cruelty which has been tempered by disquiet. Steiner's whole career is a protest against this assertion; yet, as a liberal pessimist, he doubtless secretly agrees with it.

To return to the play proper, however . . . the whole point of the narrative is to prepare for the enormous speech by the McCowen figure at the piece's end. It is relatively typical for a creator like Steiner that he *loves to hate Hitler*, and, in all honesty, his view of the German dictator is very similar to that of Norman Mailer in his last published novel shortly before his death.[5] Both of them see Hitler as not a man at all but a force, a hypostatization, a recognition of the absence of the real—even an incarnation of terror, implacability, and death.

In this regard, but in no other, they actually engage in transgression and cross over to the other side . . . if only momentarily. Neither of these mild apostates can really be accused of *Shoah* revisionism or its historical counterpart—by dint of identifying with the discourse of Harry Elmer Barnes. Not one bit of it . . . but they do, luridly, hesitantly, mesmerically (even lambently) become cultural revisionists just for a moment before snapping back into their *a priori* positions. This would amount to a post-existential and "Left" conservative in Mailer's case; a pained, enervated, diaphanous, and painfully raw (or thin-skinned) "rootless cosmopolitan" in Steiner's.

The piece itself, *The Portage to San Cristobal of A. H.*, is essentially front-end loaded. It only really exists as a prop or attainment for Hitler's great speech at the end. Some of the work's Zionist or Ashkenazic critics who said that it was poorly constructed or slightly slung together actually have a point—yet what they miss is the *deus ex machina* moment. This amounts to the *aporia* in language—the moment of apocalypse at the finale—when a demigod of inversion (literally an anti-Christ) is permitted to orate.

---

[5] Norman Mailer (1923–2007), *The Castle in the Forest* (New York: Random House, 2007).

Steiner was classically educated by his father to a very high level . . . it has to be admitted. But one of his mental conceits is that Greek tragedy, even genuine tragedy without the Grecian overlay, is impossible at this time. He wrote an entire early book called *The Death of Tragedy*[6] which is essentially on this theme. Nonetheless, I believe in delving a little bit deeper here.

The book itself is a bit of a rag-bag, primarily due to the fact that everything is fed towards (rather impatiently) getting to the end. This is the moment of high Greek drama, the play within the play which signifies the instant when the trial of Hitler begins, and that essentially resembles a playlet within a play. The main purpose of a narrative which runs for a hundred pages or so is to get all of the important characters on stage. Some of this is uneasily handled, and a good deal of it reads like some middlebrow thriller writers from the sixties and seventies, such as Hammond Innes[7] or Aleister MacLean.[8]

The *dramatis personae* are Emmanuel Lieber, the Nazi hunter and instigator of events; Simeon, the presiding judge at Hitler's mock-trial; Gideon Benasseraf, who falls ill and dies before the trial; a young Israelite, Isaac Ansell, who represents the postwar generation; and Elie Barach, an Orthodox Jew whose faith is disturbed by Benasseraf's fever-induced dream that Hitler is Jewish. Benasseraf is the holy fool of the group—the Fool or Tom o' Bedlam figure, if you like. For Benasseraf is mildly mentally ill, suffers flashbacks, and casts an alternative light on things. He even serves the dissentient role of an esoteric Hitlerist—albeit in reverse order.

There are two Gentile characters (other than Hitler). The first is John Asher (who is half-Jewish) and who Steiner basically considers to be Gentile. Like all radical liberals, Steiner is overly-drawn to the *other*. He evinces quite a lot of sympathy for this character and possibly identifies with him. Asher is fascinated by the whole affair, but not pruriently. He suffers from

---

[6] George Steiner, *The Death of Tragedy* (New York: Alfred A. Knopf, 1961).

[7] Ralph Hammond Innes (1913–1998), British novelist.

[8] Alistair Stuart MacLean (1922–1987), Scottish novelist.

no metaphysical lusts. The other Gentile is Teku, a Latino Indian or an indigenous South American . . . he is probably conceived as a largely silent witness to the trial, an incarnation of Mankind looking on.

As I say, the real purpose of the narration is to get these characters together so that the trial can occur. The elderly figure of Hitler (played by McCowen) has no real role until the trial sequence commences. When this happens he brushes aside any rudimentary defense apparatus provided by the "court" and represents himself. The whole point of the novella is really this trial.

The Hitler figure defends himself with vigor and urgency, irrespective of the fact that it's obviously not a real court case. The point here is philosophical, semi-religious, and higher in tone or intent. The whole event is primarily metaphysical in aspect—and Hitler defends himself metaphysically. Once Hitler emerges in Steiner's sequence, and despite his great age, he effortlessly dominates the scenario and virtually all the other characters lose their reality.

Hitler is really conceived of as being intimately connected to the Jewish destiny, so much so that he appears to be a part of their very development. To Steiner, he is no longer a man but an anti-god; a personal Satan not for mankind at large like the devil in Christianity or Islam. No. He is an Israelite devil; a Loki, a sprite of destruction—almost the pagan anti-god for one particular people, namely his own.

Throughout all of this we have to remember that Steiner is an uneasy co-optee; he doesn't really identify with his people that much . . . like most liberals. He admires the "hard" Jews and Israelis in his plot device—the men who have hunted down the Great Beast (666)—but he doesn't really share their passions. Unlike all of them (to varying degrees) he is not a nationalist; he strives not to allow himself group emotions.

Nonetheless, a peculiar thing occurs during Hitler's great speech (performed by McCowen) and which is quite reminiscent of the Bailiff's endless oratory in *The Childermass* (a novel by Wyndham Lewis which I have reviewed elsewhere[9]). The Leftist and Zionist critics who loathed this short book (as well as the play that came out of it via Hampton's redaction) do have a point. Hitler is the genius; they are underlings. Like the malevolent Anglo-Irish landowner Pozzo in Beckett's *Waiting for Godot*, he has the power. Steiner knows this, wills it, and lets it happen. At the deepest possible level, so to say, Steiner is a masochist who worships and adores Hitler as a negative god, albeit filtered and sublimated through aesthetic inversions (the catalog of which is multiple). In this moment of post-Christianity, he is truly a Satanist.

The arguments which Steiner/Hitler uses are less important than the way it is delivered. Hitler is not a man but a force; a diabolical instantiation; the encomium of the Word turned around. He is an avatar; an Odin in a rival religion to the one which Steiner was brought up in (Judaism) and has rejected subsequently. Like most academics with tenure, he's an Enlightenment man now.

It has to be said that in McCowen's dark threnody one comes close to a species of black metal or cacophonic white power music — of a sort that Professor Goodrick-Clarke tabulated, with little overt criticism, in *Black Sun*.[10] Steiner agrees — in a fragmentary moment or a semiotic register — with everything that Savitri Devi has ever said about the Führer,[11] but he does so as an instant of nausea and ontological victimhood. Albeit raised to a high artistic level, it is a cosmicism whereby the liberal-minded victim of a street mugging forgives his attacker, even thinks it was justified.

None of the arguments the Hitler character uses are original: moral and historical relativism, together with the fact that many Orthodox Rabbis believe Hitler to have been part of

---

[9] Reprinted in Bowden, *Reactionary Modernism*.

[10] Nicholas Goodrick-Clarke (1953–2012), *Black Sun: Aryan Cults, Esoteric Nazism, & the Politics of Identity* (New York: New York University Press, 2002).

[11] Savitri Devi (1905–1982), *The Lightning & the Sun*, 3rd ed. Complete and unabridged, ed. R. G. Fowler (San Francisco: Counter-Currents, 2014).

God's plan—i.e., to whip the chosen people for transgressing from the divine path of allegedly being Man's beacon. A role which involves waiting for the coming of Jehovah and his messiah . . . Might Hitler have been him—in the way that a sect like Jews for Jesus believe that Christians have a point?

Steiner leaves these questions unanswered, but to my mind this secularist sees Hitler as a savage god—much like Stasinopolous' view of Picasso,[12] but more importantly. The only way out of Steiner's dilemma is to attempt a caveat—and Nietzsche comes to his aid here. For in a pagan (Gentile) world Steiner believes that Jews are being punished for inventing conscience. This, although complicated, and *passim*. Nietzsche's *Geneaology of Morals* is Nietzsche's understanding of anti-Semitism as a metaphysical postulate. Didn't he partly reject Christianity as the Judaization of European gentility?

In any event, Steiner achieves an artistic madness here—in his own terms—that reminds one of Hans Prinzhorn's *Art of the Insane*. Where, following on from the manner of Kafka in *Metamorphosis*, the mild-mannered insurance salesman, Gregor, transforms into a gigantic cockroach overnight. It is the ultimate Hieronymus Bosch morphology or curdling, and at the end of the rival novella the roach-man just dies. He lowers his head plus mandibles (so to speak) for the last time, and gradually his epidermis or shell gets closer and closer to the carpet. Finally, he expires—all passion spent. It is the post-facticity of degeneration; the world-weariness, sadness in the face of Man's nature, and masochism which lurks at Humanism's heart. It, to switch one's foray into entomology, involves the endless circling of a moth around the candle flame which will devour it.

Professor Steiner seeks cessation, a Heideggerian full stop: he wishes to flop down and worship the Black Sun.

---

[12] Arianna Stassinopoulos Huffington, *Picasso: Creator & Destroyer* (New York: Simon & Schuster, 1988)

MEL GIBSON'S
THE PASSION OF THE CHRIST

Few films have been pilloried quite as much as Mel Gibson's *Passion*, yet when I last checked it was one of the ten most financially successful films of all time. Indeed, the sheer success of this piece with Christians around the world led to a de-escalation of the semi-orchestrated attack on the film. Nothing succeeds like success, and I remember with amusement watching a bus with an advertisement for Mel Gibson's *Passion* on the side of it snaking through the town where I lived at the height of the furor. But what of the film itself?

The Passion of the Christ is a highly artistic and metaphysical film from an ultra-Catholic perspective. As a director, Mel Gibson shows an impressive aesthetic sense and great artistic originality. This is reflected in every detail. Even the color palate of much of the film has an ocher tint or wash that resembles the painting of early Renaissance masters such as Giotto and Cimabue.

Several scenes are especially striking: the ravens attacking the thieves who are exposed with Christ on the Cross and Simon being made to carry the Cross on behalf of the Savior. But most assuredly the depiction of the Devil or Satan as a shaven-headed and androgynous Supermodel has to go down as one of the most startling innovations in cinema history.

Interestingly enough, the reaction to her appearance inside Italy was quite different to outside, and for a comparison try to visualize Lady Gaga as Mephistopheles in Goethe's *Faust* and you begin to get some sense of the *frisson*.

In High Christian art an artist is given free rein to depict the diabolical because it is outside the locus or expectation of human imperfection. The more perverse the depiction, the more aesthetically revelatory — so holds this particular theory.

One of the more interesting critiques of the film, particularly in Europe, was that it was blood-thirsty, sado-masochistic, and little more than a Biblical slasher movie. Yet none of the violence is gratuitous, and all of it fits in with the depiction of the Passion *per se*. During the first fifty minutes to one hour of running time, there is literally no violence, save some scuffling in the Garden.

This fits in with a very benevolent depiction of the Romans throughout the film. One is reminded that Mel Gibson's faith is called Roman Catholicism after all. The Bulgarian actor playing Pilate[1] (who bears a striking resemblance to Mussolini) depicts him, in Nietzsche's words, as the real hero of the New Testament. This could quite easily fit in with Gibson's prognosis — after all, the whole point about the film is that Christ's extraordinary moral arc or point of departure has to do with the fact that he is not a Man (*sic*).

On the issue of anti-Semitism, so-called, I have nothing to say. The film is not in the least anti-Semitic. It is a traditionalist High Catholic art film with all the suppositions which that implies. It is definitely not philo-Semitic, however. What the alleged scandal involving its release goes to show is that the implied penumbra of censorship and oversensitivity needs to be confronted and stood up to.

Gibson did nothing offensive whatsoever — even, from a classicizing point of view, the use of Latin throughout most of the feature just adds to the effect. Nothing more . . .

I recommend that people revisit this film on DVD now that the firestorm has well and truly died down. I think that Mel Gibson's film can be seen as a Christian altarpiece extension, *à la* Grünewald, to Leni Riefenstahl's *Olympia* (Parts 1 & 2). That's *Olympia* — not *Triumph of the Will*. There is a subtle difference . . .

Counter-Currents, December 1, 2010

---

[1] Hristo Shopov (born 1964).

INDEX

About the Author

JONATHAN BOWDEN, April 12, 1962–March 29, 2012, was a British novelist, playwright, essayist, painter, actor, and orator, as well as a leading thinker and spokesman of the British New Right. He was the author of some forty books—novels, short stories, plays for stage and screen, philosophical dialogues and essays, and literary and cultural criticism—including four other collections from Counter-Currents: *Pulp Fascism: Right-Wing Themes in Comics, Graphic Novels, & Popular Literature* (2013); *Western Civilization Bites Back* (2014); *Extremists: Studies in Metapolitics* (2017); and *Reactionary Modernism* (2022), all of them edited by Greg Johnson.

www.ingramcontent.com/pod-product-compliance
Lightning Source LLC
Chambersburg PA
CBHW020559030726
47497CB00007B/2012